# BLOOD
# FOUNDATION

## BY IAN CAIN

First published in the United States in 2025 by TEP

THE EMPIRE
PUBLISHERS

12808 West Airport Blvd, Suite 270, Sugar Land, TX
77478, United States

https://www.theempirepublishers.com/

Our books may be purchased in bulk for promotional, educational, or business use.

Please contact The Empire Publishers at +1 844 636-4579, or by email at support@theempirepublishers.com

First Edition December 2025

# About the Author

Ian Cain is a veteran broadcast journalist with extensive experience across television news, news-talk radio, and as a talk show host. Over a career built on on-air reporting, in-depth interviews, and live program hosting, he's developed a reputation for clear storytelling, balanced analysis, and engaging conversation that connects with diverse audiences. A skilled interviewer and communicator, Mr. Cain blends newsroom rigor with the immediacy of talk radio to inform, challenge, and entertain listeners and viewers alike. He currently resides in South Florida.

# Acknowledgment

Deepest gratitude to the team at The Empire Publishers for their tireless assistance in bringing this story to life. Special thanks to Ned Harris and Hera Abbotson for their professionalism, encouragement, and patience with the author's far too long telephone conversations. Additional thanks to Karissa Branan for her exceptional work in creating the book cover.

*In memory of Dr. Avery French*

# Table of Contents

# PART ONE

# Prologue

## Dachau, Germany - April 29, 1945

Jake fought against the grip of the nightmare, his mind ensnared in a loop of memories that refused to release him. He was back at the American Press International News Bureau in Chicago, the air thick with the scent of stale coffee and cigarettes, a haze that clung to everything in the room like a lingering ghost. The weathered oak conference table, a veteran of countless editorial battles, groaned under the weight of the reporters hunched over it. The rhythmic clatter of typewriters filled the air, a frantic symphony of urgency as headlines were hammered out, each keystroke a testament to the chaos of the world beyond the newsroom walls.

At the head of the table, News Director Dick Mercer held court, his voice rising and falling like the tide as he spoke of the Nazi strongholds still peppering Germany. "It's late in the war," he said, his words heavy with a weariness that had settled into the bones of everyone in the room. "The Nazis are pretty much spent, and a lot of higher-ups are saying this whole thing's gonna be over in a few months."

In the dream, Jake watched as Dick's words dissolved into

a blur, his voice growing distant, like the hum of a far-off engine. The pencil in Dick's hand began its relentless tap against the table, each strike a sharp, staccato beat that grew louder, more insistent, until it no longer sounded like a pencil at all. It was the rattle of distant machine fire invading Jake's sleep state and reverberating through his skull until he could no longer stand it.

With a gasp, Jake bolted upright, the remnants of the dream still clinging to him like a cold sweat. The sound that had invaded his sleep was real, not the fading echo of a nightmare. It was the unmistakable crack of automatic rifle fire, sharp and distant, but undeniably close. He shivered as the chill of the early morning air bit into his skin, pulling him fully into the present. Struggling free of his sleeping bag, Jake unzipped the flap of his pup tent and peered outside.

The German sky, a deep, unblemished azure, stretched endlessly above him, a stark contrast to the gray, snow-filled days they had endured. For the first time in what felt like weeks, the ground was clear, the snow retreating to reveal the frozen earth beneath. Today, the march would be easier. Jake crawled out of the tent, his breath puffing in the frigid air as he stood and stretched, his muscles protesting the motion after a night spent on the unforgiving ground. He took in the scene around him, the camp stirring to life in the pale light of dawn. Two hundred soldiers of Company L

3

moved with purpose, preparing for the day's mission. The air hummed with the low murmur of voices, the clatter of gear, and the ever-present undercurrent of tension.

Captain Sam Reeves, a figure as solid and unyielding as the landscape, stood at the center of it all, his voice carrying above the din as he issued orders. "Listen up! Everybody! Word has just come down from the 7th Army Corps that we're to proceed immediately to some kind of prison camp two miles southeast of here and recon with the 157th. A bunch of Nazi bastards are holding a lot of people there."

His words hung in the air like a dark cloud, casting a shadow over the men as they absorbed the news. "Apparently," he continued, "they have been holding them for months, maybe years. We don't know how many or what their circumstances are. There have been all kinds of rumors about these Nazi camps for weeks, and details are sketchy right now, so I'm unsure what we'll find. But our orders are clear. Go in there, free these people up, and take the remaining SS officers and guards as prisoners."

Reeves paused, his gaze locking onto Jake, a flicker of something unreadable passing between them. "That rifle fire you hear crackling in the background is the 157th sweeping up what's left of a bunch of Huns still holed up in the town of Dachau. Our boys have been in there since daybreak, and right about now, they're kicking some serious ass."

4

He checked his watch, the gesture precise, almost mechanical, as if the movement of time could somehow anchor them in the reality of what was to come. "It's zero-eight hundred. The 175th will wrap up quickly and be at that camp within two hours, and so will we. That's it. We move out in twenty minutes."

Reeves was just twenty-eight, yet to the young soldiers under his command, he was "the old man," a title bestowed with equal parts respect and irony. They were kids, most of them barely out of their teens, with faces that still held traces of the boys they had been before the war turned them into something else, something harder. Reeves was tough, but he was fair, a man whose steady hand had guided them through hell and back. His presence was a balm to the fear that gnawed at the edges of their minds, a reminder that someone still knew what the hell they were doing.

He shoved a cigarette into the corner of his mouth, the tip flaring as he lit it, and strode toward Jake with a purpose that brooked no argument. "Look, Cohen, this camp we're headed for could be a real horror show. I'm hearing all kinds of stories. Command up at 7th Army says there may be several thousand prisoners where we're headed. There are rumors of torture, starvation, extermination... you name it. So prepare yourself, and for Christ's sake, try to stay in the rear until we know what we're dealing with."

Jake met his gaze, his voice steady despite the tremor of dread that curled in his gut. "C'mon, Captain," he protested. "I can't stay in the rear. I have to advance with infantry. You gotta let me do my job. I'm a reporter, and I need to see it as it happens."

Reeves's eyes narrowed, the lines around them deepening as he considered Jake's words. "You just watch yer ass," he finally said, the growl of a man who had seen too much blood spilled to let another life be added to the count. "I don't want you to wind up being one of your own damned headlines."

The cigarette smoldered in the Captain's mouth, a curl of smoke rising into the crisp morning air as he made eye contact with Jake. "And Cohen," he added, his tone softening just a fraction, "I've told you before, call me 'Sam' when it's just you and me. Now c'mon. Get your gear and be ready to go."

Jake nodded, the weight of what lay ahead pressing down on him like a physical force. He turned back toward his tent, the distant crack of gunfire echoing in his ears, a grim reminder that the nightmare was far from over.

***

As the soldiers trudged down the desolate road, Jake

6

moved methodically, capturing the devastation around him with his camera. Each click of the shutter immortalized the remnants of shattered lives, a pair of tiny shoes half-buried in the mud, bombed-out houses reduced to skeletal remains, and the smoldering ruins of what had once been a church. The hollow shells of the town stood silent, as if mourning the loss of its inhabitants. The air was thick with the residue of war, a haunting quiet that wrapped around them like a shroud.

Jake's lens focused on the grim reality that lined their path: bodies, both civilian and military, lying haphazardly in ditches, their once-living forms now twisted and contorted, caught in the merciless grip of death. German civilians, Nazi soldiers, and regular Wehrmacht troops were indistinguishable in death, piled together in grotesque unity. The soldiers marched on, their faces blank and eyes vacant, as if their souls had been numbed by the relentless horrors they had witnessed. The silence was deafening, broken only by the crunch of their boots on the gravel road.

Without warning, the entire regiment came to an abrupt halt, as if they had collided with an invisible barrier. A soldier's voice pierced the stillness, filled with raw, visceral horror.

"What the hell is that smell?"

The question hung in the air for only a moment before it was answered by a collective groan of disgust that rippled through the ranks. The stench was overwhelming, a foul, noxious cloud that seemed to cling to the inside of their throats, forcing many to double over and retch uncontrollably.

"Halt!" Captain Reeves' command cut through the chaos. The men struggled to cover their mouths, choking on the sickening odor that pervaded the air like poison. Captain Reeves paused, his expression shifting from confusion to grim realization as he comprehended the source of the stench. It was coming from the camp just ahead, a place whispered about in the darkest rumors, a name that sent chills down the spines of those who dared to speak of it.

Reeves dropped to one knee, bringing his binoculars to his eyes. The scene that unfolded through the lenses was nightmarish. The camp initially appeared to be just another military outpost, an eight-foot masonry wall topped with barbed wire, a large iron gate, and guard towers that seemed eerily vacant. But as his gaze swept across the landscape, the true horror revealed itself. Near the entrance, a mound of human bodies sprawled in a grotesque heap, decomposing under the relentless sun. At first, it was difficult to comprehend, the bodies blending together into what looked like a pile of discarded, filthy laundry. But as he focused, the reality hit him like a physical blow, a wave of nausea that nearly knocked him over.

"My God. What the hell is this?" Reeves whispered, his voice thick with disbelief.

First Lieutenant Gabe Isaacs, sensing the change in his commander, called out from behind him, "Major, what is it?" Reeves turned to Isaacs, his face ashen. "Death, Lieutenant. It's the smell of death. The camp is just ahead. We're going in, but I want everyone to keep their noses and mouths covered. Those who have gas masks, use them. That's an order!"

The soldiers struggled to comply, coughing and gagging as they tried to adjust to the pervasive stench. Captain Reeves moved among his men, issuing orders, his voice steady but with an edge that betrayed his own unease.

"From what I can see, there are no signs of life up there. The guard towers seem abandoned, but we can't be sure. We'll scale the wall in groups of ten, just in case there are any Nazi forces still inside. There's a train track with about thirty cars sitting on it, abandoned. We need to be ready for anything."

Captain Reeves, Private Mike Zimmer, a German interpreter, Lieutenant Isaacs, and Jake led the approach to

9

the camp's perimeter. The smell grew stronger with each step, a rancid miasma that clawed at their senses. The iron gates loomed ahead, bearing an inscription that sent a chill through the group.

"Arbeit Macht Frei," Reeves muttered, narrowing his eyes at the foreign words.

"Zimmer, what does that say?"

"Work makes you free," Zimmer translated, his voice hollow.

They crouched near the gates, surveying the scene with mounting dread. The stench was overpowering, a physical force that made it hard to think, let alone breathe.

"We have to check those boxcars," Reeves said, his voice tight.

The men approached the train with rifles raised, tension crackling in the air. As they neared the first open boxcar, Lieutenant Isaacs staggered, dropping to his knees as his body convulsed with violent retching. His face turned ghostly pale, eyes wide with horror.

"Oh my God," Reeves gasped, stepping back as the truth of what they had found sank in.

Jake's instincts as a journalist kicked in, though every fiber of his being screamed for him to turn away. He forced himself to move forward, raising his camera. The smell hit

10

him first, a putrid wave that almost knocked him off his feet. Then, through the lens, the full scope of the atrocity came into view. Bodies were stacked inside the boxcar, piled like cordwood, their faces contorted in the final agony of death. Their hollow eyes stared out, empty and accusing.

The men moved from one car to the next, each a silent witness to the unspeakable cruelty they had uncovered. Thirty boxcars in total, each filled with decomposing bodies, twisted and broken, the remnants of lives stolen in a place where humanity had long ceased to exist. The silence was oppressive, broken only by the relentless click of Jake's camera, capturing every horrific detail. Each frame was a testament to the depths of human suffering, the faces of the dead frozen in eternal anguish.

The soldiers moved like specters through the scene, their minds reeling from the incomprehensible evil laid bare before them. Jake's hands trembled as he lowered his camera, the weight of what he had seen pressing down on him like a physical force. The images would haunt him forever, etched into his memory as a reminder of the darkest chapter of human history.

Within an hour, most of Company L had scaled the high, barbed-wire-topped wall and converged on the grim expanse of the camp. The compound, once a thriving center of unspeakable suffering, now lay eerily silent except for the sporadic bursts of gunfire. One by one, the remaining Nazi guards and officers were either killed or captured, their once-feared presence fading into the shadows of defeat. The soldiers' footsteps echoed through the vast emptiness, each sound a stark reminder of the horror they had uncovered.

The camp was a vision of desolation: an endless maze of rusting barbed wire, filthy barracks, and an oppressive quiet that hung like a shroud. Captain Sam Reeves and his men moved through the site, their expressions a mix of grim determination and profound sadness. As the sun climbed higher, casting a harsh light on the devastation, a shocking development unfolded.

From the depths of the rotting barracks emerged gaunt, hollow-faced survivors, their bodies barely clothed in rags that hung off their skeletal frames like tattered shrouds. Their eyes, though sunken and vacant, held a flicker of hope, mingled with disbelief. As they hesitantly approached the soldiers, their emaciated forms seemed to float through the filth and ruin, their presence a haunting reminder of the inhumanity they had endured.

Jake, driven by an insatiable need to document the atrocities, delved deeper into the nightmarish landscape of Dachau. He scribbled frantic notes and snapped endless photos, each click of his camera capturing the raw, unfiltered horrors that defied comprehension. Having witnessed the ravages of World War II, Jake thought he had seen the worst of humanity. But nothing could have prepared him for the depths of despair and cruelty laid bare in Dachau.

As the day waned, a chilling stillness enveloped the camp, more profound than the encroaching darkness. Weary soldiers, still grappling with disbelief, anger, and sorrow, huddled together in muted conversations, their voices barely audible over the rustling of cigarette smoke. Letters were written, cigarettes lit, but the air remained heavy with the weight of the day's revelations.

Jake, determined to piece together his thoughts and secure the harrowing images he had captured, wandered deeper into the camp. The acrid smell of decay clung to him, a constant reminder of the atrocities that had transpired. He found himself drawn to one of the furnaces, the final resting place for countless souls. The structure loomed against the darkening sky, its very presence a grim testament to the horrors of the camp.

Sitting on the cold, stone steps near the furnace entrance, Jake fumbled with a crumpled pack of Camel cigarettes. The familiar crinkle of the package brought a fleeting memory of home, a stark contrast to the horror surrounding him. "Chicago," he murmured, trying to ground himself in a place far removed from the nightmare.

He pulled out a cigarette and glanced at the Zippo lighter

given to him by Dick Mercer, its engraving reading, "Democracy is the free flow of information." Jake lit the cigarette, the flickering flame casting brief, eerie shadows. It briefly illuminated words etched into the furnace wall, but the wind quickly extinguished the light. Intrigued and troubled, Jake struck the lighter again, shielding it from the gusts. This time, the words became clear.

Jake's heart pounded as he read the inscription on each brick: "Stookton Brickworks, Stookton, Illinois… USA." The realization hit him like a physical blow. The bricks that built the inferno of Dachau, the very essence of the camp's cruelty, had come from his homeland. The clay of the bricks an actual importation of his beloved homeland to this corrupt fatherland. Stunned, Jake stumbled backward, his mind reeling from the revelation.

Desperate to verify his discovery, he shone his flashlight across the camp. Everywhere he looked, on the walls, in the floors of the gas chambers, and even in the homes of Nazi officers, Stookton bricks, and thus American soil, were embedded into the very fabric of the camp. Each discovery deepened his sense of horror and betrayal. How could such a thing happen? When did it happen? Who allowed this to take place?

Jake stood motionless, the irrefutable evidence of American complicity in this hellish nightmare weighing heavily on him. The camp's horrors seemed to echo in the dark, and Jake felt an eerie sensation of voices whispering on the cold night wind, urging him to expose the full truth.

Gazing at the cigarette lighter in his hand, Jake read its inscription once more. "Democracy is the free flow of information." A steely resolve took hold of him. This was no longer just about documenting history; it was about unveiling the dark secrets hidden within it.

In the oppressive darkness of Dachau, Jake made a solemn vow to himself. "The world will know of this," he declared softly into the night. "I will tell them." With that, he set out on a relentless mission to reveal the atrocities he had witnessed and the grim complicity of those who had enabled them.

# Chapter 1

## Summer Camp – Friday, June 12, 1936

Sophie French deftly maneuvered her sleek 1933 convertible roadster along the narrow ribbon of blacktop that led into the sleepy town of Stookton. The car, a gift from her father in celebration of her college graduation, gleamed in the fading sunlight. It was the perfect day for a drive, with the top down and the warm country breeze tousling her chestnut hair. She relished the sensation, savoring the freedom that came with this new chapter in her life. As she watched the sun slowly sink toward the horizon, fields of tall corn swayed gently in the breeze, casting long shadows across the pavement.

Just ahead, a tall wooden sign welcomed newcomers to Stookton, the words "Welcome to Stookton - Population 4,421" carved into the weathered wood. Despite the charm of the surrounding countryside, Sophie couldn't shake the memory of how isolated this town had felt during her brief visit last year for her job interview. But today, she was filled with optimism, ready to embrace the challenges and opportunities that awaited her.

As she entered Stookton, the landscape shifted from endless cornfields to a quaint collection of red brick houses and large, weathered barns. The town's center was a picture of small-town America, with tidy shops lining the main street, their brick facades glowing softly in the evening light. A lone Marathon gasoline station with just two pumps stood at the edge of town, a reminder of the slower pace of life here. At the corner of Main and Dewey Streets, a small diner named "The Cardinal Cafe " beckoned with its neon sign, the words glowing warmly in the gathering dusk.

In the town square, a stately old courthouse commanded attention, its limestone facade bearing the words "Chambers County" chiseled into the large header above the massive copper doors. The sight of the courthouse, with its towering spire and meticulously maintained grounds, brought a smile to Sophie's face. There was something inviting about the town's old-world charm, a sense of timelessness that contrasted sharply with the fast-paced life she had left behind in Chicago.

Sophie couldn't help but feel a flutter of excitement as she continued down the quiet streets. At twenty-three, she was eager to begin her first full-time teaching position at McKinley Elementary School. Starting her career in a small Midwestern town had always been her dream, and now that dream was becoming a reality. The long drive from Chicago had given her plenty of time to reflect on the journey that had brought her here, and she felt a deep sense of satisfaction as she pulled into the school parking lot.

The sight of McKinley Elementary took her breath away. The majestic red brick building loomed before her, its tall windows reflecting the last rays of the setting sun. Large oak trees, their branches silhouetted against the darkening sky, stood like sentinels on the school's sweeping green lawn. Sophie took a deep breath, trying to calm the nerves that fluttered in her stomach. This was it, the beginning of her new life. She straightened her shoulders and made her way to the school's main entrance, ready to meet her new boss, Principal Henry Wilkes.

***

Inside, the school was quiet, the halls empty save for the soft echo of her footsteps on the polished wooden floors. She found the principal's office easily enough, and after a brief knock, the door swung open to reveal Mr. Wilkes, a gentleman in his early sixties with pale blue eyes, graying hair, and an engaging manner.

"Thank you for coming so late in the day, Miss French,"

Mr. Wilkes said with a warm smile. "I know you've had a long trip, but summer school starts on Monday, and I've been here going over the curriculum."

"It's not a problem at all, Mr. Wilkes," Sophie replied, returning his smile. "I'm just so excited to be here. Besides, I'm heading straight to the house I've rented as soon as we're done here."

"And we're excited to have you here, Miss French," Mr. Wilkes said, his tone sincere. "I know your fifth graders will love you. And I can't tell you how happy we were that you agreed to arrive early to help with summer school."

"I didn't mind arriving early at all," Sophie assured him. "I've been so eager to get started. I would have been on pins and needles all summer, anxious for September, so this worked out perfectly."

*** 

As they walked back to the parking lot, the conversation became more serious. Mr. Wilkes paused, his expression thoughtful. "Miss French, there's something I should probably make you aware of regarding summer school," he began, his tone cautious. "As I mentioned, we're delighted that you could come early and assist us. However, your class sizes might be smaller than we expected this summer."

Sophie frowned, puzzled. "Oh? Why is that?"

Mr. Wilkes hesitated before answering. "Many of our families here in Stookton are sending their children to one of these new summer camps. With so many of them away, there may not be a lot of students attending summer school."

Sophie considered this information, still feeling a bit confused. "Summer camps?" she echoed, trying to understand the significance.

"Yes," Mr. Wilkes continued, his voice lowering slightly. "These camps have become quite popular around here. Since you're new to Stookton, you might need a few days to get a better understanding of our little town. I suggest you attend tomorrow's rally. It's in the town square. It might help put things into context."

"A rally?" Sophie repeated, her curiosity piqued.

Mr. Wilkes nodded. "Yes, it's sort of a political rally," he explained, though there was a note of hesitation in his voice. "You should go. It might give you some insight into our town's current... enthusiasms. Maybe I'll see you there."

\*\*\*

As Sophie drove away from the school, her mind buzzed with questions. What exactly did Mr. Wilkes mean by *"enthusiasms"*? And why did he seem so reluctant to explain? She resolved to attend the rally tomorrow, eager to understand. But for now, she pushed the thoughts aside, focusing on the task at hand. It had been a long day, and she was eager to settle into her new rental and get some much-needed rest.

*** 

The following day, Sophie arrived at the rally with a lingering curiosity about the comments from Mr. Wikes the previous night. She parked her car near the courthouse, its stately limestone façade looming large against the clear blue sky. The morning of Saturday, June 13, 1936, was sweltering. With such oppressive heat, it was stifling by mid-morning. Sophie found a seat on the giant steps of the Chambers County Courthouse, it's cool stone providing a slight relief from the intense summer sun. As she settled in, she watched the townspeople pour into the town square, their voices blending into a low, indistinct murmur that buzzed through the humid air.

Petite and attractive, Sophie was the picture of 1930s elegance. Her wavy chestnut hair, cut at shoulder length, framed a face with expressive hazel eyes that radiated warmth and kindness. She wore a simple yet stylish summer dress, its fabric light enough to flutter in the slightest breeze, though today the air was still. Despite the heat, she remained poised, her discomfort concealed beneath a calm exterior. However, as she observed the scene unfolding before her, an unsettling sense of dread began to creep over her.

The square was filling quickly, and Sophie watched with growing curiosity as more and more townspeople, dressed in their Sunday best, made their way toward a large, patriotically decorated stage. The stage was flanked by two American flags, one on either side, and in the center stood a third flag bearing the Illinois state seal. The speaker's podium, draped in red, white, and blue bunting, stood beneath a massive banner that fluttered soundlessly in the hot summer breeze. The words "German American Bund" emblazoned across the banner, stopped Sophie cold, sending a shiver down her spine despite the sweltering heat.

Her heart pounded as her eyes fell upon the symbol next to the words. It was unmistakable; the black, twisted form of a swastika, emblazoned against a stark white circle on a crimson background. Sophie's breath caught in her throat as the full weight of what she was witnessing began to sink in. The realization was like a punch to the gut, knocking the wind out of her as she stared in disbelief at the Nazi symbol, now incongruously draped over this small Midwestern town. The air, already heavy with humidity, seemed to grow even thicker with tension as the crowd continued to gather, their excited chatter rising in pitch. Further up Main Street, military music began to play, growing louder as a brass band, dressed in crisp brown uniforms, marched into view. The band's arrival was met with cheers from the crowd, who waved American flags and Nazi banners with equal fervor. The band came to a stop in front of the stage, forming a flawless line before raising their arms in unison, delivering the Nazi salute. The sight was surreal, and Sophie could hardly believe what she was seeing.

As the music faded, an eerie stillness descended over the square. A man in a business suit, his arm adorned with a swastika armband and a matching lapel pin, strode confidently to the microphone at the center of the stage. He stood silently for a moment, his piercing gaze sweeping over the crowd with an unsettling mixture of pride and vitriol. When he finally spoke, his voice boomed with an authoritarian presence that seemed to fill every corner of the square.

"We proud German Americans stand united today, under the banners of our heritage and of this great nation we now call home. Just as our revered ancestors forged the might of our fatherland, so too shall we continue to elevate America to its rightful place of greatness. The new Chancellor of Germany has shown us the path forward... one paved with the strength, resolve, and values of our Führer's great Nazi Party. We must adopt these same principles to fortify and uplift America."

As the speaker's words echoed through the crowd, the citizens of Stookton erupted in cheers, their voices joining in a feverish chorus of approval. Nazi banners and American flags were waved with equal fervor, creating a chilling blend of twisted patriotism. Sophie felt a deep, unexpected wave of disappointment as her eyes fell upon the familiar figure of Mr. Wilkes, the kindly principal who had welcomed her to town. He stood among the crowd, his face alight with enthusiasm as he joined in the applause.

The man on the podium continued, his tone growing more impassioned, his rhetoric a toxic blend of nationalism, anti-Semitism, and adulation for the Nazi regime. His voice rang out, calling for a new Germany to rise within the borders of America, warning of the impending collapse of a decadent nation if they failed to act. His words culminated in a fervent crescendo, leaving the crowd hanging on every syllable.

"I am Peter Von Stook," the man declared, his voice commanding and filled with a self-assured authority. "Most of you know me. You've toiled in my brickyards, received my wages, and reaped the benefits of your labor. But even

24

as we gather here today, our God-fearing way of life is under siege. Communist and Jewish influences conspire against us, pushing for labor unions, championing godless laws, and threatening all that we have built or will build. But we will not allow it! We will embrace the principles of nationalism, and we will defend our way of life. We will do this by preserving the moral fabric of America by embracing the precepts of our Fatherland and the Third Reich. With the indomitable spirit of our German blood and our unwavering Christian beliefs, we will continue to make this nation great!"

Von Stook's voice softened as he addressed the crowd with a measured intensity. "Today, as we send our children off to Bund Summer Camp, we are assured that they will be nurtured in the spirit of German-American freedom, learning the order and discipline of the Führer. They will form bonds that cannot be broken, ensuring that these values endure and thrive across generations. The legacy of God, America, and the German American Bund will be preserved!"

The crowd's applause rose to a deafening roar, and they surged forward as one toward the waiting caravan of buses. Dozens of children, dressed in brown shirts, shorts, and swastika armbands, marched in orderly lines, their faces aglow with fervor. Sophie watched in horror as the buses, now filled with the town's eager youth, began to roll away,

25

carrying them to a summer camp where the indoctrination would continue under the guise of *wholesome* activities.

A profound sense of unease settled over Sophie as she reflected on the scene she had just witnessed. For a moment, she had to consciously still herself for fear that she might become ill. Her thoughts turned to her father, Dr. Avery French, who had passed away only a month earlier. As a history professor at one of America's premier universities, he had devoted his life to teaching the virtues of democracy, had been a staunch advocate for equality, and a fierce defender of human rights. He had frequently voiced his concern over the rise of the Nazi Party and its many sympathizers in America. "What would Dad think of all this?" Sophie wondered, her heart heavy with sadness and disbelief.

As she rose to leave, something caught her eye: an elderly black man emerged from a nearby alley, a broom in one hand and a large canvas bag slung over his shoulder. He moved slowly and deliberately, stooping to pick up discarded cups, pamphlets, and other debris left behind by the raucous crowd. He paused briefly, glancing in Sophie's direction before offering a polite nod of acknowledgment. Sophie returned the gesture with a warm smile.

"Hey, good lookin'! Is that old darkie over there giving you any trouble?" A voice called out from behind her, breaking the moment. Sophie spun around, startled, to find a young man standing before her. He was handsome, with well-groomed hair and fashionable clothes, exuding a confidence that was at once both charming and unsettling. His presence might have been appealing, were it not for the vile comment he had just made.

Before Sophie could respond, the man continued, "I'm Andrew. So, you're the new schoolteacher at McKinley Elementary, right?"

"Yes, that's correct," Sophie replied, still reeling from the shock of his earlier words.

"I noticed you sitting here all by yourself, looking gorgeous. I asked Mr. Wilkes about you... he knows everything that happens around here. It's a small town, you know."

Sophie studied Andrew carefully, trying to gauge his intentions. "Yes, it is a small town," she said cautiously. "And yes. That's correct. I am here to teach the fifth grade at McKinley."

"Welcome to Stookton, Miss French," Andrew said, his gaze lingering on her just long enough to make her *very* uncomfortable. "Always nice to see a fresh face around here."

"Thank you," Sophie replied, though she couldn't shake the uneasy feeling that had settled in her stomach. Despite the warmth of the afternoon sun, she felt a chill run down her spine. "I arrived early because Mr. Wilkes asked me to teach summer school, too. But, as I found out yesterday, it looks like most of my students will be away for a while."

"Ah, you're talking about the summer camps, of course. And how about the rally!" Andrew exclaimed, his tone brightening. "So, what did you think?"
Not wanting to engage in a confrontation, Sophie chose her words carefully. "I'm still forming an opinion."

Andrew chuckled, seemingly undeterred by her noncommittal response. "Give it time. Once you've been here a while, you'll see. We're all God-fearing patriots here in Stookton. We look out for each other. That's why I came over, to make sure 'Old Zeb' wasn't bothering you."

Sophie glanced back at the elderly man, who was still dutifully cleaning the street. "And who is that gentleman?" she asked, a hint of challenge in her voice.

"'Gentleman?'" Andrew scoffed, his laughter sharp and dismissive. "That's no gentleman. That's old Zebediah Coal. We all just call him 'Old Zeb.' He and his father, before him, worked at the brickyard for years. A bunch of those darkies have worked at my dad's brickworks, going back forty years or more."

"He works for your father?" Sophie asked, trying to mask

28

her growing disgust.

"That's right," Andrew said with a smirk. "My dad. The guy who just gave the speech. He owns all the brickyards in this part of the state. Over the years, a lot of the blacks, and most of the low-class whites around here, have earned their keep working for my dad and my grandfather. Gramps started the brick industry around here ages ago. All the darkies and white trash live in the old village behind the brick kilns. We call that part of town the 'gulch.' You know, like a ditch?"

Sophie's face tightened with disgust as she absorbed Andrew's blatant racism. She decided to cut the conversation short, her anger barely contained.

"Nice talking to you," Andrew said as she turned away. "I'm sure we'll be seeing a lot of each other." Sophie couldn't hide her cringe as she walked off, feeling the weight of his words linger like a bitter aftertaste.

\*\*\*

As the sweltering summer day gradually gave way to twilight, Sophie settled onto her front porch, a glass of merlot in hand, her thoughts heavy with the day's events. The rally's fervent rhetoric and her unsettling encounter with

Andrew left her with a profound sense of unease. It was as if a dark cloud had settled over Stookton, obscuring its quaint charm with a sinister undercurrent.

The town's warm exterior was a stark contrast to the virulent ideology that seemed to permeate every corner. Sophie's thoughts raced with questions about the oppressive influence of the Von Stook family and what appeared to be the pervasive control of Stookton Brickworks. The townspeople, drawn by the promise of employment and the allure of the brickyards' wealth, appeared either resigned to, or complicit with the disturbing ideology of Peter Von Stook and the German Bund. It was a town where fear and loyalty seemed to be intertwined, and where moral decline had taken root long ago.

The pervasive darkness that hung over the town was akin to the black smoke that belched from the brickyard's chimneys, an ever-present reminder of the industry's grip on the community. Sophie longed for her father's wisdom and guidance. She missed the conversations they would have, his insightful perspective that always seemed to shed light on the darkest of situations. In his absence, the oppressive atmosphere of Stookton felt even more daunting, a weight she struggled to shake off.

# Chapter 2

## Madelyn

In the weeks following her arrival in Stookton, Sophie settled into her role at McKinley Elementary. The summer school session had been predictably sparse, with only a handful of students attending, making the oppressive heat of the summer days stretch interminably. But with September came the new school year, and Sophie began to find her rhythm. She was getting to know her students and the routine of her new job, and things seemed to fall into place. Almost. As Sophie got to know her students, she was increasingly troubled by some of their behavior.

The cruelty directed toward the black children was disturbing and relentless. She had taken her concerns to Mr. Wilkes, who assured her repeatedly that he would address the issue with the children's parents. Yet, he consistently changed the subject before any real action was discussed. When Sophie attempted to confront one of the parents directly, she was met with a frosty reception and a curt reminder: "In Stookton, it's the parents who teach our children their values, not the school." The attitudes of many parents and townsfolk alike were unsettling. They seemed to reinforce a culture of intolerance that Sophie found hard to reconcile with the values she held dear. The experience left her feeling ever more isolated and troubled.

Most days, Sophie lingered at school well into the evening, a quiet refuge from the oppressive atmosphere she encountered in the town. Eventually, she would make her way home to the bungalow on Brighton Avenue. The house, a charming red brick structure with white lattice trim and three Bedford stone steps leading to the front door, offered a semblance of solace. The street was lined with stately oak and maple trees, their leaves ablaze with autumn colors, yellow, orange, and red. Yet, the beauty of her surroundings did little to ease her growing sense of unease.

On this Friday night, October 30th, Sophie left school promptly at 3:30, a rare departure in sync with the rest of the staff. After a quick dinner, she anxiously awaited the end of a sudden thunderstorm, hoping to make it downtown before darkness fell. She swiftly cleared the table, bolted out the front door, and climbed into her convertible roadster. The roadster's engine roared to life as she drove toward Main Street.

Sophie parked a half-block up from Murphy's Rexall Drugstore and walked toward it with a sense of purpose. She needed Halloween candy, orange and black crepe paper, and

32

a candle to light the Jack-o'-lantern she had carved the night before. Tomorrow, her fifth-grade class will celebrate Halloween in her backyard. The streets of Stookton were eerily quiet, the recent storm having left the pavement slick and gleaming under the dim streetlights. The silence added to her unease, making the night feel unnervingly foreboding.

"Now there's a little witch who could scare me *stiff*, even if it wasn't Halloween." The voice was unmistakable… Andrew's. Sophie's anger flared at his vulgar insinuation, but she chose silence. In Stookton, avoiding Andrew's ire seemed like the only prudent course of action. Since their first meeting in June, Andrew had developed a habit of appearing unannounced, often with unwanted flirtations and inappropriate comments. His presence was a source of constant discomfort for Sophie, each encounter leaving her more unsettled than the last.

"You are just so good-looking," Andrew continued, his voice dripping with insincerity. "Stookton is lucky to have you."

Sophie quickened her pace, as she turned back, quickly deciding to return to her car. "Thank you, Andrew," she replied curtly, her gaze fixed straight ahead. At that moment, her mind flashed back to the recent, unwelcome visit Andrew had paid to her classroom. It had been late; Sophie was preparing lessons when her classroom door swung open.

There he stood, grinning like a cat with a canary, his comment as unwelcome as his intrusion. "Wow! Look who's burning the midnight oil. You know what they say? 'All work and no play makes a very dull girl.'" He stepped inside and closed the door behind him.

"I was just about to leave," Sophie said, forcing a polite smile and trying to maintain her composure.

"Then my timing's perfect," Andrew replied with a predatory grin, moving closer to her.

At that moment, the school custodian, Mr. Perkins, called out from the hallway, his voice cutting through the tension. "Everything alright in there, Miss French?"

"Mr. Perkins!" Sophie called out, her voice brimming with relief. "I was just about to see if you were still in the building. I could sure use your help with a stubborn desk drawer. The darn thing has been jammed all day."

Mr. Perkins, a burly man clad in an industrial grey uniform with a heavy ring of jangling keys at his belt, lumbered into the classroom. His eyes narrowed warily at Andrew, who was lingering in the corner. "Not supposed to be any non-employees in this building after hours," Mr. Perkins said, his tone edged with authority. Andrew's response was a haughty glare before he stormed out of the classroom without a word. "Now, let's see about that drawer," Mr. Perkins said, his expression softening into a knowing grin.

Sophie, now back in the present, could feel Andrew's presence lingering like a shadow. She glanced over her shoulder, his footsteps echoing right behind her. Just then, the bell above the drugstore's front door rang sharply, signaling someone's departure. "Please, let someone see me," Sophie thought desperately, her mind racing with fear.

"C'mon, Sophie," Andrew's voice cut through the night air, menacing and mocking. "What do you want? A trick or a little *treat*?" Panic surged through her like a jolt of electricity. In that moment, she remembered her initial excitement about moving to Stookton, leaving behind the chaotic life of Chicago for the quietude of this small town. Now, that hope seemed like a distant dream. Her hands trembling, she fumbled with her car keys, only a few steps away from safety.

Just as she reached for the car door, Andrew's hand clamped down on her wrist with a vice-like grip. The night air seemed to chill around them. "What do I have to do to get you in the *spirit of the season*?" he hissed, his breath hot and oppressive.

Sophie struggled to scream, her voice caught in her throat as a wave of pain shot through her arm. Andrew's grip tightened with each passing second, sapping her strength. He jerked her roughly, forcing her to face him. His face was a

35

mask of malevolence; his eyes filled with a lethal gleam. Sophie's mind raced, desperately searching for a way to escape the horrifying situation.

Then – without warning - her thoughts were interrupted by the sudden, screeching sound of a car coming to an abrupt halt. Tires skidded against the curb with a violent jolt, and piercing headlights cut through the darkness, creating an intense, blinding glare. A car door swung open, and a figure swiftly emerged from the vehicle.

"Take your hands off of her!" came a commanding voice, resolute and unyielding. The woman who emerged from the car moved with impressive speed and agility. She rushed at Andrew, breaking his grip on Sophie with a forceful shove. "Get out of here, now! Heir Von Stook!" she yelled, her mocking German accent giving her words a sharp edge. Andrew glared at the woman with a mixture of rage and disdain.

"Go! *Now!*" the woman continued, her voice rising. "Or I'll call the Sheriff!"

Andrew's fury was replaced by a smirk of arrogant defiance. "The *Sheriff?*" he scoffed, his tone dripping with contempt. "Sure. Why don't you just do that, Nurse Keller?" With a derisive laugh, he turned and disappeared into the alley behind the Rexall, his footsteps fading into the night.

Sophie, trembling and overwhelmed, collapsed into the arms of her unexpected savior. Tears streamed down her face as she whispered, "Oh my God. Thank you."

The woman, whose reassuring presence was a balm to Sophie's frayed nerves, held her gently. "My name is Madelyn. Madelyn Keller," she said with a reassuring warmth. "You're safe now. We need to get you home. Where do you live?"

Madelyn followed Sophie back to her bungalow, and once inside, the warmth of the fireplace provided a stark contrast to the cold fear that had gripped Sophie moments before. As the flames crackled, the two women settled in with hot apple cider laced with Sophie's favorite scotch whiskey. Over the next few hours, they shared stories and discussed the unsettling events of the evening.

Madelyn revealed that she worked as a nurse at the hospital just across the river in Shale Pointe, Missouri, and had lived in Stookton for two years. She spoke of the numerous cases she had treated, many involving severe injuries inflicted by Andrew, mostly on women. Despite the courage of a few victims who had dared to come forward, Andrew had never been held accountable. His actions remained shrouded in a dark legacy of entitlement, his family's influence, and the infamous brickyards.

"The Von Stook family has spent decades burying their

secrets," Madelyn said, her voice laden with frustration and determination. "But there's still a lot to uncover if you're willing to dig."

As the hours slipped into the early morning, a bond formed between Sophie and Madelyn, their shared experiences laying the foundation for an unexpected friendship. They spoke of the town's hidden darkness and the challenges they both faced. The night's revelations set them on a path filled with peril and intrigue that neither could have anticipated.

# Chapter 3

## Due Process

Sophie stretched her arms above her head and slowly sat up in bed, trying to shake off the lingering weight of a restless night and the unsettling remnants of haunting dreams. The memories of the previous night's terrifying encounter with Andrew flooded her mind, snapping her into full wakefulness. If not for Madelyn's timely intervention, Sophie doubted she would be waking up in the relative safety of her cozy bungalow. The bright sunlight pierced through the thin curtains, casting warm golden rays across the room, while outside, the trees lining the quiet street blazed with the vibrant hues of autumn. Their fiery reds, oranges, and yellows danced gently in the crisp morning breeze. It was Saturday. Halloween Day, 1936.

Sophie had always cherished Halloween, especially when it graced a Saturday, a day that promised nothing but joy and excitement. Today would be filled with festivities, a welcome distraction from the tension gnawing at her. She had meticulously planned every detail for her fifth-grade class. A pumpkin carving contest, a candy hunt, and the ever-popular apple dunking. The thought of her students' eager faces and their holiday glee brought a smile to her lips.

But as quickly as it came, the smile faded, replaced by a shadow of last night's horror. Sophie shuddered, trying to push past the dark memories, and reluctantly got out of bed. She reached for a simple outfit: a soft red sweater that clung to her slender frame and a gray skirt that swayed gently as she moved.

The aroma of freshly brewed coffee filled the small kitchen, mingling with the crisp scent of the autumn morning that drifted through the open window. Sophie savored the familiar ritual of stirring cinnamon and cream into her steaming cup, taking a deep breath to steady her nerves. Just as she was about to take her first sip, she was startled by a sudden knock at her door. It was rather loud, echoing through the bungalow. Her heart pounded in her chest, the coffee cup trembling slightly in her hand. She froze, her mind racing... was it, Andrew? Fear gripped her as she hesitated, then cautiously moved toward the door. "Who is it?" Sophie called out, her voice wavering slightly.

A moment of tense silence followed before a masculine but friendly voice responded from the other side. "It's Ted Betts, Miss French. I'm the Chambers County Sheriff."

Relief washed over Sophie as she exhaled the breath she

hadn't realized she was holding. She cracked the door open slightly, just enough to peer out and see a man in a crisp uniform. His presence, authoritative yet non-threatening, put her somewhat at ease. She hesitated, then offered a tentative smile as she invited him inside. "Good morning, Sheriff. I'm Sophie."

"Morning, Miss French. I know who you are," Sheriff Betts replied with a polite nod. "I'm sorry to bother you so early. I hope this isn't a bad time."

"No, it's fine," Sophie replied, stepping aside to let him in. Sheriff Betts was tall and broad-shouldered, with an air of quiet confidence that belied his youthful appearance. He looked to be in his early thirties, with a neatly trimmed mustache, closely cropped blondish hair, and pale green eyes that softened with concern as they met hers. As he removed his hat and entered the room, the sunlight streaming through the window cast a warm glow on the brightly colored sofa with bold prints, yet the atmosphere felt tense and heavy with unspoken words.

"Would you mind telling me what this is about?" Sophie asked, her voice hesitant.

Sheriff Betts sighed, a weight in his tone. "It's about what happened last night. Andrew Von Stook's assault on you."

Sophie stiffened, her heart sinking as fear wrapped

41

around her like a vise. "How did you know?" she whispered, her voice barely audible.

"Well, someone witnessed the entire incident. Someone besides Miss Keller, who I understand, intervened. I know you may be reluctant, but I'm here this morning to ask you to file charges against him."

Sophie's eyes widened, panic flaring within her. "Oh, Sheriff, I don't know. I spent the entire night talking to Madelyn about Andrew and his... his creepy history. I've only been here a few months, and *I'm just not sure.*"

"I understand, Miss French. But Miss Keller is right. Andrew has a history of assaults, but I've never been able to bring charges, much less secure a conviction. Most people in this town are scared to death of him because of his father's control over the entire county. Since coming here from St. Louis a couple of years ago, I've learned that Peter Von Stook's power reaches far beyond just the county. It has for a very long time. But I need to put a stop to Andrew. *No one* is above the law. Maybe you can help."

Sophie listened, her mind flashing back to the previous night, the way Andrew had cornered her, the paralyzing fear that had coursed through her veins, leaving her feeling like a trapped animal. She didn't need the Sheriff to remind her of the Von Stook family's stranglehold on the town. Since arriving that summer, Sophie had witnessed it firsthand. She had come to understand all too well the severe consequences of crossing Peter Von Stook.

Her voice trembled as she spoke. "I don't know if I can do it, Sheriff Betts. It's the *Von Stooks.*"

Leaning forward, Sheriff Betts spoke in a gentle yet firm tone, "I know you're afraid, but you won't be alone. There are others I'm talking to who want to come forward, who are just as frightened as you. But if we don't start taking a stand, Andrew will continue to hurt people, always under the protective wing of his father."

Sophie's mind swirled with conflicting emotions. She knew the Sheriff was right. She wanted to find the courage to do the right thing; to stand against the evil that had taken root in the town. But the thought of challenging Andrew and his powerful father sent a chill down her spine. Her gaze drifted toward the window, where the warm rays of sunlight spilled into the room, brightening the space. She thought of her father, a man of principle who had always taught her to stand up for what was right, no matter the cost. Could she find that same courage within herself?

The Sheriff's voice broke through her thoughts. "Sophie," he said, looking directly into her eyes, his expression earnest, "we need your help."

Almost as if on instinct, Sophie found herself nodding, her voice steady as she spoke. "Alright, Sheriff Betts. I'll do it. I'll give a statement and file the charges."

The Sheriff let out a relieved sigh, a hint of gratitude in his eyes. "Thank you, Sophie. You're doing the right thing. I'll do everything in my power to protect you."

His tone was grave and serious as he sat attentively, taking careful notes while Sophie recounted every harrowing detail of the previous night. She spoke for over an hour, her voice steady but her heart heavy with the weight of reliving the trauma. By the time she finished, she was utterly exhausted, emotionally drained by the ordeal of recounting it all.

"O.K., that's enough for now," the Sheriff interjected gently. "After school on Monday, come to the Sheriff's office, and we'll make the filing official. It's on the first floor of the Chambers County courthouse." He stood, tucking his cap beneath his arm. "I'll be there with Robert Hale, the Chambers County District Attorney, and a court stenographer."

Sophie nodded, letting out a deep sigh. "Alright, Sheriff. I'll be there." She paused, a thought suddenly surfacing. "Oh, by the way, Sheriff, may I bring someone with me?"

Sheriff Betts turned to her with a slight grin as he reached for the door. "If you're thinking of Miss Keller, I'm sure that won't be a problem. I saw her at the hospital early this morning, and she's already agreed to make a statement. And believe me, with her experiences patching up Andrew's victims in the emergency room, she'll have plenty to say."

A sense of relief and reassurance swept over Sophie, easing the knot of anxiety that had been tightening in her chest. As the Sheriff left, she felt a small flicker of hope, the first she had felt in a long time.

As Sheriff Betts opened the door, he gave a reassuring smile. "Like I said, Sophie, you won't be alone." His voice carried a warmth that momentarily eased her worries, but as she closed and locked the door behind him, her mind was bursting with conflicting emotions. She sank into a chair and struggled to calm herself, yet the events of the past day clawed at her composure. The terrifying encounter with Andrew, the Sheriff's visit, and now the Halloween festivities with her fifth graders, all weighed heavily on her. And above all loomed the daunting prospect of confronting Andrew, in court. She had to find strength, not just for herself, but for everyone Andrew had hurt.

When the McKinley School fifth graders began arriving, Sophie barely had time to steel herself. Their faces lit up with excitement, a welcome distraction from the turmoil inside her. She threw herself into the festivities, guiding her students through apple bobbing, sack races, and the art of carving grinning faces into pumpkins. For those few hours, the sound of children's laughter and the crunch of fallen leaves beneath their feet dulled the sharp edge of her fear. But as the day wore on, it became harder to suppress her darker thoughts. Her eyes kept drifting toward the wooden fence surrounding her yard, half-expecting to see Andrew lurking, his malevolent gaze watching her every move.

***

As the sun dipped low, casting long shadows across Brighton Avenue, Madelyn unexpectedly arrived with a smile and a wreath of autumn leaves in hand. "I thought you could use a little cheer," she said, holding up the wreath.

Sophie gave her a quick hug, appreciating the gesture but unable to shake the tension twisting inside her. "It's beautiful. Thank you, Madelyn. I'm so glad you're here."

Madelyn's eyes softened with concern. "Are you alright?" she asked gently.

Sophie glanced out at the rising harvest moon, its orange glow casting an eerie light over the porch. A chill ran down her spine. "Can you stay for a while?" she asked, her voice barely steady.

Madelyn smiled, though her eyes carried the same worry. "Of course, there's nowhere I'd rather be," she said with a smile, as she withdrew a large bottle of white Zinfandel from her shoulder bag. She settled into a large, overstuffed chair Sophie recently purchased from a second-hand store in Shale Pointe. It was a Cardinal room, but the weight of the conversation they were about to have made the air feel heavy.

"I've decided to file charges against Andrew," Sophie began, her voice trembling. "But I'm terrified, Madelyn."

Madelyn leaned forward, her voice firm but laced with empathy. "I'm scared too, Sophie. But we have to stop him. We can't let him keep *doing* this to people."

Sophie shuddered as she thought again of Andrew's hands on her skin, his twisted smile, the rage in his eyes. "His father will know the moment we step into that courthouse," she whispered, dread seeping into her words.

Madelyn nodded, her face grim. "He probably already knows. But you haven't seen the things I have, Sophie. The people I've treated in the emergency room… their bruises, the broken bones; the fear in their eyes when they talk about Andrew. All the while knowing they can't do anything about it. He'll never stop unless we make him."

Madelyn's hands trembled slightly as she reached for Sophie's. "This has been ingrained in him since he was born… that he's untouchable, that he can take whatever he wants and hurt whoever he pleases. It's time we prove that wrong."

Sophie bit her lip, struggling to find the courage Madelyn was calling forth. "What if he comes after us?"

Madelyn's gaze sharpened, her resolve unshakable. "That's why we must do this publicly, in open court. It will force him into the light, and every move he makes after that will just be more evidence to use against him. We won't be his silent victims anymore."

Sophie exhaled slowly, feeling the flicker of strength growing within her. "You're right. We have to stop him, no matter what it takes."

The conversation weighed heavy on both women as they sat in silence, contemplating the battle that lay ahead. They knew Andrew was dangerous, but together, they were determined to bring him to justice.

***

Monday, November 2, dawned bitterly cold, the first hints of winter biting through the air. Later that day as Sophie and Madelyn walked side by side up the wide stone steps of the Chambers County Courthouse, it had gotten even colder. The weight of their decision settled in with each step. The courthouse loomed above them, its tall copper doors reflecting the gray sky. Inside, the warmth was a relief, but the atmosphere was somber. The marble floors echoed with their footsteps as they passed rows of wooden benches and framed portraits of stern-faced men. Judges, past sheriffs – there was even a portrait of some Von Stook ancestor, his eyes seemingly following them as they walked the long hallway.

They entered a cluttered office where Sheriff Betts stood behind a large wooden desk, his face stern but welcoming. "Miss French, Madelyn. Thank you for coming," he said, gesturing for them to sit. The room smelled of old papers and pipe tobacco, the wooden floor creaking beneath their feet.

A man in a sharp pin-striped suit and a red and blue bowtie rose to greet them. "This is Robert Hale, the County Prosecutor," the Sheriff introduced. Hale, a neatly groomed man in his early fifties, offered a kind but serious smile. "Ladies, I want to thank you for your courage. I know this isn't easy, but I assure you, not *everyone* in Southern Illinois answers to Peter Von Stook."

Sophie's stomach tightened as she recounted the events of that terrible night for the second time in 2 days. An older woman sat at a desk across from them, her fingers flying across the dark black stenotype machine, the clacking of its keys, capturing every word. As Sophie spoke, the cold reality of what she was doing sank in, but with it came a flicker of empowerment. The weight of fear was still there, but now it shared space with a growing sense of strength.

When it was over, the prosecutor smiled. "That's what I need. You have both been incredibly brave, and we'll be ready for the next steps soon."

As Sophie and Madelyn left the courthouse, the wind whipped around them, but the chill that gripped Sophie was no longer just from the cold. It was fear mixed with something new. Hope.

Sheriff Betts escorted them down the courthouse steps, his face a mix of gratitude and concern. "Thank you, Sophie. I know it wasn't easy to relive everything again, but it's official now. These charges will be on Judge Hemming's desk first thing in the morning. Andrew will be brought in for questioning, and this time, we're going to make sure he faces the consequences."

*** 

As Sophie and Madelyn stepped onto the sidewalk, Sheriff Betts made his way back to his office. The last light of day was fading. The sun had dipped below the horizon, casting long, eerie shadows over the courthouse steps. The frigid evening air bit at their skin, their breath visible in quick, nervous puffs. The sense of relief they felt after filing

50

the charges was quickly overshadowed by a deep, gnawing fear. They had done it, taken the first step in standing up to Andrew Von Stook, but the victory felt fragile, as if it could shatter at any moment.

Just as they reached Madelyn's car, a voice cut through the stillness behind them, cold and mocking. "It's so inspiring to see Stookton's finest citizens stepping up to do their civic duty."

Sophie and Madelyn froze, their blood turning to ice. Slowly, they turned to see Andrew emerging from the shadows, his face twisted into a sneer. The dim light from the courthouse steps illuminated his expression, one of barely contained fury and malicious intent.

"Get away from us!" Madelyn's voice rang out, sharp with fear and defiance. "Sheriff Betts is just inside. Take *one step* closer, and I'll scream."

Andrew's lip curled into a snarl, his eyes narrowing into slits. "You little girl scouts really think you can make a difference? My father will crush this whole affair within a day. And who knows? Maybe you and that noble sheriff will even manage to keep your jobs." He leaned in closer, his breath hot and reeking of alcohol, his face mere inches from theirs. "But don't worry about calling for Betts. You're safe from me tonight," he hissed, the words dripping with venom. "But soon enough, I'm sure we'll all have a chance to talk...

privately." His eyes darkened with rage as he lit a cigarette, the flame flickering in the cold night air. "I swear to *God*! I'll deal with both of you personally. You have no idea what my family's capable of… what *I'm* capable of."

Sophie watched, paralyzed with fear, as Andrew disappeared back into the shadows, his parting words hanging ominously in the air. She felt lightheaded, her knees threatening to buckle beneath her. Madelyn's firm grip on her arm kept her steady, and her voice, though strained, was calm. "We have to go, Sophie. Now."

They hurried to the car, Madelyn quickly locking the doors before starting the engine. The roar of the big Ford's V-8 engine filled the silence as they sped out of the parking lot, leaving the courthouse, and Andrew, behind. Sophie's hands trembled as she whispered, "Madelyn, he is *serious*. He will *not* let this go. I could see it in his eyes. He won't stop until he's had his revenge."

Madelyn didn't reply immediately, her gaze fixed on the road ahead as the courthouse faded into the distance. She knew Sophie was right. They had just declared war on one of the most powerful families in Southern Illinois, and Andrew Von Stook was a dangerous man with a long reach. The weight of their actions settled heavily on both women as they drove in silence, each lost in their own troubled thoughts.

# Chapter 4

## Valentine's Day

Sophie stood at her kitchen window, staring out at the snow-covered world beyond. The warmth of her small bungalow was a stark contrast to the icy scene outside. Deep snowdrifts buried cars, sidewalks, and driveways along Brighton Avenue. She glanced at the thermometer mounted beyond the ice-glazed window, shivering at the sight of the needle hovering at sixteen degrees. Cupping a steaming mug of tea between her hands, she tried to let its warmth seep into her bones, but the chill of the past few months was hard to shake.

The conversation with Sheriff Betts the night before replayed in her mind, each word echoing with a cold finality. She hadn't slept; the fear and uncertainty gnawed at her all night. As she tried to find the right word to describe what the sheriff had told her, only one came to mind: chilling. The sudden ringing of the telephone jolted her from her thoughts, and she quickly answered. "Hello?"

"Good morning, Miss French. I hope you're staying warm this morning." It was Mr. Wilkes, the school principal.

"Good morning, Mr. Wilkes. Not as warm as I'd like to be," she replied, forcing a light tone.

"Well, you won't have to brave the cold today," he continued. "This snowstorm has paralyzed the entire area. We're canceling school for today, and maybe tomorrow, too - depending on how things go."

"Oh no, the children will be so disappointed to miss the Valentine's Day party," Sophie said, her voice tinged with regret.

Mr. Wilkes sympathized but encouraged her to enjoy the unexpected day off. "Try to relax and stay warm, Sophie. And Happy Valentine's Day."

"Thank you, Mr. Wilkes. You too." As she hung up the phone, the prospect of a day off did little to lift her spirits. If anything, being alone with her thoughts all day was daunting. She had been looking forward to the distraction of her fifth graders, especially after last night's unsettling conversation with Sheriff Betts.

Pouring more tea, Sophie picked up the phone again. She needed to talk to Madelyn. Over the past few months, their friendship had deepened, born from shared fear and a need for mutual support. They had become nearly inseparable. As it turned out, the charges filed against Andrew by Sophie and Madelyn had emboldened women from both Stookton *and* neighboring Shale Pointe to come forward. It resulted in Andrew's conviction of five counts of assault and a four-year prison sentence. But the victory had come at a price. The Von Stook family had not taken kindly to the verdict, and Sophie specifically had been the target of their intimidation ever since.

The hospital switchboard operator transferred Sophie's call to the emergency room, and soon Madelyn's cheerful voice came through the line. "Sophie! Can you believe this weather?"

Despite everything, Sophie smiled. Madelyn's unshakable optimism was a beacon of light in these dark times. "Looks like the weather didn't give you a day off," Sophie replied.

Madelyn laughed, her voice a welcome sound amid Sophie's worries. "No rest for the wicked... or the ER staff. I was here at 5:30 this morning. But I heard the schools are closed, so it looks like you're a woman of leisure today, right?"

"Not by my choice," Sophie sighed. "I'm not thrilled about spending the day cooped up here, staring out the window. Madelyn, we really need to talk. Have you spoken to Sheriff Betts since last night?"

"No, I haven't," Madelyn replied. "He usually stops by the hospital every morning before I start my rounds, but I haven't seen him today. With this unexpected winter storm, I'm sure he has his hands full. Why do you ask?"

"Oh my God, Maddy, you won't *believe* what's happened," Sophie said, her voice trembling with urgency. "You have to talk to him."

"Hold on," Sophie said, "Ted's walking in right now. Let me call you back."

"Yes, please do. And brace yourself for some really shocking news," Sophie added before hanging up.

Sophie stared out the window at the frozen world outside, still struggling to process last night's revelations by Sheriff Betts. Richard Keeling, the district Congressman for Stookton and personal attorney to Peter Von Stook, had managed to secure Andrew's release from Clayburgh Penitentiary pending a new trial. Sophie had long known Keeling's political career was intertwined with the Von Stook family's influence, but she had hoped that the justice system would hold. Instead, Keeling's close ties to the mining industry, and his dependency on the Von Stook family's financial support, made him a powerful ally for Peter Von Stook. With Keeling in Washington for his third term, thanks to Von Stook financial backing, it was clear that Peter was calling in favors. Sophie shuddered at the thought of Andrew's impending freedom and wondered where he was now.

Twenty minutes later, Madelyn called back. Her tone was soft. "Sophie, Ted told me everything. Now look. I know you're scared. So am I. But I'm coming over as soon as I can. We'll get through this together, okay?"

Sophie's eyes filled with tears, the weight of everything pressing down on her. "Oh! Thank you, Madelyn. When does your shift end today?"

"At two this afternoon," Madelyn said." "I can be at your place by three. We need to meet as soon as possible. Ted wants all three of us to get together later. He'll probably be tied up most of the day escorting county trucks to clear the snow drifts. But like I said, he will be available until later. In the meantime, you and I can go someplace public, where we feel safe until Ted shows up. We should head downtown to the Cardinal Café. He thinks it's best if we wait for him there. If he gets delayed, we can return to your place and hunker down. But right now, no one really knows Andrew's whereabouts."

"Madelyn, I don't know what I'd do without you," Sophie whispered.

"You'll never have to find out," Madelyn assured her. "I'll be there soon."

\*\*\*

When Madelyn and Sophie arrived at the Cardinal Cafe, the night air was bitterly cold. Stookton had turned into a frozen landscape of drifting snow, with icicles hanging from storefronts like giant stalactites. Valentine's Day decorations and ornately heart-shaped boxes of chocolates adorned shop windows. The uncomfortably 's neon sign flickered erratically, casting a warm glow that beckoned, "Come inside." The diner's interior offered a stark contrast to the frigid air beyond its large, frosted windows, filled with the comforting hum of friendly conversation and the clatter of dishes.

Madelyn brushed snowflakes from her hair and settled into their booth. Her crystal-blue eyes sparkled with a hint of mischief. Laughing, she teased, "Well, if nothing else, I have the perfect remedy for this cold. I brought a little flask of peppermint schnapps to mix with Cardinal's famous hot chocolate. Nothing says 'Happy Valentine's Day' like a bit of extra warmth!"

Sophie reached across the table, squeezing Madelyn's hand gratefully. "You are such a great friend, Maddy. I don't know how I would have gotten through these past few months without your support."

"Same here," Madelyn said brightly. "Who would have thought two city girls would end up together in this small town? It feels like fate to me."

Sophie's smile faded as she glanced around the cafe, her mood darkening. "Madelyn, I can't *believe* Andrew is out! He was supposed to serve four years in Clayburgh."

"I know," Madelyn replied, her voice laced with concern. "Ted says Andrew's release has Peter Von Stook's fingerprints all over it. And no one knows exactly where he is now," she said, her voice noticeably strained. "I can't get his threat out of my mind. *And –* He's had months to plot his revenge."

Sophie's expression grew somber. "The Richard Keeling connection is terrifying. He's not just the Von Stook family's attorney; he's a U.S. *Congressman.* With that kind of influence, how can we ever be sure we're truly safe from Andrew?"

After two hours in the place, and too much schnapps, cocoa, and dessert, Sheriff Betts had still not arrived. They paid for their meals, bundled up, and prepared to leave for Sophie's bungalow on Brighton Avenue.

***

Outside, they trudged through the snow toward Madelyn's car. The night air was even colder than when they had arrived, and the streets were deserted. Sophie glanced around, feeling exposed and shivering as Madelyn rummaged through her purse for the car keys. Once inside the car, Madelyn turned on the windshield wipers and adjusted the heater, waiting for the engine to warm up.

"Well, it looks like the intersection at Main and Dewey streets is closed because of the snow," Madelyn said. "I'll have to take the old Coal Road and circle back to Brighton Avenue. Give it a few minutes, and this damned car will eventually warm up."

A block away, a shadowy figure remained hidden behind the wheel of a large, dark-colored sedan, its engine purring softly. The figure's eyes, hidden beneath a wide-brimmed Beau Brummel hat, had tracked them since they stepped outside the café. As Madelyn pulled away from the curb, the dark figure behind the wheel smoothly maneuvered for position behind Madelyn's Ford, following, but maintaining a cautious distance.

As Madelyn navigated the narrow, winding stretch of blacktop, she watched the distant lights of the town square fade in the rearview mirror. The courthouse clock, distant but clear in the still night, chimed ten times, marking the passing of another hour.

The drive to Sophie's house was usually brief, but tonight the road was treacherous. The narrow ribbon of pavement, flanked by cliffs and ridges of old shale pits, was barely visible through the snow and ice. Madelyn's cautious pace was a testament to the hazardous conditions. She leaned forward, squinting through the frosted windshield, straining to see through the wintry veil.

Sophie sat quietly, glancing occasionally at the side view mirror. For a fleeting moment, she thought she saw a brief flicker of headlights behind them. Her heart skipped a beat. Doubt gnawed at her. Was she imagining things, or was there truly someone following them? The isolation of the road and her growing anxiety made her question her perception.

Without warning, Madelyn's voice trembled, "Sophie, I think someone's tailing us, and it looks like they're speeding up."

Sophie whipped her head around to peer through the back window. There was no denying it now. The headlights were closing in, maintaining a relentless pace. The growing sense of dread in Sophie's chest was replaced by full-blown panic. "Maybe they just want to pass us," Madelyn suggested, a slight quiver in her voice. "But why the urgency in weather like this?"

Madelyn's eyes were locked on the rearview mirror as she approached the narrowest section of Coal Road, a narrow little bridge that spanned a frozen creek. The headlights behind them grew brighter, more insistent. Determined to escape, Madelyn pressed the accelerator, urging the car to go faster. The pursuing vehicle matched their speed effortlessly, closing the gap with chilling precision.

The increasing brightness from the headlights cast eerie shadows across the dashboard, heightening the sense of impending danger.

"Sophie, this guy is right on top of us. I can't push the car any faster; it's too dangerous in these conditions."

The first violent jolt came without warning, causing the car to lurch. Sophie gasped, "Oh my God!"

"Is it him?!" Madelyn yelled, desperately trying to keep control.

The big sedan rammed them again with force, sending Madelyn's car spinning uncontrollably onto the icy bridge. The impact with the cement abutment was jarring, a brutal shock that seemed to rip through the car's frame. Before Madelyn could fully process what was happening, a final crushing blow sent the car off the road. The metal groaned and screeched as it collided with the pavement, a spectacular shower of sparks and shattered glass exploding into the night.

In the aftermath of the collision, silence fell, broken only by the relentless hiss of leaking fluids, the ticking sound of an overheated engine cooling, and the screech of a slowly spinning wheel. Madelyn's car had flipped onto its roof. The disorientation was overwhelming. Pain surged through Madelyn's body, making her cry out in agony. The acrid smell of gasoline, antifreeze, and motor oil filled her nostrils, causing her to gag. She turned to find Sophie beside her, both women now thrown into the rear seat, half-sprawled on the floorboard.

The eerie stillness was interrupted by the sound of a car rolling to a stop nearby. The crunch of tires on the icy road. Fear washed over Sophie as she saw the terror mirrored in Madelyn's eyes. "Sophie, stay calm and stay put!" Madelyn urged through gritted teeth, despite the excruciating pain. She struggled to free herself from the wreckage as the sound of approaching footsteps grew louder. A figure emerged from the shadows, silhouetted against the car's headlights.

"Stay in the car," Madelyn whispered urgently. "Can you move? We need to get out."

But it was too late. The figure moved with swift, determined steps toward the wrecked vehicle. He wrenched open Madelyn's door and grabbed her coat with a menacing grin.

Driven by a primal instinct to survive, the two women fought through their pain, struggling to escape the wreckage. They managed to scramble out of the car, their movements clumsy and uncoordinated as they slipped and stumbled on the icy road. Sophie's hope flickered bricfly as she suggested, "If we can reach the woods, we might find somewhere to hide."

But the icy ground betrayed them. They fell hard onto the pavement, their injuries flaring in agony. The figure advanced once again with predatory precision. He was back on Madelyn in an instant, her futile struggles overshadowed by his brutal strength. As he brought a heavy object down upon her skull, Sophie looked away, unable to bear the sight. The sickening crack of the blow echoed in the night, followed by the disturbing sound of liquid dripping, signaling Madelyn's demise.

Sophie, paralyzed by terror and resignation, fought weakly to stand. She stumbled, collapsing again. The man seized her by the hair, dragging her closer to Madelyn's lifeless body. As she lay mere inches away from her friend, Sophie's eyes locked with Madelyn's vacant stare, the terror and silent plea in her friend's eyes fading into an empty gaze. As Sophie felt the cold grip of the man's hand on her throat, a chilling sense of finality overcame her. With the darkness closing in, fleeting memories of her father, her fifth-grade students, and a childhood memory of a merry-go-round swirled through her mind, each one fading as the darkness overtook her.

In the oppressive silence of the cold night, the dark figure stood over the lifeless forms on the icy pavement. Snow began to fall in earnest, covering the scene of brutality with a deceptive veil of peace and beauty.

In a voice that was disturbingly gentle, the man whispered into the cold night air, "Happy Valentine's Day."

# Chapter 5

## River's Edge

The morning after Valentine's Day was bleak in Stookton. The sun barely made an effort to pierce through thick, overcast clouds that blanketed the sky, casting a gray, damp pall over the small town. Sheriff Ted Betts stood at his office window, staring out at the empty streets lined with snow-covered houses. The silence of the town felt unnatural, and Ted's mind was weighted with anxiety as he thought about the two early morning calls that had shaken him to his core.

Sophie and Madelyn were missing. Sophie hadn't shown up at McKinley Elementary to teach her fifth-grade class, and Madelyn had missed her shift at Shale Pointe Hospital. The two women, both young and vibrant, and except for the Von Stook family and their cronies, were beloved by everyone in town. The last time anyone had seen them was leaving the Cardinal Café the night before. In a place like Stookton, news like this spread fast, and Ted could feel the collective fear rising in the community, thickening the tension in the air. He knew his own emotions were far too close to this case. The pang of knowing how dear both women were to him urged him to reach out for help from someone who could bring an objective eye to the investigation.

He picked up the receiver and reached for the telephone, hesitated just a second, and then dialed the number of the only person he trusted to help him see things clearly.

"Ted Betts!" a gruff yet familiar voice answered. "Hell, I heard you were dead."

A slight smile tugged at Ted's mouth, even though his heart was heavy. "Abel," he said, his voice tight. "I need your help."

There was a pause, and Ted could imagine Abel Stark on the other end, sitting in his cluttered office, perhaps doodling on a pad while thinking about the cold Pabst Blue Ribbon waiting for him that evening. Abel was an aging but sharp-witted homicide investigator with a knack for cutting through to the truth. Right now, Ted needed that more than ever.

"Still hanging on in that two-bit sheriffless town, huh?" Abel's voice held a hint of a smile, but Ted knew his friend could sense the urgency in his voice.

"Couldn't escape it if I tried," Ted replied with a forced chuckle. But then he let the heaviness of the moment sink in. "Listen, Abel, I've got a double missing person's case… two young women who are close to me. Sophie French, a schoolteacher, and Madelyn Kellar, an ER nurse. They've been gone since last night, and I'm too close to this. I need your objectivity, your experience... I need you here, Abel." The humor faded from Abel's voice. "What's going on, Ted?"

Ted's throat tightened, and he had to swallow before he could speak. "They're twenty-three and twenty-five. Sophie French is the teacher, and Madelyn Kellar is... she's a nurse over at Shale Pointe Hospital just across the state line." He struggled to say her name without his voice breaking. Madelyn meant something more to him than most people realized. Abel likely picked up on that unspoken sentiment. "They're both beloved here, Abel. The town's in a panic already."

Abel's tone shifted to a deep seriousness. "Is this personal for you, Ted?"

Ted didn't answer. He didn't have to.

"Alright, Ted. I'll be there by six tonight," Abel said, his voice resolute. "We'll figure this out."

Ted sank into his worn, squeaky desk chair, feeling the weight of the situation pressing down on him. His gaze drifted to a framed photo of Madelyn on his desk, her bright smile, the image frozen in time. He clenched his jaw, determination welling up inside him. He would not stop until he found her and Sophie. His mind drifted to Andrew Von Stook. Dangerous as hell, and freed from Clayburgh Penitentiary only two days earlier. The timing was too coincidental, and Ted couldn't shake the nagging suspicion. "I won't rest until I find you," he whispered to Madelyn's photo.

His eyes moved to a worn old map of St. Louis. He treasured it like the photo of a beloved family member. The tattered map exhibited dozens of colored pins. Locations of cases marking the scenes he and Abel had long since solved. The map of St. Louis felt like a living thing. Each street and corner brought memories of Abel Stark rushing back. *Too* many late nights, drinking *too* much Scotch and soda. Cases solved, loves lost – but mostly, the bond they had forged over years of fighting crime in a city that never made it easy.

Ted had met Abel back when prohibition was law, and Abel was a relentless detective in the Special Crimes Unit. Abel had a reputation as a man who didn't tolerate a single drop of illegal booze on his beat. He was tough. A stickler for the law, and damn proud of it. Standing at 5'10" and built like an unbreakable wall, Abel commanded respect and attention. He had grown up in a rough part of New York City, but at sixteen, had moved with his family to St. Louis, where the blues clubs and breweries were as common as churches in smaller towns. The city had made Abel street-smart. It had given him a resilience and determination that would serve him and others throughout his life.

During World War I, Abel had enlisted and served with distinction, earning commendations for his bravery and tactical skills. After the war, he returned to St. Louis. He joined the Missouri State Police Department and, within five years, was known as a detective who went after only the biggest bootleggers in illegal liquor. Whenever the FBI was in St. Louis working a case, J. Edgar's boys wanted Abel Stark on the case with them.

Then, in December 1933, the 18th Amendment was repealed, and Prohibition ended. After having a few drinks, Abel transitioned to homicide. His sharp instincts and unwavering principles became his trademarks. Ted admired his mentor's sense of duty and carried much of Abel's no-nonsense style into his own work. Now, three years after leaving St. Louis, Ted faced one of the most personal cases of his career. The irony? It was in the very town he initially thought would be a reprieve from the violence and corruption of the big city. Abel heading to Stookton was the only hopeful thought he was capable of conjuring.

71

The biting chill of winter seemed to creep straight to the bone as Ted and Abel Stark plodded through the thick snow lining the frozen banks of the Missouri River. Their breath crystallized into misty puffs that hung briefly in the frigid air before disappearing. Abel had been in Stookton barely two hours when they'd received an anonymous tip directing them to this spot on the river's edge. Ted's gut was already screaming that this was anything but routine.

The river lay blanketed in ice, its stillness disrupted only by the distant sound of water flowing beneath. The eerie silence blanketed the scene, broken only by the crunch of their boots in the snow. As they approached the spot described in the call, Ted felt his pulse pounding, his steps burdened by a sense of foreboding.

"There," Abel murmured, gesturing to a clump of reeds protruding from the snow.

Ted's gaze followed Abel's finger, and as his eyes fell on the figures nestled within the frozen brush. His heart sank. Two pale, almost ghostly shapes lay twisted and contorted in the ice, their forms frozen in lifeless, eternal stillness. Ted's breath caught as he recognized one of them. His knees

72

felt weak.

"No...," he choked, his voice a hoarse whisper. "Madelyn..."

Her name slipped from his lips, barely audible, as he fought back the grief threatening to consume him. Her face, usually so full of life, was now ice-covered. Frozen into a macabre, haunting grin. Ted dropped to one knee beside her, his fingers hovering just above her, as if touching her might somehow break the spell and bring her back. Tears stung his eyes, freezing on his cheeks in the brutal cold.

"Madelyn, I'm so sorry..." His voice cracked, emotion spilling out despite his efforts to stay composed.

Abel crouched beside him, laying a steady hand on Ted's shoulder, a silent gesture of support. Both men were seasoned officers, hardened by years of confronting death, but this, finding Madelyn like this – it was a nightmare. This wasn't just a case. It was personal.

"Ted, we need to document everything carefully," Abel said softly, his tone grave. "Someone wanted you to find them here."

Ted's gaze hardened, shifting from Madelyn's still form to the untouched snow beyond. "You're right," he replied, voice steadying. "This is a message," He paused. From someone."

Ted scanned the area, eyes sharp and determined. That's when he noticed them, a set of footprints leading away from the bodies, still crisp and unblemished by the snowfall. "Look," he said, gesturing toward the tracks, "they're fresh. Whoever did this didn't go far."

Abel's eyes followed Ted's gesture, and he nodded. "Let's see where they lead."

They moved with urgency, following the trail through the snow, their breaths quickening with each step. The tracks eventually led them to a narrow path where a car had clearly been parked, its tires leaving deep impressions in the snow. "Damn," Ted muttered, frustration clawing at him. Whoever had done this was gone, but he felt that, without any evidence, it might be close.

Abel placed a hand on his shoulder, grounding him. "We'll get them, Ted. We'll pull every record, talk to every contact, turn over every damn stone. We won't stop until the people behind this pay."

Ted nodded, his resolve hardening. "For Sophie. For Madelyn. They deserve justice."

As they returned to the scene to finish gathering evidence, Ted's mind raced with memories, of Madelyn's laughter, her smile, the whispered promises they'd shared. He would stop at nothing to find those responsible.

Back at the Chambers County Sheriff's Office, the

atmosphere was thick with tension. The murders of Sophie French and Madelyn Keller had shaken the department to its core. Desks were littered with files, phones rang with tips, and Ted's office was a whirlwind of activity. Yet Ted himself sat in silence, staring at a photograph of Madelyn.

The door creaked open, and Abel stepped inside, closing it behind him with a solemn look. He crossed his arms, watching Ted with understanding eyes. "Ted," Abel said gently, "we need to talk."

Ted looked up, his eyes red-rimmed from grief. He nodded, setting the photograph aside, but the pain lingered, hanging between them like a shadow.

"Madelyn and I… we were in love," Ted began, his voice barely audible. "We kept it quiet; thought we could protect her by keeping things under wraps. But now… it feels like I failed her."

Abel took a seat across from him, his gaze steady. "Ted, there was no way for you to know. The Von Stooks… they're dangerous people. They've hurt a lot of good folks. But don't let them make you think this is on you. If they did have anything to do with this, we'll find out. We'll make this right."

Ted's jaw clenched, a flicker of anger joining his grief. "She was threatened after she and Sophie testified against

Andrew Von Stook in court. They *both* were. And now, a *day* after he's released from Clayburgh, she's gone. Sophie, too. This isn't just a coincidence."

Abel nodded. "Then we follow that lead. If he's involved, he's not getting away with it."

Abel nodded, his gaze steady. "Then our next step is to secure a court order to question Andrew's attorney and his father. If they have any involvement or know anything, we'll make sure they realize the consequences of staying silent. We also need to go back over the witness statements and talk to anyone who saw Sophie or Madelyn at the café the other night."

Before they could continue, a deputy appeared in the doorway, breathless. "Sheriff Betts, Detective Stark… you're not going to believe this. Mr. Murphy from the Rexall Drug Store just called. He said Andrew Von Stook showed up an hour ago, looking like he owned the place, and got a prescription filled. Murphy figured, with all the rumors flying around, he'd better call us. Apparently, Andrew's back at the Von Stook mansion right now."

Ted's jaw tightened, exchanging a quick look with Abel. "Get the car. We're heading over there."

\*\*\*

The Von Stook mansion sat at the end of a long, treelined driveway just off of Dewey Street, its ornate architecture imposing against the winter sky. Within minutes, Ted and Abel were at the door, ushered in by the butler, who seemed uneasy as he led them into the study.

***

An hour later, Abel sat across from Andrew in the stark interrogation room of the Chambers County Sheriff's Office. Andrew Von Stook's perfectly styled dark hair, tailored jacket, and polished shoes gave him an air of privilege and arrogance. He was strikingly handsome with cold blue eyes that hinted at something ruthless beneath the charm. He looked more like someone just back from a luxury vacation than a man who'd recently been behind bars.

Abel studied Andrew's posture and demeanor, noting the smug smile playing on his lips as he looked from Ted to Abel, seemingly entertained by the proceedings. Ted watched him as well, his expression controlled but his jaw set. Abel's calm voice broke the silence.

"Mr. Von Stook, I'm glad you chose to cooperate with us," Abel began, his tone steady. "We have a few questions about the recent murders of Sophie French and Madelyn Keller."

Andrew's smirk widened, and he leaned back in his chair with a casual arrogance. "Well, Detective Stark, I knew you'd be wasting my time, so why should I waste more by having my father's lawyers drag me in here? Better to get this ridiculous game over with now."

Ted's voice was cold as he asked, "Andrew, where were you last night?"

Andrew's eyes flicked to Ted, his smirk deepening. "As you should know, Sheriff, I was just released yesterday afternoon. I spent most of the ride home sleeping in the back seat while our driver took me back to my father's house. I've been there ever since. Where you both found me. If you wanted to confirm that, you should have asked the driver while you were there."

Abel kept his gaze steady. "We'll be verifying that alibi, Mr. Von Stook. In the meantime, can you confirm if you had any contact with Sophie or Madelyn after your release?"

Andrew's smirk turned to a sneer. "Sure. I called them both and invited them over for a little celebration." His tone dripped with sarcasm as he added, "Hell no, Detective. I didn't have any reason to speak to those... women."

Ted kept his voice even, though his anger simmered just

below the surface. "We have witnesses who say you threatened both of them after they testified against you. Care to explain that?"

Andrew laughed, his eyes gleaming with mockery. "Oh, come on, Sheriff. People love to talk. Sure, I may have had a few choice words for them, but threats? Isn't that a bit dramatic?"

Abel leaned forward, his voice now carrying a sharper edge. "Andrew, this isn't a game. Two women are dead. Show some respect."

Andrew's smirk faded, replaced with contempt. "Respect? For what? Two nobodies who apparently got on someone's shit list? Look, their deaths are unfortunate, but don't expect me to get sentimental."

Ted's hands clenched under the table, but he kept his face calm. "You really think you're untouchable, don't you? That your family's money and influence will shield you forever. But we'll get to the truth, Andrew. And when we do, you'll face the consequences."

Andrew chuckled, his tone icy. "You're welcome to try, Sheriff. After all, isn't that what you're paid for?" He shot a mock salute, leaning back in his chair.

Without breaking eye contact, Abel leaned in so close that their faces were nearly touching. "Don't leave town, Andrew. We'll be in touch." His voice was low but intense, carrying the weight of an unspoken threat.

Andrew stood with a smug smile, buttoning his jacket. "Always a pleasure, gentlemen. I'll be sure to keep my calendar clear."

As he left, the silence in the room was heavy. Ted's gaze followed Andrew until the door closed, his frustration evident. He turned to Abel, his expression grim. "He's guilty, Abel. I can feel it."

Abel's face was thoughtful, though he shared Ted's anger. "Oh, he's hiding something. That's certain. But I don't know Ted. We need to be prepared for a dead end. If the chauffeur who picked him up at Penitentiary confirms his alibi, the time Andrew left the prison and the time he arrived home? We might be left with nothing."

The two men left the room and walked out into the biting winter night. They made their way to Ted's place, where they spent the next hours poring over the case and sharing memories from years past. Perhaps too much prompted them to bounce from absolute resolve to solve the case, or - if Andrew's alibi held, complete uncertainty.

# Chapter 6

## A Tiny Favor

Peter Von Stook stood at the towering bay windows of his opulent office, his broad frame silhouetted against the eerie glow of the industrial town below. The landscape of Stookton sprawled out before him, a labyrinth of soot-streaked brick factories, narrow alleyways, and towering smokestacks. The cold winter sun sank lower on the horizon, its waning light casting jagged shadows across the town's cobbled streets. Each brick seemed to carry the weight of history and exploitation, silent witnesses to the relentless ambition of the man who now surveyed his empire.

The office itself was a testament to Peter's wealth and ego. Rich mahogany walls bore the weight of ancestral portraits; each face etched with the same stern determination that now carved deep lines into Peter's own. A grand, polished desk dominated the room, its surface cluttered with ledgers, correspondence, and a gilded photograph that drew the eye. The air was thick with the scent of leather-bound volumes, aged wood, and a faint undercurrent of the brandy swirling in Peter's hand.

Peter himself was the embodiment of ruthless capitalism. His barrel chest and commanding posture exuded the confidence of a man who had built an empire on the backs of the laborers who toiled in the roaring brickyards below. His sharp, predatory eyes betrayed a mind perpetually calculating, seeking opportunity even in the misfortune of others. To the townsfolk, he was a tyrant cloaked in respectability, a man who controlled not just the bricks they made but the very air they breathed, polluted and heavy with the smoke of his coal-fired kilns.

The brickyards roared day and night, their towering chimneys belching thick plumes of black smoke into a perpetually gray sky. The unrelenting rhythm of industry drummed in the distance, a sinister symphony underscoring the lives of the workers who labored under conditions as harsh as the furnace temperatures. The town, though alive with industry, bore the scars of Peter's unyielding grip, a community both sustained and suffocated by his greed.

On his desk, a photograph from an extravagant Capitol reception, a tableau of wealth and power that reflected his partnership with Congressman Richard Keeling. Peter's thin lips curled into a sardonic smile as his eyes lingered on the image. Keeling wasn't just an ally; he was a pawn, a puppet dancing to Peter's tune. Their alliance, forged in the dark corridors of mutual gain, allowed Peter to fortify his dominion, shielding him from scrutiny while advancing policies that made him increasingly rich.

But Peter's ambitions were not confined to Stookton. His ideology, fed by the fervent nationalism spreading across the Atlantic, had found a disturbing resonance in the rhetoric of Adolf Hitler. Articles praising Germany's economic revitalization under a strong regime littered his desk, each one devoured with rapt attention. Peter saw in Hitler not just a leader but a reflection of his own philosophy: control through strength, order through fear, and prosperity through the subjugation of the weak.

As the twilight deepened, painting the town in shadows, Peter turned away from the window. His thoughts were restless, circling a problem that gnawed at his carefully constructed world. His son, Andrew.

Andrew had always been a source of frustration, his reckless behavior an unwelcome contrast to Peter's calculated ruthlessness. Recent events had spiraled out of control, and despite Andrew's alibi holding firm for now, the rumors surrounding him threatened to unravel everything. Law enforcement, emboldened by the arrival of the seasoned Detective Stark, was closing in, their investigation threatening to drag the Von Stook name into scandal.

The sharp click of heels on the polished floor announced the arrival of Peter's secretary. "Congressman Keeling is here, sir," she said, her voice steady despite the tension that hung heavy in the air.

"Show him in," Peter replied, setting down his glass with a deliberate motion.

Keeling entered cautiously, his tailored suit failing to hide the unease that shadowed his every move. Peter rose, extending a hand that no longer trembled as it had in his youth.

"Richard," Peter greeted, his voice steady but laden with the gravity of the situation.

"Peter," Keeling replied, his tone measured as he settled into the offered chair. Adjusting his jacket, he tried and failed to mask his nervousness. "To what do I owe this late invitation?"

Peter wasted no time. His gaze was unyielding as he spoke. "I'll get straight to it. My son, Andrew. You've heard the rumors, I trust."

Keeling shifted uncomfortably, attempting to feign ignorance under Peter's penetrating stare. "The investigation?"

"Yes, and it's only a matter of time before these rumors become problematic for us both," Peter continued, his tone sharpening. "Our local Sheriff and this heavyweight Detective Stark, whom he brought in to assist in the murder of our little town's 'favorite darlings,' are all over this investigation. It could cause me real problems. You owe me, Keeling. And I need a favor."

Keeling's throat tightened as the weight of old debts pressed heavily on him. "What are you suggesting?"

"For now, Andrew's alibi is holding solid, but I want him out of Stookton. Washington, specifically," Peter leaned in, his voice dropping to a razor-sharp whisper. "I need you to employ him as a Congressional aide. Keep him busy and out of trouble. Most importantly, out of town."

Keeling hesitated, the thin ice beneath him all too clear. "Peter, Washington is a different beast. Can Andrew even manage there?"

"That," Peter replied, his voice brooking no argument, "is not my concern. You will make it work."

The dim glow of the ornate office lamp threw long shadows, casting Peter Von Stook in a sinister light as he leaned back in his imposing leather chair. The faint creak of the chair punctuated the silence, his fingers steepled beneath his chin in a pose of calculated authority. The pungent aroma of cigar smoke clung heavily to the air, mingling with the faint scent of brandy emanating from the glass on his desk. Behind him, a stern portrait of his father loomed, the man's unforgiving gaze seeming to oversee the unfolding tension like a ghostly judge.

Rising from his chair, Keeling paced relentlessly over the intricate patterns of an opulent Persian rug. His usually composed demeanor faltered, the gleam of sweat on his brow betraying his unease. Each step he took was measured yet frantic, his polished shoes brushing softly against the woven threads beneath him.

"You can't be serious about this, Peter," Keeling burst out, his voice tight with anxiety. He paused mid-stride, turning to face the other man, his eyes wide with disbelief. "Taking Andrew to Washington? What if this backfires? The press is already sniffing around, and the last thing I need is more controversy right now."

Peter's lips curled into a slow, calculating smile, the kind that froze the room in its tracks. "Controversy?" he repeated, his voice low and menacing, each syllable dripping with disdain. He let the word linger in the air, allowing the silence that followed to stretch unbearably. The only sound was the faint hum of a distant clock, ticking away in sync with Keeling's rising discomfort.

Peter's dark eyes locked onto Keeling's, pinning him in place like a predator toying with its prey. "You misunderstand me, Richard," he said with a deliberate calm that made the hairs on the back of Keeling's neck stand on end. "This isn't about what *you* need. It's about what *I* can offer you… a lifeline, a way to control the narrative before it spirals into chaos. And most *importantly*, a way out of this little mess in which you find yourself and which has found its way *right to my door*! And You. You know better than anyone that, *at this particular moment,* taking Andrew away benefits you as much as anyone!"

Keeling stiffened, the weight of Peter's veiled threat hanging between them like a guillotine ready to drop. "You're threatening me," he said after a pause, his voice trembling slightly despite his attempt to appear composed.

Peter chuckled, a dark, guttural sound that filled the room like an ominous echo. "Threatening? No, Richard," he said smoothly, leaning forward, the flicker of the desk lamp catching the cold glint in his eyes. "I'm merely... reminding you of the precarious nature of your situation, and the threat it is to our arrangement. Loyalty in politics is a fragile thing, easily shattered by misplaced confidence or a loose tongue." Keeling resumed pacing, his movements more frantic now. His hand drifted to the edge of Peter's massive desk, gripping it for stability as his thoughts raced. "I have a family," he said, his voice breaking slightly. "If this... if Andrew's presence in Washington blows up, it could ruin everything."

Peter rose slowly from his chair, his imposing frame casting a shadow that seemed to consume the room. He stepped toward Keeling, his every movement deliberate, predatory. "And who do you think will light that fuse, Richard?" he asked softly, his voice a sinister whisper. "You talk of ruin as though you're immune when you are right at its epicenter."

Keeling froze, his breath hitching as Peter loomed over him. "You think you're untouchable?" Peter badgered, his tone now icy, each word a blade cutting through Keeling's defenses. "But every king has pawns, and pawns, my dear Richard, are expendable. Refuse me, and I will ensure that every whisper about your dealings becomes a shout heard in every corner of this country. Your 'respect' in Washington will vanish faster than you can say 'fall from grace.'"

Keeling's face blanched, the color draining as Peter's words coiled around him like a noose. He tried to speak, but the lump in his throat refused to budge.

"You don't have a choice," Peter said, his voice low and final. "Andrew goes to Washington. You will take him under your wing, give him an inconspicuous position, and keep him out of trouble. This is not a request, Richard… it's an ultimatum."

Keeling's hands trembled as he finally found his voice. "And if I do this?" he asked, his tone laced with reluctant resignation.

Peter stepped back, a satisfied smirk spreading across his

face as he returned to his chair. "If you do this," he said, swirling the glass of brandy in his hand, "you'll remain in my good graces. The whispers will stay whispers, and your life will continue as it always has… uncomfortably able, secure, and intact."

The room fell into an uneasy silence, the tension crackling like a live wire. Keeling's chest rose and fell with shallow breaths as he grappled with the weight of his decision. Peter leaned back, exuding an air of triumph, his gaze fixed on the Congressman as though daring him to defy the inevitable.

Keeling lowered his eyes, his defeat palpable. "Fine," he muttered, the word barely audible. "I'll do it."

"You bet your ass you'll do it," Peter said with a wide smile that possessed no warmth. Only the cold satisfaction of a man who had won yet another game in his ruthless pursuit of control.

The fire in the wrought-iron fireplace crackled, casting an amber glow that struggled against the shadows creeping across the vast library. Every surface of the room spoke of wealth and power, the rich, handwoven carpet underfoot, the floor-to-ceiling bookshelves lined with leather-bound tomes, and the gleaming mahogany desk dominating the space. Yet, despite its opulence, the room felt cold, a mausoleum for the living.

Keeling swallowed hard, the weight of Peter's words pressing against his chest like a lead vest. He had long danced at the edges of compromise, but this felt different, darker, more final. He nodded slowly, his movements robotic, like a man walking willingly into his own grave.

"Consider it done," he muttered, the words tasting like ash in his mouth. He straightened his tie with trembling fingers, an unconscious effort to mask the cracks forming in his facade.

Peter's lips curved into a smile that didn't reach his eyes, a hunter relishing the moment the prey stopped struggling. "Good. And welcome to the game. One from which we both profit – handsomely."

The fire flared for a moment, its light painting jagged shadows across the room, as if mocking the pact just made. Both men sat in silence, the weight of their choices settling like a thick fog, binding them together in a web of corruption.

***

The heavy oak door creaked open, the sound echoing through the cavernous library like a warning. Andrew Von Stook entered cautiously, his footsteps hesitant on the plush carpet. The grandeur of the room, with its towering bookshelves and glimmering trinkets, felt suffocating, a reminder of the legacy he could never escape. He adjusted his tie, his crisp suit doing little to hide the tension radiating from his frame.

"You wanted to see me?" Andrew's voice was steady, but there was an edge to it... a note of defiance carefully veiled in respect.

Peter looked up, gesturing toward the chair opposite him. "Sit," he commanded, his tone sharp enough to carve stone. Andrew hesitated, his gaze darting to the fireplace where the flames seemed to writhe in warning. Reluctantly, he sat, the leather chair creaking softly under his weight. He shifted uncomfortably, the distance between him and his father feeling far greater than the desk separating them.

"What's this about?" Andrew asked, his voice tight. "If it's about Sophie and Madeline, I've told you, I had nothing to do with their deaths. They were like family to me."

Peter chuckled, a low, mirthless sound that sent a chill through the room. "Your alibi might buy you sympathy, Andrew, but it won't erase the whispers. The Sheriff and that damn Detective Stark are circling like vultures. And let's not forget your past indiscretions. This family doesn't need another scandal."

Andrew stiffened, his fists clenching in his lap. "I didn't kill them," he said through gritted teeth. "I'd never hurt them. And as for my past… those were mistakes. I've moved on."

Peter leaned forward, his gaze piercing. "Mistakes have consequences, Andrew. And right now, the consequence is suspicion. This family can't afford that kind of attention. Not now. You're going to Washington, D.C., to work under Congressman Keeling. You'll stay out of sight and out of trouble."

"No," Andrew said firmly, shaking his head. "I'm not leaving. This is my home. I can handle the rumors. I'm not running away."

Peter's expression darkened, the firelight reflecting ominously in his eyes. "You think this is a choice? This is survival, Andrew. Yours and mine. The longer you stay here, the more they'll dig. And if they dig deep enough…" He let the implication hang in the air, a silent threat that spoke volumes.

Andrew shot to his feet, anger blazing in his eyes. "I'm not your pawn, Father! I'm not running off to D.C. just to make your life easier!"

Peter rose slowly, his imposing frame towering over his son. "You'll go because I said so. Or you'll find there's nothing left for you here… not the family name, not the business, not your so-called friends. You think defiance will protect you? It won't. It'll destroy you."

Andrew's breath came in ragged gasps, his fists trembling with barely contained fury. "This is bullshit," he spat.

"Enough!" Peter's voice thundered, silencing the room. "You'll leave tomorrow. The first train out. I've made arrangements. Congressman Keeling will handle you, and you'll follow his orders to the letter. Do not cross me on this, Andrew. You've seen what happens to those who defy me." Andrew's defiance faltered, the weight of his father's ultimatum crashing down on him. He lowered his gaze, his voice barely above a whisper. "When do I leave?"

"Tomorrow morning," Peter said, satisfaction lacing his tone. "Pack your bags. Someone will accompany you to ensure there are no... complications."

The flames crackled, filling the silence that followed with an eerie rhythm. Andrew turned on his heel, storming out of the room, the sound of his footsteps fading into the distance. Peter remained where he was, a faint smile curling at the edges of his lips as he stared into the fire, the flickering light dancing in his cold, calculating eyes.

# Chapter 7

## Andrew's Little Secret

The night settled over Washington D.C., its veil of darkness accentuating the glow of streetlights and the hum of life in the nation's capital. Andrew stood at the entrance of Congressman Keeling's grand office, a place where power and ambition coalesced into an almost palpable force. The richly decorated room spoke of influence wielded with precision, a fitting reflection of the man who occupied it.

Andrew, with his easy charm and striking looks, was no stranger to commanding attention, but tonight, resentment simmered beneath his polished exterior. His presence in Washington was not of his choosing but a favor his father had wrung from Keeling. The arrangement left no doubt about where he stood in the congressman's hierarchy of importance.

Keeling looked up from his desk, his piercing gaze devoid of warmth. "Andrew, take a seat," he said, his tone curt and businesslike.

Andrew sauntered to the chair, masking his emotions with a façade of indifference. "Congressman," he replied coolly.

94

Leaning back in his leather chair, Keeling surveyed Andrew with thinly veiled disdain. "Let's get one thing clear," he began, his voice steady but menacing. "You're here because your father asked me to keep you occupied and away from Stookton for a while. That's it. Don't mistake this for an invitation to meddle in my affairs."

Andrew's lips curved into a thin smile, sharp with irony. "I understand, Congressman. So, what exactly am I supposed to do here?"

Keeling's smirk widened, cruelty flickering in his expression. "You'll be paid handsomely to enjoy the city. Visit the clubs, make friends, do whatever you want." He leaned forward, his voice dropping to a mocking whisper. "Might I suggest 'The Silver Spur'? Exclusive, very private, and from what I hear, offers the kind of entertainment which appeals to people of your – uh, shall we say *proclivities*?"

Andrew's stomach churned at the insinuation, but his smile only broadened, an icy gleam in his eyes. "Thank you for the suggestion. I'll be sure to check it out."

As he left the office, his jaw clenched with a hatred that ran deeper than he had anticipated. Walking along Pennsylvania Avenue, the Capitol's silhouette looming behind him, Andrew's mind drifted to the moment he realized the depth of his father's betrayal. There was no doubt now that Peter Von Stook had confided in Keeling, sharing the very secret that had shattered their relationship years earlier.

***

As Andrew walked along, he thought back. It had been a sweltering summer afternoon, the kind that made the air ripple and shimmer. The Von Stook estate sprawled across acres of manicured grounds, the brick mansion standing as a testament to his father's legacy of wealth and power. Inside, however, the atmosphere was stifling, not with heat, but with tension.

Andrew reclined on a leather sofa in the grand foyer, flipping through a magazine with feigned disinterest. His father's pacing, the sharp clack of his shoes against the marble floor, created an unbearable rhythm.

"Andrew!" Peter's voice sliced through the silence like a whip.

Andrew looked up, startled but defiant. "What is it, Father?"

Peter's expression twisted with anger, his features hardened. "I've received troubling news about you. It seems you've been... God Damned *disgusting* behavior with one of my foremen."

Andrew's heart leapt into his throat, as he made a poor attempt to feign confusion and irritation. "What are you talking about? What behavior?"

"Don't lie to me!" Peter barked, his voice echoing off the vaulted ceilings. "Mike McKinney. You've been seen with him. Do you have any idea what this could do to our family's reputation?"

Andrew's cheeks flushed with equal parts anger and shame. "It's none of your business who I spend time with! You don't own me!"

Peter's laugh was sharp, devoid of humor. "Own you? You're my son, and you bear my name. Every move you make reflects on this family. And this... this *filth*... is unacceptable! And yes, *I do by God own you!*"

Andrew rose to his feet, his defiance blazing. "I'm not ashamed of who I am, and you can't control me forever!"

Peter's voice dropped to a low, menacing growl. "You think the world will accept you? In 1936, Andrew? At this dangerous moment in history? Your 'appetites' would destroy you... and us. The newspapers would have a field day. You'd be ruined; maybe murdered."

Andrew faltered, the weight of his father's words sinking in. He had seen how merciless society could be.

"I didn't mean for it to happen," Andrew muttered, his

voice barely audible.

Peter advanced on him, his towering presence almost suffocating. "It happened because you're reckless and weak," he spat. "You've tarnished the Von Stook name, and for what? A moment's indulgence in an impossible lifestyle? You're pathetic, Andrew."

The words struck like physical blows, each one stripping away another layer of Andrew's bravado. He fought to maintain composure, but tears stung his eyes. Andrew didn't respond. He couldn't. The weight of his father's condemnation was too great. "You're a liability. A spoiled, petulant boy who has squandered every privilege life handed him," his father had said. Do you know how many men would kill for the opportunities you've thrown away? And for what? A white trash *foreman*? A cheap, sordid fling?"

Andrew's chest burned with humiliation, but he refused to let his father see his tears. Turning away, he stared at the polished marble floor, his hands clenched into fists. "I'm not ashamed of who I am," he muttered, his voice trembling but resolute.

Peter closed the distance between them, his towering frame casting a menacing shadow over Andrew. His voice dropped to a menacing whisper. "Then you'd better learn to be ashamed. I won't allow your disgrace to destroy everything I've built. You will keep your dirty secrets buried, or I swear, Andrew, I will make you regret it every day of your miserable life. You want to play at being a man? Then start acting like one. But hear me clearly: if you ever bring shame to this family, I will erase you. Do you understand?"

In that moment, Andrew understood that whatever bond had once existed between him and his father had been severed. Peter Von Stook didn't see a son before him, only a reflection of his own ambitions, tarnished by the unbearable truth of Andrew's identity. The shame and anger in his father's voice echoed in Andrew's mind, leaving him hollow, stripped of dignity.

Now, walking through Washington's dimly lit streets, Andrew felt that weight anew. But with it came a resolve, hardened by years of rejection and ridicule. If his father had sent him here to keep him out of sight, Andrew would make himself impossible to ignore.

# Chapter 8

## The Silver Spur

The crisp November air stung Andrew's face as he stepped onto the cobblestone streets of Georgetown, Washington, D.C. The bustle of the capital provided a stark contrast to the turmoil that churned within him. He adjusted his tailored Brioni suit, its immaculate cut giving him an air of confidence he didn't quite feel. The Silver Spur, an elite and clandestine nightclub, loomed ahead, a sanctuary for Washington's power brokers and those who reveled in the city's undercurrents of secrecy and seduction.

The club's dim lighting and rich mahogany interior exuded an exclusivity that made Andrew momentarily forget his father's venomous words. As he took a seat in a secluded corner, the hum of murmured conversations and the clinking of crystal glasses enveloped him. The Silver Spur wasn't merely a nightclub; it was a meeting ground where deals were whispered, alliances were forged, and indiscretions were buried under layers of gilded charm.

For the first time since arriving in the capital, Andrew allowed himself to relax, letting the intoxicating ambiance of the club ease the tension in his shoulders. He nursed a glass of whiskey, savoring the warmth that spread through him as he observed the room. The elite of Washington moved with calculated grace, their polished exteriors concealing the machinations that defined the city.

A sudden hush fell over the room, drawing Andrew's attention to the entrance. A man stepped inside, commanding the space with an effortless charisma that turned heads. He was tall and impeccably dressed in a black Hugo Boss suit with crimson pinstripes, his blonde hair slicked back to reveal a face that seemed sculpted for dominance. On his lapel, a small pin glinted under the dim light, a swastika, its stark red, black, and white colors both shocking and mesmerizing.

Andrew's breath caught as the man's piercing blue eyes scanned the room, finally landing on him. The man's gaze was both assessing and inviting, a silent challenge that sent a thrill of anticipation coursing through Andrew.

Henry, the club's host, approached with his usual elegance, breaking the spell. "Andrew Von Stook," he began, his voice smooth and professional. "May I introduce Reichsbank Führer Heinrich Müller of Berlin? Herr Mueller, this is Andrew Von Stook, newly appointed aide to Congressman Keeling."

Andrew rose instinctively, smoothing his suit and

extending a hand. "A pleasure, Herr Mueller," he said, masking the nervous energy that thrummed beneath his composed exterior.

Mueller's grip was firm, his smile sharp as he studied Andrew with unsettling intensity. "The pleasure is mine, Mr. Von Stook. I understand you're the son of Peter Von Stook. Your family's contributions to rebuilding Germany after the Great War have not been forgotten."

Andrew inclined his head, a polite smile tugging at his lips. "My family has always valued its connections to Germany. My grandfather spoke often of the pride he felt in aiding the restoration effort."

"Indeed," Mueller said, his tone laced with something Andrew couldn't quite place: admiration, perhaps, or something more sinister. "It seems we share more than just a heritage. Perhaps you and I have much to discuss."

As Mueller's words hung in the air, Andrew felt a mix of intrigue and apprehension. The man's presence was magnetic, drawing him into a world that promised both opportunity and danger. In that moment, Andrew knew that his time in Washington would test him in ways he had never imagined.

Mueller chuckled, the sound carrying a calculated edge beneath his affable demeanor. "Yes, I am aware of your family's history. It was, indeed, a testament to the resilience and pragmatism of American industry. As the emissary of international trade relations, I have come to America on behalf of our Führer to establish partnerships that will benefit both our nations."

Andrew felt a surge of intrigue as Mueller's piercing blue eyes met his, a gaze brimming with unspoken promises. The air between them seemed to hum with possibility, a mixture of professional opportunity and something far more personal.

Henry returned, placing two crystal flutes of champagne on the table with practiced ease. "Compliments of the house," he murmured, offering a discreet smile before retreating to attend to another group of patrons.

Andrew lifted his glass, meeting Mueller's gaze as their flutes clinked softly. "To new alliances," Andrew said, the words carrying a dual meaning he couldn't ignore. "Especially those founded on shared values and ambition."

The dim glow of the chandeliers above bathed the room in warm light, enhancing the sense of intimacy that had enveloped their conversation. The low hum of laughter and the soft murmur of voices around them faded into the background as the weight of their exchange deepened.

Leaning forward slightly, Andrew broke the silence. "You mentioned that your visit to America is on behalf of the Führer. My father speaks highly of your leader's efforts in restoring Germany's economy and pride. What exactly brings you to the States?"

Mueller's lips curved into a small, enigmatic smile, his tone rich with measured candor. "Ah, Andrew, the essence of diplomacy lies in such questions, does it not? One of my primary objectives here is securing resources... resources critical to Germany's continued resurgence." He paused, letting the weight of his words settle before adding, "Bricks, in particular."

"Bricks?" Andrew echoed, his brow furrowing. "I would've assumed that Germany's brickyards were more than capable of meeting domestic demand, especially given the remarkable economic recovery under your Führer's leadership."

Mueller's expression darkened slightly, his voice dropping to a conspiratorial whisper. "If only that were true. The truth, Andrew, is that while our brickyards are operating at full capacity, the scope of our national transformation is vast. Reconstruction efforts, the expansion of infrastructure, and, shall we say, other pressing projects have stretched our resources thin. We require a reliable partner to bridge the gap."

Andrew's pulse quickened at the implications. "Are you suggesting Stookton Brickworks could once again supply Germany with the materials you need?"

"Precisely." Mueller leaned back, his demeanor calm yet commanding. "Your family's reputation for quality precedes you. The bricks produced by your company could play a pivotal role in ensuring Germany's progress. Of course, these are delicate matters, and the details would require careful negotiation. But think of the mutual benefits, Andrew. It would not only elevate your family's influence but also solidify a partnership that transcends borders."

Andrew hesitated, his mind racing. The idea of aligning with a figure as charismatic and powerful as Heinrich Mueller held undeniable allure, yet the implications were unsettling. "I appreciate your confidence in my family's enterprise, Herr Mueller," Andrew said carefully. "But any decision of this magnitude would rest solely with my father. His experience and discernment are unparalleled, particularly when it comes to matters of international trade."

Mueller's smile widened, his tone tinged with subtle persuasion. "Oh, I have no doubt about your father's understanding of the opportunities before him. His appreciation for Germany's cultural and economic resurgence is well-known, and it is precisely why I am certain he will see the merit in this endeavor."

Mueller leaned closer, his voice dropping to a level meant only for Andrew. "Let us speak plainly, shall we? The Germany we are building requires a foundation that extends

105

beyond bricks and mortar. It is a cultural and racial renaissance, one that will secure the purity and strength of our people. But certain elements within our society resist this progress."

Andrew froze, a chill running down his spine as Mueller's words sank in.

"There are those," Mueller continued, his tone smooth yet cold, "who must be...removed for the good of the Fatherland. Our Jewish population presents a challenge that cannot be ignored. What we seek, Andrew, are the resources to construct facilities... camps, if you will... where these individuals can contribute to the greater good through labor. Your family's bricks could help us build these facilities, paving the way for a brighter future for Germany."

The calculated detachment in Mueller's voice was chilling, and yet Andrew found himself captivated, his emotions a storm of fascination, fear, and something dangerously close to admiration.

"Congressman Keeling spoke highly of your father," Mueller added, his tone softening. "He assured me that Peter Von Stook is a man who values cultural preservation and the prosperity of our shared heritage. Imagine the favor your family could garner, both abroad and here in America, by contributing to this noble cause."

Andrew's breath caught; the weight of Mueller's proposition settled heavily on his chest. The allure of ambition and the excitement that came with understanding the darker implications of the man's words thrilled him.

"Your father is a pragmatic man," Mueller said, his voice steady and confident. "I trust he will see the wisdom in supporting this endeavor. And you, Andrew, could play a vital role in facilitating this alliance. After all, what is progress if not the courage to embrace bold choices?"

Andrew struggled to find his voice, his thoughts a whirlwind of conflict. In that moment, he realized that the path before him was fraught with peril, but also a path that he instinctively knew would be the fabric of his identity.

"Have you spoken to anyone else about this?" Andrew pressed, his voice carrying a hint of skepticism, which contrasted with the allure of the moment.

Mueller chuckled softly, a glimmer of amusement sparking in his eyes. "Ah, my dear Andrew, such matters require delicacy. One does not simply present an idea of this magnitude without first establishing the right foundation. It's a bit like a waltz, you must find the rhythm before you take the first step." He sipped his champagne leisurely, the corners of his mouth curving into a smile. "Congressman Keeling seemed... interested, though I sensed a certain reluctance. That is why I sought you out. When I discovered that we share a particular taste for fine establishments like this one, I saw it was a - 'sign'?"

Andrew's mind churned, balancing the weight of strained relations with his father against the intoxicating prospect of an alliance that could restore his position within the family. Keeling's hesitance was an opportunity, a chance for Andrew to take the lead and secure a deal of immense proportions for Stookton Brickworks. But as his thoughts swirled, his focus was momentarily stolen by a vision of grace.

A statuesque brunette, her green eyes like emeralds, glided past their table. She wore an exquisite black sequined Elsa Schiaparelli evening gown, her presence commanding attention, as all eyes turned to her.

Mueller, ever observant, leaned in slightly, his voice lowering to a conspiratorial murmur. "Ah, a true American beauty. Do you admire women more than men, Andrew?"

Andrew's breath hitched. Before he could form a reply, Mueller continued, his tone playful yet laden with subtext. "Don't look so startled, my friend. I enjoy *both*. My instincts tell me you do as well."

A flood of conflicting emotions rushed through Andrew: excitement, trepidation, and a newfound vulnerability that left him momentarily unmoored. He met Mueller's gaze, those piercing eyes drawing him in, until the next words escaped his lips almost instinctively. "What do you want me to do?" he asked, his voice barely above a whisper.

Mueller's hand, impeccably manicured, drifted across the table to brush the back of Andrew's fingers, a touch both intimate and calculated. A devilish grin played on his lips. "What do I want?" he repeated in the most effeminate manner. "Oh, Andrew. A great *many* things."

Andrew's voice trembled with anticipation. "A meeting... with my father. Should I arrange it? Serve as a liaison?"

Mueller's smile deepened, his tone turning smooth and coaxing. "Precisely, my dear Andrew. A meeting is exactly what I desire. Your father is a man of influence, a figure who understands the tides of history. And you, my friend, are the key. I know more about you than you might imagine. You see, I never approach a potential ally without knowing their story."

He leaned closer, his voice dropping to a velvety whisper. "This is your chance, Andrew. You can rise above the shadows of doubt, reclaim your family's trust, and secure your legacy. Together, we can carve a new path... one that history will not forget." Mueller paused, staring deeply into Andrew's eyes. Then, in a tone oozing false humility, he said, "Oh Andrew. You *must* forgive me. I almost forgot. We must do things in their proper order. Before any meeting with your father, you and I must have a little meeting of our own." Mueller then turned to summon Henry. "Henry. I'll have the check now, please. Andrew and I are retiring to our room."

*** 

The golden hues of morning bathed Georgetown in a soft, radiant glow. Along cobblestone streets framed by ivy-draped façades, the Presidio Arms Hotel stood resplendent, a beacon of old-world charm. Inside, the polished marble floors reflected the sunlight streaming through towering windows, while the aroma of freshly brewed coffee mingled with the buttery scent of croissants wafting from the dining room.

Andrew strode into the opulent space, his heart pounding with the anticipation of seeing the Riechsbanker again this morning. The intimacy he and Heinrich Mueller had shared the long night before, still danced in his mind. Now, the weight of his decision felt both exhilarating and unnerving.

At a secluded table by the window, Heinrich sat with a posture of practiced ease, a newspaper folded neatly beside him. His tailored suit was a testament to German precision: sharp, immaculate, and commanding. As Andrew approached, Mueller's expression shifted, a warm smile breaking through his otherwise composed demeanor.

"Ah, Andrew! Good morning," Mueller greeted, his deep baritone voice carrying a note of genuine pleasure but no mention of the night before. "You look as though you've had a revelation. Come, tell me… what news do you bring?"

Andrew slid into the chair across from him, his resolve firming. "Good morning, Heinrich," he began, his voice steady but tinged with excitement. "I have excellent news. As a result of an early morning telegram, I can tell you my father has agreed to meet with you. He wishes to personally host you in Stookton for your assessment of our shale and coal mining facilities as well as the brickworks."

Mueller's eyes gleamed with satisfaction, his fingers steepling as he leaned forward. "And this will allow us to discuss everything?"

"Everything," Andrew confirmed. "You'll tour the operations, as well as a key part of any arrangement, our rail system, which we use to transport goods to Mississippi River and Missouri River ports. My father is eager to finalize the logistics and secure the necessary contracts. He understands the scale of what you're proposing."

Mueller raised an eyebrow, his smile widening. "Ah, Andrew, you've surpassed my expectations. This is not just good news; it's extraordinary. With Stookton's resources, Germany's ambitions can be realized in ways previously

111

unimaginable. And most importantly, unnoticed by U.S. trade regulators. These are, after all, tricky times in terms of international trade."

He lifted his glass of orange juice, his expression one of triumph. "To new beginnings, my friend. To partnerships that change the course of nations."

Andrew mirrored the motion, their glasses clinking softly. "And to us, Heinrich. May this be the start of something remarkable."

Mueller's grin turned almost predatory, his voice dropping to a tone laced with ambition. "Mark my words, Andrew… this is not just business. This is history in the making."

# Chapter 9

## The Covenant

## Good Friday, March 26, 1937

The unusually warm air hinted at the coming spring as Heinrich Mueller's train slowed to a halt at the Stookton railroad depot. The sight awaiting him was nothing short of an orchestrated spectacle. Townsfolk, young and old, gathered en masse, their faces alight with excitement. Red, white, and black swastika flags rippled crisply in the breeze, and the rhythmic cadence of marching boots punctuated the jubilant cheers. For Mueller, it was a scene reminiscent of his homeland's precision and fervor.

At the forefront of the crowd stood Andrew and Peter Von Stook, the young heir vibrant with anticipation, his father exuding the measured dignity of a man who had weathered the storm of uncertainty for decades. Both raised their arms in welcome as the train door swung open, revealing the impressive figure of Heinrich Mueller. His tailored coat and confident stride bespoke a man accustomed to commanding respect.

Stepping off the train, Mueller was first greeted by Keeling, who extended in an overtly obsequious manner. "Welcome to Stookton, Herr Mueller," he said, his voice as smooth as the campaign promises he so often delivered. "I trust your journey was comfortable?"

Mueller clasped Keeling's hand briefly, his sharp eyes already surveying the bustling crowd. "Thank you, Congressman. The journey was quite satisfactory," he replied, his tone clipped but courteous.

Keeling, eager to assert his role in the proceedings, gestured toward the Von Stook patriarch. "Allow me to introduce Peter Von Stook."

Peter extended a firm handshake, his steady gaze implicit that he expected respect in return. "Herr Mueller, it is an honor to host you. Andrew speaks highly of your vision for our mutual benefit." Mueller flashed an approving smile as he turned toward Andrew. "Your son is a credit to your name, Mr. Von Stook. His insight and ambition have been instrumental in bringing us together today. You should be very proud."

Peter nodded appreciatively, but it was Keeling whose expression tightened at the seeming exclusion of his role. Eager to reclaim the spotlight, the Congressman interjected, "Of course, Herr Mueller, our mutual efforts over the next few days will ensure the outcomes we all desire.

114

Collaboration, after all, is key."

Mueller's gaze flicked briefly to Keeling, his smile unchanged, but his attention unmistakably focused elsewhere. "Indeed, Congressman. But I am most eager to see firsthand the facilities and operations that young Andrew has described with such enthusiasm. The Reich values efficiency and ingenuity, and I trust my report on Stookton Brickworks will reflect nothing less."

Andrew stepped in smoothly, firmly asserting himself into the narrative. "Herr Mueller, we've prepared a comprehensive tour of our brick yards, mining operations, and logistical hubs. I'm confident you'll find everything up to the standards you're expecting."

Mueller inclined his head. "I have no doubt, Andrew."

The party moved toward a sleek 1936 Duesenberg limousine waiting to whisk them through the town. The vehicle fell into formation behind a small motorcade, part of a grand procession organized by the local chapter of the German American Bund. Streets lined with banners and fountains dyed in red, black, and white underscored the gravity of the visit. Townsfolk waved enthusiastically as the procession advanced toward the brickyards.

As the limousine rolled past the expansive facilities, Mueller observed with a practiced eye. Endless rows of kilns billowed smoke into the crisp sky, their industrial rhythm underscoring the workers' efficiency. Stacks of bricks, neatly aligned for shipment, hinted at the scale of production, while coal and clay operations visible in the distance underscored the resources at their disposal.

"Impressive," Mueller murmured, his gaze sharpening as he leaned forward. "This operation speaks of tradition, yet I sense there's room for growth."

Peter Von Stook, seated beside him, nodded solemnly. "There is always room to expand, Herr Mueller. With the Reich's resources, I believe we can elevate Stookton Brickworks into an enterprise of global significance."

Mueller offered a small, approving nod but said nothing further, his thoughts clearly occupied with calculations and potential.

The convoy finally pulled into the sweeping driveway of the Von Stook mansion. A monument to wealth and endurance, the grand estate stood framed by manicured lawns and towering oaks. Its stately façade of red brick, adorned with intricate carvings, spoke of meticulous craftsmanship and old-world influence. As Mueller stepped out, his discerning eye appreciated the mansion's understated opulence.

"This is a home built to last," Mueller remarked, his voice carrying an almost reverent tone as he ascended the marble steps. "Just as I hope our partnership will be." Peter gestured toward the massive oak doors, which swung open to reveal a grand foyer gleaming with polished wood and gilded accents. "Herr Mueller, welcome to our home. Tonight, we dine as allies. Tomorrow, we build a legacy."

\*\*\*

Inside the Von Stook mansion, the atmosphere was an intoxicating blend of luxury, history, and quiet power. Rich tapestries hung on the walls, their intricate patterns telling stories of generations past, while the furniture mixed antique elegance with sleek designs of the 1930s, an embodiment of old-world wealth meeting the aspirations of a new order. In the grand drawing room, a large fireplace crackled warmly. The marble dining table was a sight to behold, laden with sumptuous dishes. Fine crystal gleamed in the flickering firelight, and silver cutlery caught the last glimmers of the setting sun as it poured through the expansive windows. As the clinking of glasses filled the air, the laughter and chatter seemed to hold a celebratory lightness.

The Reichsbanker held his glass raised high, paused as a moment of gravity settled over the room. His face grew serious, and with a measured tone, he spoke. "To a prosperous partnership between the Von Stook family and the Third Reich. May our collaboration bring success to us both."

Peter Von Stook, his hand clasping Mueller's firmly, said, "Indeed, Mr. Mueller. We are honored to contribute to the advancement of our shared goals. Stookton will play its part in the great forward march of progress."

Mueller's gaze never wavered, and he raised his glass in a solemn toast. "Your bricks will build the future, brick by brick, so desperately necessary to the Fatherland. Imagine the structures that will rise from Stookton clay... monuments to our efforts, our strength."

As the evening unfolded, the atmosphere shifted between genuine merriment and intense conversation. Plans were sketched out, flowing like the fine wine that filled their glasses.

"The logistics are fixed," Peter said. "In keeping with our trade agreements, I have devised a plan to ensure the smooth export of our brick shipments. The shipments will bypass the usual interference from the railway officials. We will transport the bricks from all five of Stookton Brickworks' kilns to barges on the Missouri River. From there, they will be transported via the Mississippi River, reaching the ports along the Gulf of Mexico and New Orleans. The flow of materials will be seamless, uninterrupted."

But beneath the surface of celebration, there was an unspoken darkness. The weight of their collaboration carried with it the knowledge that it was about more than just bricks and mortar; it was about shaping a new world, one rooted in death, destruction, and control.

Later that evening, as the fire in the drawing room crackled, casting long shadows, Peter and the Reischsbanker sat alone. The air was thick with the scent of cigar smoke, and the soft glow of candlelight flickered, adding to the oppressive atmosphere of the room. It was here, in the quiet of the mansion, away from the revelry, that the true nature of their alliance would be laid bare.

"Peter," Mueller began, his voice lower now, edged with the weight of unspoken truths. "The time has come for us to discuss the true purpose of our alliance. You must understand fully the significance of your role in this partnership. The bricks from Stookton Brickworks will be integral to the Reich's infrastructure, not just for buildings, but for a much more significant goal: the reshaping of Germany." He stepped closer to Peter, his voice growing colder, the firelight casting harsh shadows over his features, emphasizing the predatory glint in his eyes. "You know what I mean. It is the Jewish problem. The vermin corrupted our bloodline for centuries, tainting our society and controlling the global economy. We will build the foundations of the

Reich's purification with the very clay and soil that form the bricks from Stookton. Our two countries will be bonded forever."

Peter met Mueller's gaze, unwavering, as he waited for him to continue. "I understand the stakes, Heinrich," he replied, his tone steady, his resolve firm. 'The final solution.' I am ready to play my part."

The covenant formed, it was a declaration of power, of a new empire. One built on foundations of clay, stone, and blood.

# PART TWO

# Chapter 10

## Friday July 17, 1959 - Boys Night Out

Nearly fifteen years had passed since the end of World War II, and Andrew had more than regained his father's favor. Peter often reflected on the irony of it all. It was Andrew's behavior, and sexual proclivities, which Peter found so detestable, that eventually led to a business venture with Reichsbanker, Heinrich Mueller and the Third Reich. Despite Nazi Germany's horrendous defeat, the war had made the Von Stooks very rich; more wealth and power than Peter would have thought possible. And for Andrew - his privilege and entitlement only increased, right along with his cruelty and ruthless ambition. Now in his late 40s, he was heir-apparent to the Von Stook empire, and days away from taking the reins from the aging Peter Von Stook.

The air in Peter's private study was thick and cool. And despite the otherwise foreboding atmosphere, it offered a welcome reprieve from the oppressive summer heat. A single bronze lamp cast a cone of dim, amber light across the desk, casting the rest of the room in deep, expansive shadows.

Peter sat behind the desk, his eyes focused and

calculating despite his advanced years. He cleared his throat and reached for the brandy glass before him. He raised it slightly in Andrew's direction. "You've done well, Andrew. *We* have done well. And this move we're about to make into public utilities? Well, it gets us out of coal and bricks permanently. Leave all that shit to the cheesy companies that make their fortunes from the sweat, blood, and wrecked health of poor white trash. The Von Stook family is finished with all of that. Our acquisition of Clayburghh Valley Power Company is the right investment at the perfect time. CVPC provides electricity for homes and businesses throughout Southern Illinois and most of Central Missouri. It's a smart move. And now, with Congressman Keeling Chairing the House Oversight Committee on Public Utilities, our road to expansion is paved in gold."

"Keeling!" Andrew spat. I still hate that son-of-bitch. He's a cutthroat who can never be trusted."

"Maybe so. But he's been indebted to me for years, and most of the time he's come through for us." Peter sat silently for a moment, staring at the brandy as he swirled it in the glass. "Besides," Peter began slowly. "You may be more indebted to Keeling than you ever knew."

"Bullshit!" Andrew hissed. "Keeling couldn't find his ass in the dark if all ten fingers were flashlights! I owe that prick exactly *nothing*. And! The asshole is almost sixty years old. How much longer are we gonna carry his ass?"

"As long as he's useful! Peter shot back. "And right now he's very useful." Peter stopped for a moment, then said, "Just like he was twenty-three years ago, when he saved your ass."

Andrew was out of his chair in a split second, leaning across the desk. "What in the *hell* are you talking about?" Andrew shouted.

"You sit your ass back in that chair, shut your mouth, and get control of yourself!" Peter demanded.

Andrew anxiously raked his hands through his hair and reached for the brandy decanter. "Alright," Andrew said, pulling himself together. "Are you going to tell me what the hell you're talking about?"

Peter poured another brandy. He sat back and, after taking a long swill, looked directly at Andrew. "Do you remember Valentine's Day, 1937?

"How could I forget?" Andrew said with a smirk.

"Alright then. You sit there and listen," Peter began. "Don't interrupt. Not a word."

Andrew lifted his glass toward his father. "The floor is yours."

"Before you were released, it had been decided that

there would *never* be another trial. Keeling and I had information that Sheriff Ted Betts and his old war hero, Able Stark, were gathering information that would have implicated you in at least a half-dozen other assaults."

Andrew leaned forward to speak. "Not a word!" Peter snapped. "I told you, don't interrupt. This is an old business that threatens new business. It *has* to be discussed and *resolved.*"

Andrew settled back into his chair without a word.

"If a new trial had been granted, and our two little local darlings had made it back to the witness stand, you faced twenty years in prison. I wasn't having it. We were about to acquire Southern Missouri Rail to transport the raw materials we needed for the brick business. We would never have survived the scandal. Whatever happened, the nurse and schoolteacher could *never* testify."

Andrew stood slowly and moved toward his father's liquor cabinet and retrieved a fresh bottle. "I think I'm going to need this," Andrew said.

"Probably," Peter said. He sat silently for a moment before continuing. "It was Keeling who came up with the plan. You have to understand something. Back then, the US Congress was starting to get nervous about the activities of the Ku Klux Klan. At the time, they were more popular than they are today. Even *with* all this 'civil rights' horseshit currently going on in the South. At one point in the 1930s, Klan membership was estimated between five and eight million. Between the great progress of our beloved German Bund party and the tensions between the darkies and the Klan, the goddamned do-gooders and liberals in Washington were about to piss themselves. That was when one of Keeling's colleagues in D.C. approached him with some very disconcerting news. None other than Wesley Kleg from right here in Stookton was on a federal watchlist. Kleg was facing federal prosecution for his alleged racial violence. I mean, what the hell? He is the Grand Dragon of the Missouri Ku Klux Klan, for Christ's sake."

"Wesley Kleg?" Andrew interjected. *Our* Wesley Kleg?"

"None other," Peter said. "He was my regional foreman for the brickworks here in Stookton and over in Shale Pointe. Wesley had been - how shall I say it? A valuable assistant in a variety of important and rarely discussed areas. Just as his father before him. But at that point, he was in real trouble. The feds had him in their crosshair. That's when Keeling and I approached Wesley right here in this office. The deal was simple, straightforward. If Wesley made the nurse and the schoolteacher go away, so would his problems with the feds.

126

We guaranteed him that we would see to it. And- the possibility of those two women getting back on the witness stand – well, it was never going to happen.

Silence fell between the father and son as they reflected on how Peter's story would end, but need not be uttered. Andrew didn't react with horror, but with a sudden, cold calculation. He had always known his father was a brute, but this... this was crisis management wrapped in murder.

"So," Andrew responded flatly. "It was a situation that required a quick resolution. Problem solved."

"That's what Keeling and I always believed," Peter agreed. "With 'nurse and teacher' out of the way, no witnesses for a retrial on the assault charges. In the meantime, you had an ironclad alibi for the murders, *and you were in D.C. being 'a good citizen'* in service to your local Congressman. In a matter of weeks, the whole thing just... went away."

Andrew's next question came with a tone of trepidation. "So why are we discussing this now?"

Peter knocked back the rest of his drink. "Like I said. Keeling and I thought it was all old business. Until last week." Peter said, the immediate pivot filled Andrew with a sense of dread. Peter retrieved a silver cigarette case, snapping it open with sharp finality. "It looks like the past -

a seemingly *stubborn corpse* - is unwilling to stay buried."

Peter lit the cigarette, inhaling deeply before continuing. "After all this time, Wesley Kleg, may be proving to be a liability. He drinks too much, talks too much, and is frequently violently abusive to his wife, Mulysa. In one of his increasingly frequent tirades, he unburdened himself of the entire history... the money, the Keeling connection, the murder of the two women... to her."

Andrew inhaled sharply, the news of the unearthed conspiracy suddenly feeling more alarming than the original crime. "Jesus Christ!" Andrew snapped, "And what about Mulysa? "

"Oh, Andrew," Peter smirked. "This is where it gets *really* interesting. You know who Isaac Coal is, right?"

"Sure," Andrew said grimly. "That's Zeb Coal's boy. Just like his ole pappy before him, he's one of our firemen stoking coal for the brick kilns."

"Well...Mulysa has been having an affair with Isaac for almost two years. Apparently, they are very much in love. A *white* woman, married to the former grand dragon of the Ku Klux Klan, with a *black* man!"

Andrew grew pale and silent as he contemplated the implications of what his father was saying.

"It's a relationship that, even without the secret, is a

treasonous offense to all of us in Stookton and everything we stand for. And from what I have learned, in a moment of pillow talk, Mulysa told Isaac everything."

Peter took another drag, his eyes… usually cold and steady, flickering with rage. "And here's the real 'ball-buster.' Isaac Coal has his own history with the Von Stooks. His father, Zebediah, was the man lynched back in 1936 for having information about those same two murders. Isaac has carried that scar for twenty-three years. He now has the full truth. He will definitely try to get to Sheriff Betts with this information. He has powerful motives to do it."

Peter ground out his cigarette violently in the crystal tray. "If he does, everything… your freedom, Keeling's career, and our impending takeover of the Clayburgh Valley Electric Company, collapses into a bonfire of scandal and criminal charges."

Andrew's features hardened into a mask of pure, vicious resolve. This was a challenge he understood: eliminate the threat.

"History repeats itself," Peter continued, rising slowly from the chair. "So, here's what happens next. You will meet Wesley Kleg. I've already talked to him. He knows the drill. You two must make Isaac Coal disappear. Tonight. Before the sun rises on Stookton, Isaac Coal must be gone, utterly and irrevocably. And then, we have to discuss what to do about Kleg."

\*\*\*

Stookton Brickworks was a brutal place to earn a living, especially on this summer night in 1959. The flames that baked the unfired clay into the final product of durable bricks reached temperatures up to twenty-seven hundred degrees Fahrenheit. The air, already a wet, suffocating blanket, was boiled to an agonizing extreme by the massive, roaring kilns.

Isaac Coal, stripped to the waist, his dark skin slick with coal dust and sweat, worked in the relentless, rhythmic dance of a man resigned to the inferno. He was a creature of shadow and toil, his silhouette thrown into exaggerated relief every time he leveraged the heavy shovel and cast another payload of coal into the open mouth of 'Kiln #4'. Inside, the bricks baked in a dry, silent heat that felt, to the flesh, like the scorching surface of his old granny's pot-belly stove.

Exhaustion was a constant companion, but tonight, it was tempered by a grim, hard resolve. He had the truth. The names: Sophie, Madelyn, Kleg, Keeling, and Von Stook. They seared into his consciousness, a devastating echo of the wordless knowledge that had cost his own father, Zebediah, his life twenty-three years ago. Every shovel full of coal was a countdown. He just needed to make it to dawn, get to Sheriff Betts, and finally settle the generational debt of Stookton's corruption.

Lost in his thoughts, Isaac at first failed to see the car- a big, heavy American sedan. It glided silently into the dusty clearing near the loading dock. But the twin beams cut through the gloom.

Isaac stopped, the shovel suspended, his breath catching in his throat. It wasn't one of the nightshift foremen. This was something else.

Andrew Von Stook emerged, looking immaculate and utterly alien against the backdrop of industrial grime. He was in a crisp, light suit that might have been lined. His movements betrayed his fastidious distaste for the dust that at once clung to his shoes.

Beside him, materializing from the shadow, stood Wesley Kleg.

Wesley was the opposite of Andrew: sweaty, disheveled, and radiating a volatile, drunken aggression that the heat only seemed to amplify.

"Coal," Andrew's voice cut through the air, cool and sharp, carrying effortless authority despite the roar of the kilns.

Isaac let the shovel drop with a resonant, metallic clang. He knew instantly and put it together. Andrew, son of the political machine, and the hired butcher.

Wesley took two steps toward Isaac, the years of repressed violence bubbling to the surface. He saw not a man, but the walking embodiment of his own weakness, the secret confessed to Mulysa, the proof of his cowardice.

"The Boss needs a word, boy," Wesley snarled, the words slurring slightly. He didn't use a weapon. He didn't need one. His very presence was a weapon, the smell of cheap whiskey and cheap murder.

Andrew, however, pulled a heavy, matte-black object from his jacket pocket. It was a small, lead-weighted club, a tool of efficiency, not passion.

"Save the dramatics, Kleg. We're here to work," Andrew instructed, his eyes not on Wesley, but fixed with icy focus on Isaac. He moved swiftly.

Isaac understood he would never make it to dawn. The fire of the kiln behind him felt less like heat and more like the grave opening. He saw his father, Zebediah, in his mind's eye—the rope, the crowd, the silence after the snap. This was the same silent conspiracy, now being executed a generation later.

He made one desperate, futile lunge, not toward escape,

but at Wesley Kleg. Wesley moved with surprising, brutal speed, a reflex honed from years of back-alley violence. A sickening, wet crunch resonated in the humid air as Wesley's fist connected with Isaac's temple.

Isaac went down instantly, his struggle ending not with a roar of defiance, but with a limp collapse into the gritty coal dust.

Andrew paused, looking down at the felled man, then at the bloodied knuckles of Wesley Kleg, a flicker of disgust crossing his face.

"Good. Quick and clean," Andrew murmured, wiping his own hands on a handkerchief he instantly discarded onto the filth-caked ground, a final, tiny act of defilement.

The disposal was swift. The kilns were vast, purpose-built furnaces, designed to consume. Working together—Andrew, his suit now irreversibly ruined, forcing the work with the cold rage of entitlement; Wesley, grunting and sweating, driven by the fear of his own discovery—they dragged the body across the dock.

The heat radiating from Kiln #4 was overwhelming now, a physical force that scorched the lungs. The opening, where Isaac had just shoveled fuel, glowed a vibrant, eye-searing white. It was more than a furnace; it was a hungry, consuming void.

With a final, terrible heave, they tipped Isaac Coal into the inferno. The sound was muffled, yet profound, followed by a momentary, almost imperceptible surge in the heat. There would be no body to find, no forensics, no gravesite for Sheriff Betts to dig up. Only ash, consumed by a Von Stook industry.

Andrew stepped back, breathing heavily, the smell of burnt coal and burnt flesh acrid in his nostrils. He looked at Wesley, the man who had bought him his freedom twice.

"The matter is settled, Kleg," Andrew stated, his voice now a low, chilling whisper. "The Von Stooks are clean. You did your work. Now go home and keep your mouth shut."

Andrew turned, leaving Wesley standing alone, sweating, shaking, and tainted by the hellish glow of the kiln. The silence of the night, broken only by the bellowing roar of the brickworks, had just secured the Von Stook dynasty for another generation.

# Chapter 11

## Bad Memories

Mulysa Kleg sat alone in the dimly lit room, the only sound a soft hum from a rotating fan on the table beside her. The air was thick with heat and humidity, the half-open window providing a languid breeze to stir the stagnant air. She stared out into the night, her eyes unfocused, lost in thought. The wine in her glass seemed to offer little comfort as she sipped it slowly, her mind consumed by the familiar ache of her marriage.

Sixteen years of living in the little wood-framed house at the end of Perry Street with her husband Wesley had taken its toll. The verbal and emotional abuse, the physical blows, the constant walking on eggshells, never knowing when the storm would unexpectedly blow in. As she reflected on her miserable existence, Mulysa thought back to her childhood when she watched her mother-the only person who had ever truly loved her, and whom Mulysa had loved so dearly-suffer endlessly at her father's hand. The way she now found herself the victim of Wesley. Unsuccessfully, she struggled to free herself from the memory that swept over her, as she thought back to a summer night so long ago. A humid evening not unlike this one, when her father had beaten her mother one last time. The memory still lingered, a visceral reaction that tightened her chest even now. It had been another night when her father, too inebriated to understand or care, had injured her mother badly. Finally, he had passed out on that horrible baby-crap-brown colored sofa that Mulysa had always hated and could never forget. It was where her failed-in-life, drunken, angry father always collapsed into unconsciousness after his brutal tirades. That horrible night back in Canton, Ohio, her mother had finally decided, enough was enough. Mulysa had hidden in the hallway closet. It was her regular place of refuge during daddy's declarations of war.' That's when she heard it. An ear-shattering explosion filled the still night air like a cannon blast. Next came the awful sound of liquid gushing out onto the wooden floor. Well, wouldn't you know? Earlier that evening, Mother had discovered Dad's loaded 12-gauge Remington at the back of a closet. No more beatings for mommy.

An hour later, the Ohio State Police arrived. "Why did you do it?" one of the officers had asked her mother. All she told them was, "Well… I guess I was havin' one of 'my old dark days.'" Mulysa was ten years old. She saw her mother twice a month until she was twelve. On Mulysa's thirteenth birthday, her mother died at the notorious Cleveland State Hospital.

As the wine assisted Mulysa's drifting in and out of deep reflection, her thoughts turned to Isaac Coal. A warmth spread through her chest, a stark contrast to the cold dread that usually accompanied her thoughts of Wesley, and those awful recurring thoughts of mommy and daddy's final 'little spat.' Isaac was a happier and much more recent event. She basked in the thoughts of his gentle touch, his kind eyes, and his words of encouragement that had awakened something deep within her.

But with the memories of Isaac came the crushing weight of reality. She was a married white woman secretly but truly in love with a black man in Stookton, Illinois. A town festering in hatred and racism. All while bound to a man who would stop at nothing to destroy her if he ever discovered her secret. The thought of being caught, of being seen with a black man, sent a shiver down her spine. It was dangerous. Yet, she couldn't help the way she felt. Isaac had become her sanctuary, her escape from the hell that was her marriage. With him, she felt seen, heard, and alive. But at what cost? The risks were enormous, and the price of discovery could be her life, Isaac's life, or their freedom.

As she sat there, lost in the turmoil of her thoughts, the

137

fan's soft hum seemed to mock her, a reminder of the secrets she kept hidden, the lies she told, and the danger that lurked in every corner of her life. Still, she couldn't bring herself to regret the time she spent with Isaac. He was her light in the darkness, her reason to keep going, even when everything seemed hopeless.

But the thought that haunted Mulysa the most, that nagged her relentlessly, was the secret she had shared with Isaac about Wesley's role in the murders of Sophie and Madelyn. Isaac harbored unspeakable hatred for the men who had left him without a father, after Zebediah had attempted to present the same information that Isaac at long last had securely in hand. Mulysa's mind reeled as she thought about Isaac's threat to go to Sheriff Betts. "I will by *God* finish what my father started." She had begged him to reconsider, to think about the danger he was putting himself in. But Isaac was resolute, driven by a sense of justice and a need to expose the truth about Wesley's past. She knew he was tired of living in fear, tired of being treated like a second-class citizen in this town that seemed determined to keep him in his place.

But she knew the Von Stooks, knew what they were capable of. And Wesley, her own husband, was a monster. She had seen it firsthand, the way he brutalized those he deemed beneath him. If they found out about Isaac's plan, if they even suspected that he was going to the sheriff... She couldn't bear the thought of what might happen. The image of Isaac, beaten and broken, flashed through her mind, and she felt a cold sweat break out on her skin.

She thought about the way Wesley had been acting lately, the way he'd been watching her, the way he'd looked at her with a mixture of contempt and suspicion. Did he know? Had he figured out about her and Isaac? She knew she had to warn Isaac, to get to him before it was too late. But how? She was trapped in this house, trapped in this marriage, and she never knew with certainty when or how she would see him next.

The fan on the table seemed to spin faster, its hum growing louder in her ears as her anxiety spiked. She had to do something, but what? The weight of her fears threatened to overwhelm her, and for a moment, she felt like she was drowning in a sea of uncertainty.

A sudden pounding on her front door jarred Mulysa from her ruminating. She quickly moved to answer the rapping on the door. Her heart sank as she saw Dougie Nettles, his dark face etched with worry and urgency. Dougie was Isaac's closest friend and the only person who knew about her and Isaac. What is it, Dougie?" she asked pleadingly.

"It's Isaac," Dougie said, his words tumbling out in a rush. "He disappeared from his shift at the brickyard. I was talking to some of the guys, and they said he left with Wesley and Andrew Von Stook. They drove away in Andrew's car."

Mulysa felt like she'd been punched in the gut. She stumbled backward, her hand grasping for the doorframe to steady herself. Dougie's words replayed in her mind like a cruel mantra: Wesley, Andrew Von Stook, Isaac.

She collapsed back into her chair, her body numb, her mind racing with worst-case scenarios. Just as quickly, an unexpected but all-encompassing calm settled over her. She was astonished by the immediate sense of clarity. Fatal retribution echoed in her thoughts, a cold, calculated promise. She would make Wesley pay for what he'd done to Isaac. Oh, she would make him pay dearly.

As the darkness closed in around her, Mulysa's thoughts turned icy and detached, her mind fixating on one thing: revenge. The fan on the table whirred softly, a gentle hum that seemed to mock her anguish. In that moment, she knew she would stop at nothing to avenge Isaac's disappearance, even if it meant sacrificing her own life.

# Chapter 12

## Mulysa's Dark Ole' Day

The creaking of the front door echoed through the small wood-frame home, a stark contrast to the silence that had filled the space just moments before. Wesley stumbled in, his eyes bleary, his words slurred. The stench of cheap whiskey and stale cigarettes clung to him like a bad omen.

"No more chocolate for you, 'sugar bear'," he sneered, his voice dripping with malice. "Your darkie lover just joined his old Pappy in the 'big brickyard on the other side!'"

The words were like a slap to Mulysa's soul. She felt her heart sink, her vision blurring as tears welled up in her eyes. Wesley's face twisted into a cruel grin as he took a step closer, his hand raised.

The sound of his palm connecting with her cheek was like a wooden match snapping. Mulysa's head jerked back violently, her body crumpling onto the sofa. She lay there, weeping uncontrollably, as Wesley stumbled towards his easy chair.

He collapsed into it with a grunt, the worn fabric sagging under his weight. The chair seemed to swallow him whole, its dirty, overstuffed arms embracing him like a grotesque lover. Wesley's snores soon filled the room, a harsh, guttural sound that seemed to mock Mulysa's anguish.

As the minutes ticked by, Mulysa's sobs slowly subsided. The icy cold clarity she had felt earlier that evening slowly returned like a dearly missed friend. Her anguish was replaced by a calculating fury that simmered just beneath the surface. The room seemed to darken. The deepening shadows danced merrily on the walls like a troop of grotesque performers on a dark stage. In the midst of it all, Mulysa's eyes locked onto Wesley.

Except for the sound of his snoring, the room grew deadly silent, amplifying his labored exhalations and disgusting sounds of wet wheezing.

Mulysa's gaze drifted to the fireplace poker, its metal gleaming in the faint moonlight that filtered through the windows. The calm now washed over her like a warm and soothing bath.

Without another thought or sound, she picked up the poker and moved slowly toward Wesley. Her hands were steady, her heart beating with a slow, deliberate rhythm. She raised the poker, feeling its weight, its balance. And then, with a swift, powerful motion, she brought it down.

The sound was sickening, But not to Mulysa. For her, it was a perfectly delightful dull crunch that seemed to echo

142

through the room like a melody. Wesley's body jerked violently, his arms flailing wildly as he tried to sit up. But Mulysa was having too much fun to notice his dying body instinctively reacting to her handywork. She raised the poker again and again, each blow landing with precision, each impact sending a shockwave through Wesley's body.

Blood sprayed and splattered everywhere, a piece of abstract art appearing on the walls. Mulysa felt a surprising sense of relief, which quickly turned to glee that made her momentarily giggle aloud. Then, for some unknown reason, as the poker continued to find its mark, Mulysa found herself singing a little melody. Something from her schoolgirl days that just popped into her head.

"Mares eat oats, and does eat oats, and little lamb eats ivy - a kid'll eat ivy too, wouldn't you – wouldn't you?"

As the poker rose and fell, the blows grew weaker and more erratic until they finally ended. Mulysa was startled by the sound of her own voice as she said, "Whoa! I'm about out'a breath."

She stood over the now departed Wesley, her chest heaving, the poker still clutched in her hands. Relief and exhaustion washed over her. She looked down at his battered, bloodied face. She slowly lifted her gaze, catching sight of her blood-soaked reflection in the mirror that hung just above Wesley's final resting place. She grinned as she spoke to the image in the mirror in a prissy tone. "Well! I guess I'm just having one of my 'old dark days.'"

*** *** ***

The night pressed down on Perry Street, thick and suffocating. For nearly two hours, Mulysa sat on the sofa, silent and motionless. The blood on her, and Wesley's essence on the floor, had begun to cake into an ugly brown. Periodically, a chill ran through her, causing her hands to tremble uncontrollably. Except for a horrible ringing in her ears, her mind was numb.

Across the street, parked beneath the drooping branches of an ancient oak, a black sedan idled with its lights off. Inside, two men watched the house with predatory patience. They were a couple of Peter Von Stook's 'executive assistants.' Marcus McBride, local- doing the Von Stooks' bidding in exchange for cash and promises. The other was Peter's man from St. Louis, Eddie Pritchard. Their faces unreadable, they watched the Kleg house, eyes cold and calculating.

"Pritchard broke the silence. "It's been more than two hours since she did him, and she's still in there. We need to

144

let the old man know," he said, as he wheeled away from the curb.

# Chapter 13

## Ashes to Ashes

It had begun to rain. It mixed with the heavy black smoke from the chimneys of the nearby brickyard, making the night air thick and barely breathable. Blood still congealing on the floor, Mulysa had begun to slowly emerge from the stupor that had gripped her since dispatching Wesley. Slowly pacing her ruined living room, she barely registered the sound of tires crunching gravel outside. Bright headlights sliced through the gloom.

A heavy knock rattled the front door. Mulysa froze, her breath caught in her throat. Before she could move, the door burst open, splintering against the wall. Peter Von Stook entered first, his silhouette broad and commanding, flanked by two men. Andrew followed, his face pale and drawn.

Peter surveyed the room, his gaze lingering on Wesley's corpse.

"So it's true," he murmured, voice low and dangerous. "Wesley's finally outlived his usefulness."

Andrew stepped forward, glancing at Mulysa with a mixture of contempt and pity.

"Father, let's finish this. We don't have all night."

Mulysa backed away, her hands trembling.

"You don't have to do this," she whispered, desperation creeping into her voice.

Peter's lips curled into a thin smile.

"I'm afraid we do, Mulysa. You know too much. And you've proven yourself... unpredictable."

One of the henchmen moved swiftly, grabbing Mulysa by the arms. She struggled, but the grip was iron. Andrew watched, expressionless.

Peter leaned in, his voice a chilling whisper.

"You should have kept quiet."

Mulysa found a surge of defiance. "I hope you burn for what you've done."

Mulysa's final scream was muffled. Peter turned to Andrew.

"Torch this place."

All loose ends tied. All past crimes concealed beneath a blanket of ash.

# Chapter 14

## The Last Battle

The sun rose over Stookton, dragging the heavy, humid air up with it. The faint smell of burnt wood and coal dust still hung in the air, but the scene was eerily quiet. Sheriff Ted Betts, stood alone on the scorched earth where the Kleg home once stood.

Stookton was abuzz with rumors and speculation. *The Stookton Gazette*, ran the headline exactly as Peter Von Stook had dictated:

**TRAGEDY ON PERRY STREET: AUTHORITIES CONFIRM MURDER-SUICIDE IN KLEG HOME**

Reporters repeated the official story: Wesley Kleg, driven mad by drink and jealousy, had murdered his wife, Mulysa, before setting the house ablaze and turning the weapon on himself. The Von Stook name was nowhere to be found, and Congressman Richard Keeling's involvement remained buried beneath layers of influence and intimidation.

He had walked the perimeter of the brickworks, where Isaac Coal had disappeared. He had interviewed the terrified night foreman, who nervously swore Isaac had simply left his shift early. Betts had seen the kiln, the radiating heat forever searing the true story into oblivion.

He had tried to get a warrant. He had appealed to the state police. But his calls went unanswered, his evidence deemed circumstantial, and his witnesses nonexistent. Betts had only his memory: the sight of Zebediah Coal—Isaac's father, lynched for what he knew of the 1936 murders. The memory of a ten-year-old Isaac watching from the shadows. Ted could still feel the rage, a dull, grinding pain in his chest.

The investigation into the "accidental" house fire was closed within seventy-two hours. Peter Von Stook's influence, silent and absolute, was everywhere. The insurance investigator ruled it a drunken accident. The County Coroner, a man who owed the Von Stook family more than he could ever repay, signed off on the two badly charred bodies. Cause of death: smoke inhalation and severe burns.

Ted knew better.

\*\*\*

A few days later, Ted drove to the courthouse one last time. Sitting at his desk, the weight of twenty-three years of failure bore down on him. The file on Sophie and Madelyn's murders lay open before him, the pages yellowed and brittle. He had tried—God, how he had tried—to bring the truth to light. But every time he got close, the Von Stook machine crushed his efforts, twisting facts, silencing witnesses, and buying loyalty with money and fear.

He ran through the names again. Sophie French and Madelyn Kellar (his beloved Madelyn) in 1936. Wesley Kleg, Mulysa Kleg, Zebediah Cool in '36, and now Isaac Coal, twenty-three years later. Who really knew how many others?

He stared at the resignation letter on his desk, the words blurring as he blinked back tears. He had aged beyond his years. Far too old for 55. The town belonged to the Von Stooks and always would.

A few hours later, in the late afternoon heat, Ted Betts pulled his beat-up Ford sedan out of the Sheriff's parking spot. He drove slowly through the dusty streets of Stookton. He passed the gaudy, ornate gates of the Von Stook estate, then the monolithic, smoke-stained walls of the Stookton Brickworks, and finally, the vacant lot where the Cook home had once stood.

As he drove out of Stookton, the fields and brickworks receding in the rearview mirror, Ted felt a strange sense of relief. For the first time in decades, he was free.

He didn't look back.

# PART THREE

# Chapter 15

## Present Day- The Whittacres

The persistent ring of David Archer's telephone sliced through the predawn silence of his sleek, minimalist Chicago apartment. His eyes snapped open to the glowing blue numerals of his bedside clock... "4:32 AM," he groaned, his mind foggy from the remnants of sleep, but his instincts kicked in as he grabbed the phone.

"Archer," he answered, his voice gravelly from interrupted rest.

"David, it's Carl Meyer," came the clipped, no-nonsense voice from the other end. Carl, the National News Producer out of New York, wasted no time. "We've got a breaking story in Stookton, Illinois. I'm putting you on it. Get a crew together out of the Chicago bureau. You're the closest."

David swung his legs off the bed and sat upright, his body already awake, adrenaline starting to surge. The mention of a breaking story had his mind immediately engaged. "Carl, where the hell is Stookton, Illinois?"

Carl's voice tightened, the urgency clear. "Who the hell

knows? That's what makes this story so damned bizarre. It's a little town of about five thousand people, where the most serious crimes are typically porch pirates or shoplifting. But last night, a family of four was found dead in their trailer just after midnight. A single mother and her three teenage sons. And apparently, it's pretty brutal. Shotgun deaths. Close range. Not much more than that right now, but I can tell you, it's going to explode. A mass murder in a one-horse farming town? This thing that won't remain a local story. It's gonna go national in about a heartbeat. I need you down there fast. We want you *live* on 'America This Morning' at ten a.m. That's about four hours from now. Get moving."

David's mind kicked into gear. "On it," he said. He grabbed a pen and a notepad from the nightstand, scribbling down the scant details Carl had given him. Stookton. Four dead. Shotgun deaths. Mass murder. The urgency felt heavy in the air.

Carl continued, "The chopper will be at the helipad at 5:30 AM, and you'll be on the ground by around 9:00. I already have Linda Car on this. She'll be feeding you info during the flight down. Just get there, get set up, and go live with whatever you've got. Don't wait for the details… this is breaking. Headline with detail to come will suffice for the early reports. This is gonna be the topic of conversation

154

around every water cooler in the country by Noon."

David hung up, already moving. He quickly dressed in the dark, with practiced efficiency as he mentally mapped out the operation. Jerry Marsh, his field producer, would be his right-hand man, always calm and collected, the one who could manage chaos like a seasoned pro. Mark Allen, the photographer, would be their third. Mark had an incredible eye, able to capture the heart of a scene with a single shot, whether it was witty, gritty, or heart-wrenching. Together, they had covered some of the most harrowing stories in the country.

With his crew in mind, David grabbed his jacket and his bag, checking his watch as he moved swiftly toward the door. The workday had already started.

By 5:30, the team was standing on the helipad atop the Grady Building, a towering monument to modern journalism. The city stretched out below them, lights still blinking faintly in the distance. A cold wind whipped across the rooftop, biting and sharp, as the helicopter's blades spun, making the wind howl in unison. Despite the frigid air, there was no hesitation in their movements.

Jerry was already there, his usual easy grin replaced with a seriousness that matched David's own. His calmness in the face of pressure was one of the reasons David trusted him

155

implicitly.

"Where to, boss?" Jerry asked, voice tight, ready for the chaos of what was to come.

"Stookton, Illinois," David replied, his voice slightly edged with the intensity of the situation. He was already thinking about the logistics of the job ahead. "This one's going to be a real trip. I'll brief you guys in-flight. I don't even know where the hell Stookton, Illinois is. But based on what Carl told me, I do know it meets the 'if it bleeds, it leads' criteria. And ladies, we're going live at 10 this morning, no matter what."

David's years on the job had prepared him for the unexpected, for situations where time and information were both in short supply. But his team was sharp. They'd handle whatever came their way.

The blades of the big chopper kicked to life with a deafening roar. The force of the spinning rotors whipped the air, sending a gust that tousled David's hair.

"Three hours and twenty minutes, gentlemen," the pilot called over his shoulder, his eyes fixed on the horizon, his voice calm and detached. "That's how long it'll take to get there."

As they all settled into the plush seats of the sleek Bell 407 helicopter, Mark Allen, his photographer, broke the silence, his voice laced with disbelief. "I can't believe we're the first ones on this," he said, adjusting the heavy camera equipment on his lap. His fingers worked swiftly, the gears of the machine as familiar to him as breathing. "Normally, the vultures are already circling by now."

David glanced over at him, his mind racing through the familiar cycle of fast-moving news stories, each one devoured by the media machine within hours. But this one felt different. The weight of it - the brutality. "We may be the first crew live, but trust me, every network in the country, including ours, is going to be reporting on this within hours. We need to get there, set up, and get the Chief of Homicide, or a forensics guy, or hell – the local dog catcher. I don't give a dam. For this first live shot, I'll take anything we can get." David leaned back in his seat, watching the cloud-filled sky pass by, imagining the chaotic scene awaiting them below. His mind already worked through the logistics, how to approach the police, how to get a handle on the story, and how to navigate the rawness of it.

As the heavy thrum of the engine drowned everything else, David once again went over a few facts they had so far. Four dead in a trailer. A shotgun massacre. A town on the edge of nowhere. He was already thinking about Stookton, and the monstrous tragedy he was about to see up close and personal.

The steel-and-glass skyscrapers of Chicago soon gave way to endless stretches of green farmlands and patchwork fields, the pulse of the city fading behind them. He watched it all with a practiced eye, each shift of the landscape a reminder of the kind of chaos he had become accustomed to. He found comfort in it… this endless churn of stories, the unrelenting pace of television news. "I wonder if that's healthy," he thought to himself, but quickly dismissed it. He would think about it later.

\*\*\*

The sun over Stookton, Illinois, seemed slow to break through the clouds, casting a sickly, pallid light over the landscape as the helicopter made its descent. The chopper dipped below the cloud cover and began to slowly descend, sending a gust of wind across the road below. Stones skittered across the gravel, and swirling dust devils danced in the wake of the landing. The helicopter came to a rough stop about a hundred yards from the crime scene, rocking on its skids before settling into stillness.

David could feel the cold air pressing in around him as he stepped out of the helicopter. Mist clung to the earth, and a dense fog hovered just above the rocky surface of the road, wrapping everything in an eerie veil. The chill of the morning and the dampness of the fog seeped into his bones as he led the way toward the looming crime scene. They hiked toward a long, winding dirt driveway. At the end of it was an old, battered mailbox, its faded white paint chipped and peeling. Written in the haphazard strokes of a paintbrush were the words *The Whittacres.*

"This is it," David said.

Ahead, in the distance, the faint hum of police radios mixed with the chatter of reporters, all gathered in a disorganized cluster. Bright lights from multiple spotlights were trained on a small, dilapidated house trailer, illuminating the whole area like it was noon. Until a few hours ago, it was the makeshift home of Mary Whittacre and her three teenage sons. David's heart pounded with a familiar combination of dread and anticipation. He had been to crime scenes before, but this one felt heavier, more immediate. "Stay close, guys," David instructed, his voice firm. Jerry Marsh, his field producer, pulled his jacket tighter, his eyes scanning the scene, already assessing how best to handle the situation. Mark adjusted his camera and sling bag, the heavy equipment a constant companion, ready to capture the unfolding chaos.

As they moved closer, the acrid smell of gunpowder reached them, a bitter reminder of the violence that had erupted just hours before. The trailer, a weathered relic of a bygone era, stood alone in a field of knee-high grass and overgrown weeds. It was the kind of neglected rural property that had become all too familiar in stories like this. The scene was quickly becoming a cacophony of loud conversation, snapping cameras, and the ubiquitous crackle of two-way radio chatter. A small army of reporters, police vehicles flashing red and blue lights, and, to David's relief, forensics vans parked haphazardly around the area. He would have a credible interview for his live shot after all. The word was obviously out. Reporters continued to stream onto the property, each jostling for position, eager for the best angle, the best shot, while the first responders moved with grim purpose, their faces hard with the weight of the job.

David's eyes swept over the scene, taking it all in. "Look at this place," he murmured to Jerry, his gaze lingering on the grisly tableau before him. "It's like a nightmare come to life.

The door to the trailer was open wide. A huge yellow canvas draped across the entire entry, intended to block the view of inside. The bodies were apparently still in there. "Mark. They haven't extracted the remains. Get a wide shot of the trailer and then zoom for the tightest shot possible." David could already see it: the sun barely rising, the flashing lights. The unseen, but all too present, dead, somewhere beyond the yellow canvas. Perhaps already haunting the emptiness of this place. It would be the opening image for the morning live shot. At moments like this, David thought about the irony of the term "live shot." In his experience, most of the images captured by the camera seemed to be of people who were dead.

"We have about forty minutes to get something for the live shot," Jerry said. "We'll be using the local affiliate's news unit. I'll go find them."

David nodded and watched as Jerry broke off to find the network affiliate. He would do his first report using their satellite uplink. His eyes returned to the trailer. The yellow crime scene tape flapped in the wind, separating the living and dead. The man-made boundary between the known and the unknown.

The forensics team had already begun processing the scene, methodically combing through the chaos, while the police worked to keep the area secure.

Mark worked steadily capturing images. Most of it the viewer would never see. David inhaled deeply, the sharp scent of wet earth and gunpowder filling his lungs, continuing to mentally prepare for the live broadcast. The camera, the lighting, the shot, and the interview. He walked toward the nearest officer, a man who looked as though he hadn't slept, his face drawn and creased with stress.

"Excuse me, Officer," David began. "What can you tell me what you know about the situation?"

The officer exhaled sharply through his nose, his eyes scanning the area before meeting David's gaze. "Not much yet. We're still processing the scene. The bodies were discovered just after midnight. Shotgun wounds, up close to the head or torso of the victims, five that we know of. It's a straight-up massacre. Really horrible shit." His voice was quiet, almost mechanical, as though he had repeated the words a hundred times since the grisly discovery.

David read the policeman's brass name tag. "Sgt. Andrews." "So- how are *you* doing, Sargent?" David asked. Andrews exhaled again, exasperated. "I've just *never* seen anything like it," he said flatly. The oldest kid in there? I knew him. Our fathers used to work together out at the shale pit. They were both heavy equipment operators."

Andrews paused for a second, looking right at David, and said, "I just can't get my head around it. It's brutal stuff." "Any suspects?" David asked.

Andrews shook his head slowly. "Not yet. We're

162

canvassing the area, speaking with people who might have seen or heard something. But... nothing solid." He glanced around uneasily, as though haunted by the unanswered questions that lingered in the fog. Andrews pointed to a uniformed officer standing next to a man in a business suit and said, "If you want information or to do an interview, you should talk to those guys. The 'uniform' is State Police Major, Dale Phipps, and the 'suit' is a state boy, too. He's Captain Alex Boyd. He heads up the homicide unit."

Mark, ever the professional, moved closer, angling his camera to capture the officer's pained expression, hoping to convey some fragment of the despair hanging thick in the air. He was careful not to intrude too much, knowing how easy it was to make such tragedies feel like a spectacle. The challenge, as always, was to find the right balance between telling the story and respecting the pain that came with it.

Minutes passed, stretching out in silence, and it became apparent that the bodies had yet to be removed. David stood still, his mind working through the logistics of the live shot. He mentally cataloged every detail, mentally rehearsing his introduction, his questions, and the brief but necessary bit of background that would anchor the story in a way that felt respectful but urgent.

Just then, a murmur ran through the crowd. Reporters

163

began to shuffle aside, and David turned just as a man, face slick with sweat, pushed through the gathered bodies. His clothes hung off him loosely, and he looked nervous; his every movement seemed deliberate yet unsure, as if he wasn't sure he belonged in the scene he was entering.

"David Archer?" The man's voice was shaky, as if saying the name out loud required more courage than he could summon.

"That's me," David responded, narrowing his eyes as he sized the man up. There was something about him… an energy, a desperation, that piqued David's curiosity despite his reservations.

"I can't believe I'm meeting you. I watch you on TV all the time. My name's Emile Fletcher," the man stammered, his hand shaking as he extended it toward David. "I might know something about this… something you should hear. It's not just random. There's more to it."

David froze, instinctively cautious. His first impulse was to brush the man off; he'd seen plenty of people like this before, eager to insert themselves into the narrative, sometimes out of desperation, sometimes for reasons more complicated. But something in the way Emile spoke, hesitant yet urgent, tugged at David's attention.

"You from around here, Mr. Fletcher?" David asked, his

tone even but probing. "Most of my life. My family came here when I was a kid. My father was the doctor here for years," Emile replied, his voice lowering as if the very mention of the town might provoke unwanted attention. "I know this place better than most. But if you're serious about finding out what happened, you've got to understand the real story behind it. This town... it's like a maze. The closer you get to the truth, the harder it becomes to find it." He glanced over his shoulder, his eyes darting nervously as if expecting someone to overhear.

David studied him carefully. Something didn't feel right, but it wasn't uncommon for leads to come from unexpected places, and in a town like this, things weren't always what they seemed.

"Alright, Mr. Fletcher," David said after a moment, his voice calm but carrying an edge of skepticism. "What do you know?"

Emile leaned in, his eyes widening with urgency. "Not here," he muttered, his gaze flicking nervously around. "Meet me later. Down at the 'Pour House,' on Dewey Street. It's the only bar in town. You can't miss it. Tonight, about eight?" He straightened up, his voice suddenly more assured. "We can talk over drinks. I'll tell you everything, but you have to listen... really listen."

David observed Emile closely, questions swirling in his head. Something about the way Emile spoke, both desperate and cryptic, triggered a warning signal in David's gut. But he had learned long ago that following his instincts was often the best course of action, even when those instincts pulled him into the unknown.

"Alright," David said, glancing at Jerry and Mark, who exchanged wary looks. "We'll meet you there."

Emile nodded, his expression tightening with both relief and apprehension, before he turned and melted back into the crowd of reporters and flashing cameras, disappearing as quickly as he had appeared.

"Strange guy," Jerry murmured, his voice tinged with doubt as he adjusted his jacket, trying to shake off the uneasy feeling that lingered in the air.

"Could be nothing," Mark added, his hands hovering near his camera as he adjusted his lens, eyeing the crowd with practiced caution.

"Maybe. Maybe not," David replied, his mind already turning the encounter over. He glanced toward the crime scene again, mentally preparing for the live broadcast. "Let's get through today first. We'll meet the old guy later. What the hell, it's been a long day already." He glanced back at the team. "By the end of this, we'll all need a drink."

166

Jerry and Mark exchanged a knowing look, both silently acknowledging the stress that came with the job, the urgency of the story, and the strange feeling that the day was far from over.

# Chapter 16

## Happy Hour

As dusk settled over Stookton, the fading light of day melted into a deep, inky blue, and the first few stars began to twinkle faintly in the sky. The neon sign of The Pour House Bar and Grille flickered to life, casting a warm, yellow glow that spilled across the cracked pavement, a beacon of light in the quiet town. The air, heavy with the remnants of a long day, was still. The world seemed to hold its breath, but inside the bar, life pulsed on.

David, accompanied by Jerry and Mark, their minds still spinning from the gut-wrenching scene they had witnessed earlier that day, stepped into the bar. Immediately, the sound of chatter and laughter from the patrons hit them like a wave. The wooden floors creaked beneath their feet as they crossed the threshold, and the atmosphere shifted. A hundred pairs of eyes turned their way, as if the arrival of the news team had altered the very energy in the room. Conversations slowed, but the buzz of excitement surged.

"Look! It's him!" someone shouted from across the room, and suddenly, David found himself at the epicenter of a storm of questions.

"Mr. Archer! What can you tell us about the Whittacre murders? Are there any suspects?"

"How can something like this happen in Stookton?" "Do you have any information on potential arrests?"

The barrage of inquiries came from all sides, the voices rising with both curiosity and fear. David felt the weight of each question, but he stayed composed, raising his hands in a placating gesture to calm the growing crowd.

"Well, we're still gathering information," he said, his voice steady but weary, hoping his response would momentarily slow the tide of questions.

Mark nudged Jerry, both watching David with a mixture of amusement and concern. The energy in the bar was palpable, an unsettling mix of excitement and unease, the kind of buzz that came with something horrible happening in a place where nothing usually stirred the surface. The patrons, still grappling with the reality of such a brutal crime in their small town, couldn't help but look to David for answers, even if he didn't have them yet.

As the crowd closed in, the situation quickly became overwhelming. David could feel the press of bodies around him, the tension mounting. Just as he was beginning to lose his patience, a familiar voice broke through the clamor, sharp and commanding.

"Alright, folks, a little order, if you don't mind. These boys have had a long day."

The crowd parted, and from the murmur of voices, Emile Fletcher appeared. His presence was strikingly calm amidst the chaos. The older man moved with an ease that belied his years, his weathered face a study in wisdom and quiet authority. He placed a firm hand on David's shoulder, a gesture of solidarity, and guided him through the crowd toward a table at the back of the bar, away from the press of the curious.

"Thanks, Emile," David said, the relief evident in his voice. "I didn't expect this kind of chaos."

Emile gave him a knowing smile. "It's a small town, eager for news," he replied, his tone matter-of-fact. "Especially with something like this."

Once they sat down, the noise of the bar fell away, replaced by the low hum of conversation from the surrounding tables. Emile leaned in, his hands clasped in front of him as his bright blue eyes gleamed with a youthful energy that contrasted with his age. He spoke quietly, but with a sense of urgency.

"Right now, there's a storm of rumors blowing through Stookton... and the town doesn't quite know how to process it," he began, his voice low but steady, as though he'd been waiting for just the right moment to speak.

Before David could respond, a waitress approached their table, her notepad at the ready. She flashed a quick smile at Emile, her familiarity with him clear.

"What can I get you, gents?" she asked, her eyes flicking from David to Emile.

"Beers all around, please," Emile ordered, his voice warm but authoritative. The waitress nodded and disappeared into the bustling crowd, weaving through the patrons with practiced ease.

Emile settled back into his seat, his eyes never leaving David's as he continued. "Now," he said, "before I get into the details, I thought you might wanna know a little about me."

David, intrigued, studied Emile carefully. Despite the thick silver hair that framed his face, the brightness in his eyes suggested a vitality that one might not expect from someone his age. Emile had an engaging presence, articulate and thoughtful, as though he had the kind of education and life experience that may make him an invaluable source.

"Absolutely," David replied, his tone open, his curiosity piqued. "Take your time. I'm always ready to hear from a source who can assist me with an accurate backstory."

171

"Well, David I've been for here *most* of my life. My father moved the family to Stookton back in 1949. Hell, I was only five years old. It was just a few years after the end of World War II, and the baby boom was in full swing. Dad had just finished medical school and wanted to start private practice in a small town. For some reason, he chose Stookton. But I remember how much my mother always hated this place, patiently awaiting the day we would leave. Originally, my family planned to stay only a few years. You see, Dad wanted to have some time in private practice as a general practitioner on his resume, then return to school and become a surgeon. But time passed, Dad never returned to school, and we just sort of settled in. So, here I am."

"How did you manage to spend *your* life here?" David asked.

"I graduated from high school in 1962 and went off to Missouri M & T. It was the big school for mining and metallurgy back then. I did my undergraduate and graduate work there. After school, I came back here and took a job as a geologist over at the Stookton Brickworks in Shale Pointe. That is just across the river in Missouri. In those days, Peter Von Stook was running the show, but his son Andrew was fully involved and heir apparent. Now, let me tell you, Andrew was a vicious little weasel. I could tell you stories about him that would make your hair stand on end. And now, fast forward to the present, Victor, Andrew's son, controls everything around here. Not just the businesses. He has his hands in politics too, including bankrolling the local Congressman's campaigns. And *that* Congressman? None other than Phillip Chambers. He's Victor's personal cupbearer in D.C."

Emile stopped for a moment, his eyes flicking to the side as though recalling a memory that had lingered with him for years. "But as I was saying," he continued, "right after the war, Peter Von Stook was hell-bent on putting brickyards all over southern Illinois. My job was doing geological surveys. Peter Von Stook and the Chambers Mining Company were looking for clay, shale, coal, everything needed for brick manufacturing. And, let me tell you, we found it. These hills down here are loaded with minerals that'll make you a small fortune if you're willing to search for it. And old man Von Stook? He was determined to own every damned bit of it. He spent a fortune to find it."

Emile's face grew momentarily distant as he looked off into the distance, the weight of his years in the industry evident in his gaze. "I worked for Chambers Mining across the River in Shale Pointe, Missouri, *and* here for Stookton Brickworks. I spent more than fifty years before finally retiring, finding rocks, shale, clay, you name it. I turned eighty-one last month, but I only retired last year... well beyond when I should've. In that time, I've become something of the regional historian around here, a keeper of the secrets, if you will."

Jerry and Mark listened intently, clearly absorbed in Emile's story. The weight of his words seemed to hang over them, connecting past to present, revealing a deeper undercurrent in the small town of Stookton.

"You said you've been here most of your life, so did you know the Whittacre family?" Jerry asked, leaning forward with a mixture of curiosity and urgency. "And what can you tell us about these horrible murders?"

"I want to address *all* of that," Emile quickly responded. "But - before we take the deep dive into Stookton's shadowy past," he said. "Allow me the luxury of a few moments to tell you a story that has nothing to do with your coverage of the Whittacre murders. But I promise, if you indulge me, it will put the pervasive attitudes that permeate this entire region into context. It will make it easier for you to digest a lot of what I'll tell you this evening."

"You have my undivided attention," David replied.

"I was just a kid - about seventeen years old, when I witnessed something with my own eyes that affected my

174

outlook to this very day," Emile said.

"It was back in 1961. It was in August. I'll never forget what a miserably hot, humid summer night it was. There were still very few homes with air conditioning in the early 60s, so that night, the windows of damned near every house in town had all the windows opened. The hum of those giant old rotating fans they had back then, could be heard up and down about every street in Stookton. A lot of the families sat on their front porch, lazily fanning themselves with those big cardboard fans stapled to a wooden handle. That's probably not something you young fellas remember. But back in the day, those old cardboard fans were a staple for any household in the heat of a Midwestern summer. A lot of the kids were riding their bicycles out in the street. It was a typical small-town summer night.

That evening, the Pritchards, a black family, were driving through Stookton. We later learned they were returning to their home in Jefferson, Missouri, having attended a funeral here in Illinois. They were traveling west on Highway 50, a particularly treacherous road. No interstate in those days. The old road was narrow, with sharp curves and deep dips; lots of accidents. Well, Mr. Pritchard apparently didn't anticipate the narrowness of the concrete bridge that crossed Little Runyon Creek. It was a bridge just outside of Stookton, and over the years, it was the scene of some nasty ass car wrecks. By God, Mr. Pritchard slammed smack into the bridge's concrete abutment. From the look of that car, he hadn't even *touched* the brake pedal. Judas Priest! The poor Pritchard family. All four of them were *seriously* injured. Broken, bleeding, - three of them trapped in the wreckage. Mr. Pritchard, the father, got the worst of it. He was thrown from the car to the side of the road. He landed face up on a patch of maple saplings, I'd guess about two inches in diameter. Earlier that week, the Highway Department had trimmed them down to a height of a couple of feet. It was like a patchwork of sharp spears, sticking right up out of the ground. And Mr. Pritchard, well, he had been impaled by at least a half-dozen of the damned things. The poor guy was lying there near death, moaning and crying out loud - *begging* for someone to help him."

Emile stopped suddenly and took a long swill from his beer, and then just sat quietly.

Mark and Jerry had been listening intently, hanging on Emile's every word. David's grip on his beer glass tightened, his expression grim. "So, for Christ's sake, Emile, what the hell happened next?" David asked.

"Well first you gotta' understand something. As far back as anyone knows, Stookton has always had a *fully volunteer* emergency rescue unit. After all, it's needed. The only paid first responders the town has ever had are the Chambers County Sheriff and two deputies. That's the way emergencies are handled to this very day. As a doctor, my dad was a natural addition to the unit. And for some *damned* reason, every time the town's emergency siren blared, summoning the rescue squad, my dad would drag me along to those awful sites. I was just a *kid*! My Mother used to protest like hell. But dad, thoroughly convinced that I would someday be a doctor, just said, 'Dammit, he's old enough to start seeing things close up – no matter how ugly it is. It's a good experience for him.' To tell you fellas the truth, after a while it started getting pretty interesting."

"On the night of that horrible car crash, the town siren went off. Within ten minutes, the entire rescue squad had gathered down at the Sinclair station to meet the Sheriff. That was the way it was done. Meet the Sheriff and then rush to the scene."

"So how many of these rescue guys were there?" Mark asked.

"Great question," Emile responded enthusiastically. "And it takes me right where this story is going."

"Wow, Emile," David interjected. "No one could *ever* accuse you of breviloquence."

"'Brev' what?" Emile asked.

"Ignore him," Jerry chimed in. "He's just showing off. Continue your story."

"To answer your question, Mark," Emile continued. "There were ten of us who showed up that night. I remember it like it was yesterday. My dad was there, of course, and the Sheriff at the time. A guy named Ed Byers. For some reason, he was driving the town's only ambulance. There was also a young lawyer who had just moved to town. His name was Michael Hart. Then, there was a young minister there, too. I remember his last name was Helton. He came here about the same time as the young attorney. He pastored the Methodist congregation out on Coal Road. He only stayed in Stookton for a couple of years.".

"Excuse me a moment," David interrupted, as he summoned the waitress over to order another round.

Mark rubbed his hands together rapidly, smiling broadly and gleefully said, "O.K., Emile, go on. This is getting *really* interesting."

Addressing David, Emile said, "I know I'm probably not being 'brev'- whatever that word is that you used, but you'll see in just a moment that all the details about who was there that night is the *crux* of the story."

"No. It's cool," David responded. "Go on. I agree with

Mark. It's getting interesting."

"Alright, Emile continued. "So eventually five of the Andrew Von Stook lackies also showed up. Not that he gave a dam about helping *anyone* in need. It was just Andrew's way of keeping tabs on every damned thing that happened in Stookton. Just like Peter before him, and now *Victor* Von Stook is the all-seeing eye.

So here we all are at the scene of this horrific car wreck. Dad goes immediately to aid Mr. Pritchard, and I'm shining a flashlight into the mangled wreckage to try to ascertain the condition of the other family members. Eventually, my father advises the group that we all have to find a way to lift Mr. Pritchard off those damned saplings, and *quick*. It was horrible. The things had penetrated his insides so deeply, Dad was sure he would die if we didn't all work together immediately.

As the minister, my dad, and the young lawyer moved forward to try to maneuver Mr. Pritchard…"

Emile suddenly stopped in mid-sentence. He sat silently for a long moment, staring at nothing.

Sensing that recalling the story had become difficult for him, David said, "It's alright Emile. Just take your time."

Emile continued, voice laced with a mix of anger and sadness. "But the others did *nothing*. They all just *stood* there. They would *not* assist with Mr. Pritchard or the other injured family members. I couldn't even get Sheriff Byers to train the ambulance spotlights on the scene. They all just *stood* there. They refused to lift a *damned finger* to help!"

"For God's sake, why?" Jerry asked, his eyes widened in horror. "Why?"

Emile's gaze locked onto Jerry. "Because. Because the Pritchards were black."

Everyone just sat silently.

"And the '*rescue*' unit?" Emile said. "They didn't hide their feelings about the situation a *bit*! The Sheriff, and Andrew Von Stook's five 'great humanitarians' seemed to be sure that their racism was on full display *that* night."

Emile paused again. Everyone sat quietly.

"Jesus Christ!" Mark exclaimed. "That's unbelievable."

"And after countless racial slurs, and even *jokes*!" Emile went on. "They let that family lie there and *bleed* and *suffer*. All because of the *color of their skin*. By the time the young lawyer was able to get to a phone and call the Illinois State Police, who promptly responded with a real, professional rescue team, well, hell, Mr. Pritchard had already died. Right there on the *roadside*, on that awful night. I'll *never* forget it."

The  uncomfortably 's neon sign outside flickered,

180

casting an eerie glow on the faces of the four men around the table. David's eyes never left Emile's, the weight of the story hanging heavily between them.

"I told you, gentlemen, that terrible story to underscore the most important fact before you. The racism, the brutality you just heard about? That, in a nutshell, is the ubiquitous spirit in Stookton. Whatever you investigate or discover, you'll find that despicable evil at the heart of it. And - it goes back for generations."

For several moments, no one spoke. David looked around observing the people in the little bar, in this small town. Until a few days ago, he had never known this place even existed. As he reflected on what the elderly gentleman sitting across the table from him had just shared, he began, for the first time, to truly feel the weight of it. That such hate, such inhumanity to man, did not reside solely in large cities, or in some distant war zone, places more familiar to David, seemed hard to grasp. Evil could seemingly find a home anywhere.

Emile's expression shifted as he regarded them thoughtfully, his eyes narrowing slightly. "Yes," he said.

"What?" David asked.

"Yes," Emile said again, responding to the question Jerry had asked earlier. "I did know the Whittacre family.

181

Particularly, Mrs. Whittacre. And yes, I can tell you a few things that might point you in the right direction when you start looking for answers."

He hesitated for a moment, his tone shifting to something deeper, more somber. "But let me tell you this. As horrific as the murder of that entire family is, there are darker stories here. Stories that run through the very fabric of this community."

Emile's gaze flicked around the bar, as if to make sure no one else was listening too closely before continuing.

"Stookton has seen more than its share of shadowy figures," he said quietly, his voice lowering. "Let's go back to Congressman Phillip Chambers for a moment." He paused for effect, his eyes locking with David's. "He is a powerful man, as deeply rooted in this area as an ancient oak. He has two sons. Robert Lee, the eldest, is twenty-one. A.J. is seventeen."

Emile leaned in closer, his voice dropping to a near whisper, a conspiratorial gleam in his eye. "Those boys? They're no angels."

David's pen hovered over his notepad, documenting every word. He leaned forward, his attention laser-focused. "What exactly do you know about them?"

"First, let's put the two of them into perspective," Emile

began, in a conspiratorial tone. "They're the great-grandsons of Peter Von Stookton, the man who built this town. You see, the two most powerful families around here are the Von Stooks and the Chambers family. For decades, these two families have been intertwined, doing business together in ways that shaped this entire region. When the Von Stooks started building the brickyards, the Chambers family was right there, supplying them with coal and clay. And Stookton Brickworks, the company owned by the Von Stooks, was the place where the final product was made. Over the years, the two families grew incredibly wealthy and *very* powerful."

Emile paused, looking at Mark as if to emphasize the point. "And that wealth and power? *Both* are still very much present today."

Mark furrowed his brow and interjected, his voice filled with confusion. "Wait a minute, Emile. Stookton, where we're sitting right now, isn't this this Chambers County?"

Emile nodded, leaning forward slightly as if to ensure Mark understood the significance of what he was about to say.

"*Exactly!*" The county is named after the Chambers family. And not far from here, just across the river is Shale Pointe, Missouri. Originally known as Chambers Township. So, understand. These two young men I'm talking about, are the product of heritage, wealth, and power. He leaned back in his chair, his hands folding in front of him as he spoke with an almost imperceptible smirk. "And let me tell you, those boys are notorious around here… vicious little bullies, each of them carrying a massive load of unchecked entitlement."

David, stopped taking notes for a moment as he tried to piece together what Emile was saying. "Okay, Emile. So, we have these two powerful families whose roots run deep in this area. They have close business and family connections Then there's the two spoiled kids, and a congressman who may – or may *not* have a somewhat dubious past. And these circumstances in a place where racism exists is out in the open for all the world to see. I get all of that, I don't want to imply those are not important facts. But what does any of it have to do with the Whittacre murders?"

Before I answer that," Emile said. "Allow me to go on. You may find yourselves drawing some conclusions of your own."

"Wait a minute Emile," Jerry's voice cut in, sharp and direct. "*Are* you saying you believe they might be involved in the murders?"

Emile didn't answer right away, instead pausing to let the question settle. After a moment, he spoke, his tone laced

184

with careful thought. "I've just been mulling over a few facts all day, ever since I heard about this awful tragedy. You see, Mrs. Whittacre... Mary, that is, was a hardworking widow, raising three sons from two different marriages. Her first husband died in a fire at Stookton Brickworks, and just two years ago, her second husband, Walter Gates, died in a freak accident at one of the mines over in Shale Pointe."

Emile's voice took on a more somber tone as he recalled the details. "Mary and I've known each other for years. She used to work at the Post Office, and we'd often chat. We even shared a few cold ones right here, in this very bar. About a month ago, I ran into her at The Food Barn, our local grocery store. She told me something that really stuck with me. When Walter Gates died, the life insurance from Chambers Mining Fidelity, the company that was supposed to look out for the miners, didn't pay out. The family was already struggling, poorer than Job's turkey. So, Mary's oldest son, Jerome, starts pressing for that insurance settlement, trying to get some justice and much-deserved finances for his mother and two younger half-brothers."

Emile's voice dropped, and his eyes flicked around the room, ensuring he had everyone's full attention. "Well, Jerome started digging around in earnest and discovered that Walter had been involved in unionizing the mine workers.

185

He'd been pushing for better pay and working conditions. And that, my friends, is when things started getting ugly."

David's pen hovered over his notepad, eyes narrowing as Emile's words took on a darker edge.

"Two weeks ago," Emile continued, his voice quiet but heavy with meaning, "Mary told me about an encounter Jerome had with the Congressman's sons. It happened at the drugstore, not two blocks from here. Mary told me Jerome was picking up a prescription for her, and out of nowhere, one of the Chambers boys made a comment. Something about how the Whittacres would never see a penny of insurance money, *or* a miner's union. She told me that after that run-in, the congressman's sons started following him around town. Whenever they saw Jerome out on the street, they'd drive by and throw empty beer bottles out the window at him, and shout racial slurs. One night, they parked their car at the end of the Whittacre driveway and just sat there for hours."

Emile leaned closer, his voice low and deliberate. "I've been thinking about that a lot. Jerom may have inadvertently gotten his family caught up in something bigger than they knew. And I truly believe, if you're going to get any answers about what happened to the Whittacres, you're going to have to look in that direction. Of course, you'll be grabbing a rattlesnake by its tail. Trust me, the ties that bind these families run deep, and they don't let go easily."

David's question hung in the air for a moment. "Did she say whether she had talked to the cops, or anyone else, about what was going on? About the harassment?"

Emile shifted uncomfortably in his seat, his fingers idly tracing the rim of his glass. "I asked her the same thing," he replied, his voice lowering as he seemed to reflect on the conversation. "She just said that no one would listen to a black woman struggling to feed her kids, especially when it means going up against the damned Chambers clan. I mean, think about it. The poor woman already has two dead husbands. *Each* of whom had worked at the Von Stook or Chambers businesses. And hey, *ain't* that a helluva' consequence. Remember. When he died, *Walter* was embroiled in a pissing contest with the Chambers family over their attempt to unionize. It's not like he woman didn't have a reason to be scared shitless, for Christ's sake."

He paused, his expression darkening, his gaze flickering to David. "And she was. Mary was scared to death. I could see it in her eyes. She didn't even want to talk about it, but she had to, you know? That's the thing about fear... sometimes it drives people to speak when they'd rather stay silent."

187

David nodded slowly, processing the weight of Emile's words. Jerry and Mark sat in silence, their thoughts tangled in the gravity of it all. The tension in the air was palpable, but Emile's next words only added to the growing sense of unease.

Almost in a whisper, Emile said, "I know it just sounds like a couple of spoiled rich kids throwing their weight around, messing with a poor family. But around *here*? It's never that simple. I just told you guys. I've seen the viciousness and racism firsthand; the way the Von Stooks and the Chambers family control everything. For decades, the people in Stookton, most of the town, really… have been living as servants to them. The Von Stooks and the Chambers... they've built their empire on blood, sweat, and the misery of people like the Whittacres. And trust me, if you dig deep enough, you'll find that the skeletons in their closets go way back. All the way to the days when rival brickmakers disappeared without a trace. There were whispers then of witch hunts, of dark secrets buried under these bricks, and some say those ghosts are still around. The entire place is riddled with corruption. I've seen things you wouldn't believe... things no one ever talks about."

He paused, letting his words sink in before continuing, his voice even lower now. "Take a look at Victor Von Stook.

188

Start with him, and you'll start to peel back the layers. The more you discover, the more you'll see how deep and dark Stookton's secrets run."

The air in the room felt heavier after Emile spoke, the weight of his words lingering like thick fog. As the minutes passed and the evening dragged on, David and his team absorbed the gravity of what they had just learned. Their curiosity had only grown, but so had their unease.

When Emile finally excused himself and sauntered toward the exit, David watched him closely, his mind racing. After a long moment of silence, he said, "I don't know if you guys picked up on it, but with all that Emile said tonight, he left the door open for more conversation. He knows more. He's holding something back."

Jerry nodded, his expression serious, a deep concern settling in. "If he's right about all of this... we're dealing with one helluva' story. And I'll tell you something for certain. The Chambers family, the Von Stooks... these aren't just two families with a history. This is something that's been festering for decades. It's all connected."

Mark, who had been quiet for most of the conversation, finally spoke up, his voice quiet but filled with thought. "What did he mean when he said that the Whittacre murders would make some of this area's history 'look like Sunday

School'?"

David leaned forward, his elbows on the table as he gathered his thoughts. "That's exactly why we need to dig deeper into Stookton's history. It's becoming pretty clear that the more we learn about the past, the better we'll understand what's happening now. Emile's right. This is all tricky stuff."

Suddenly, the door to the tavern swung open, a gust of chilly wind sweeping in and cutting through the warmth of the room. The unsettling silence of the night beyond seemed to press in against them, heightening the tension of the evening. David shivered, not from the cold, but from an instinctive feeling that they weren't alone.

"Let's get out of here," Jerry said as he stood up. "Back to the hotel. "We need to regroup and figure out our next steps. Maybe we can get our hands on some police reports or public records about the Whittacre family and the Chambers boys. See what we're really up against."

As they stepped out of the Pour Hose Bar and onto the dark streets of Stookton, the small town seemed even quieter than before, the shadows cast by the streetlights stretching long across the deserted roads. David couldn't shake the feeling that they were being watched. He glanced around, but the night was still, the only movement the soft rustling of leaves in the wind.

***

Back at the hotel, David settled into the worn leather chair at the desk, the quiet hum of the fluorescent lights overhead filling the room. He pulled out his laptop, eager to get started.

"I have to call New York," he muttered, more to himself than anyone else, as the screen blinked to life. "Carl's probably going to want a detailed backstory on the towns before we go live. I'll need everything we can find on the Whittacres, the Chambers family, and the history of the brickworks."

Jerry paced the small room, his footsteps soft on the carpet. "Let's not forget about Emile's claims," he added, his voice edged with concern. "If those boys are involved, we need to connect the dots. What do we know about their family? Congressman Chambers has been in politics for a long time. There could be a lot of skeletons in that closet. If we're going to make this story stick, we need to dig deep."

Mark, ever the pragmatist, set up his camera in the corner, adjusting the lens with careful precision. "You're right, but we clearly can't use any of it in tomorrow

191

morning's live shot. Not yet, anyway. But I can start going through the archives for any past incidents related to the Chambers family or the brickworks. That might give us a more comprehensive view of the town's past."

David nodded absently, his eyes already glued to the screen. "Let's split up the research. I'll focus on the Whittacres and the Chambers family to see if there's anything unusual in their history. You two dig into the history of the brickworks. We need to find a way to explain how this seemingly quaint little town could harbor such darkness beneath its surface."

Jerry stopped pacing for a moment and nodded in agreement. "Got it. Let's make sure we don't miss anything."

The room fell into a comfortable rhythm, each man working with quiet intensity. The only sound was the tap of keys, the occasional flick of a page, and the faint rustling of papers.

Hours ticked by as David sifted through countless online articles, public records, and old news clips, piecing together bits and pieces of the town's past. As it turned out, despite almost crippling financial struggles, the Whittacre family had always been respected by much of the community. Apparently, Mary had received a community service award on the tenth anniversary of her volunteering at

Shale Pointe Hospital. Her name had appeared in the town's small newspaper several times over the years, always with positive connotations. The brutality of her family's murders seemed like an impossible contradiction to the image of kindness and respectability they had worked so hard to maintain. It didn't make sense... none of it did.

Meanwhile, Jerry and Mark worked on uncovering the history of the brickworks, sifting through old company records and town archives. They found scattered mentions of labor strikes and a few rumors about shady dealings, but nothing concrete enough to draw a clear line to the present. Still, something about the way the pieces were falling into place didn't sit right with them. The deeper they dug, the murkier the situation became.

It was already 5:30 the next morning. David was exhausted. Suddenly, his phone buzzed sharply on the desk. It was a text from Carl Meyer.

"David, I need you to stay in Stookton. Take as much time as you need. This story is garnering an incredible amount of attention. People are asking questions, and they want to know why or how something like this could happen in such a small community. Research the history of both towns, Stookton and Shale Pointe, and explore potential connections between the Whittacres and the Chambers. The guys in programming are thinking we may have a documentary here."

David stared at the message for a long moment, processing the urgency in Carl's text. "Wow," he said aloud. The story was taking on a life of its own, and he needed more information, faster. He pulled out his phone again and dialed Linda Carr, his diligent research assistant back at the Chicago bureau. Linda had been a rock since the Whittacre murders had first hit the news, working tirelessly to feed him any scraps of information she could find. As the phone rang, David glanced at the screen and saw again how early it was in Chicago. Likely too early for Linda.

Just as he'd expected, he got her voicemail. "Linda, I need your help," David said, his voice low and urgent. "I've got a few more leads to follow up on here in Stookton, but I need you to dig deeper into the history of the Chambers family, especially Congressman Chambers. Look for any ties to corruption, or anything that sends up red flags. I also need a full background on the Whittacres, everything we can find. Check police records, obituaries, and anything that might give us more insight into their family. And don't forget about the brickworks. I want to know everything about their dealings over the years. This story is bigger than we thought. Thanks so much. Now, go work your magic."

He hung up the phone, his mind already racing with the tasks ahead. A sense of weariness settled over him, but he knew that he couldn't stop now. The team was counting on him, and the deeper they dug, the closer they would come to uncovering the truth about Stookton.

David stood up and stretched, his muscles stiff from hours of sitting at the desk. He could feel the weight of the story pressing down on him. With a final glance at his laptop, he gathered his things, preparing himself for another long day ahead. This was only the beginning.

# Chapter 17

## The Good Ole Days

An hour later, David was barely out of his steaming morning shower, a long day ahead with very little sleep. With Beads of water clinging to his skin, the insistent buzz of his phone startled him. He grabbed the towel slung over the door, quickly patting himself dry as he glanced at the glowing caller ID on the screen. His heart gave a small jolt. Linda Carr.

"That was quick," he muttered under his breath, swiping to answer. He pressed the phone to his ear, his voice carrying a blend of excitement and lingering unease. "Linda. What do you have for me?"

Her voice came through sharp and purposeful, wasting no time. "David, I just got your voicemail. I was going to call you later this morning, anyway. I'm way ahead of you. I've already come up with some really interesting stuff on our sleepy little Midwestern towns of Stookton and Shale Pointe. You were right to suspect there's more to Stookton than meets the eye," she began, her tone taking on a darker edge. "And the whole Von Stook legacy? Well, that's just creepy. And it's still very much alive."

David, still standing by the sink, felt a familiar rush of anticipation coursing through him. His investigative instincts flared to life, sharpening his focus. He leaned forward, his free hand gripping the edge of the counter. "What do you mean?" he asked, his voice low and measured. There was a slight pause on Linda's end, deliberate, as though she were letting the weight of her words sink in. "Their history of power and greed runs deep, and they're still at it, pulling strings in politics. It's almost unbelievable, but over the years, they've shifted their focus from coal, clay, and bricks to, are you ready for this? Nuclear energy."

David froze, the implications tumbling through his mind. "Nuclear power?" he repeated, his voice tinged with intrigue and caution. "So what are you telling me?"

"Get this," Linda said, her voice tightening with urgency. "They're currently pursuing the contract for the construction of a new nuclear power plant right alongside the Missouri River. The Stookton Nuclear Power Plant. Apparently, the Chambers and Von Stook families liquidated all their interests in coal and brick industries a few years ago when the coal industry started going south. They consolidated all their efforts into a newly formed power company incorporated as Clayburgh Valley Power Corporation

(CVPC). Ever since, they've had their eye on the prize. The new nuclear power plant. We're talking about a price tag of fourteen billion dollars for two reactors, David. And to secure the deal, they're apparently playing for keeps."

David straightened, pacing slowly around the small bathroom, towel now forgotten on the floor. His mind raced as he tried to piece together the fragments of information swirling around him. Images flashed through his thoughts: the Whitacre family murders, the shadowy legacy of the Von Stooks, the unchecked influence of money and power. It all began to crystallize into a dark, foreboding picture.

"And there are ties to the government?" he asked, the words spilling out as his thoughts accelerated.

"Absolutely," Linda replied without hesitation. "There are plenty of people in power, including some federal lawmakers and other mid-level agency bureaucrats who owe their positions to the Von Stook family. It's like an old boys' club that hasn't gone away. When Peter Von Stook was around, he had a congressman named Richard Keeling bought and paid for. And now, it's Victor, Peter's grandson, who's cementing his power over Congressman Phillip Chambers. The cycle continues."

David let out a breath, running a hand through his damp hair. "Yeah. I keep hearing the congressman's a lot. This is all feeling like a rotting tree that just won't fall," he muttered. "Rather than withering away, they've adapted, found new ways to entrench themselves."

"Exactly," Linda said, her voice carrying an edge of frustration. "It doesn't matter if it's the twenty-first century or the early twentieth; when it comes to Stookton, it's still the good old days."

David stopped pacing, leaning back against the counter, his reflection in the mirror looking as tense as he felt. A flood of thoughts cascaded through his mind, a thousand questions begging for answers. He took a steadying breath before speaking again.

"Okay, Linda," he said, his tone sharpening with purpose. "This is great information. So where do we go from here?"

"Well, finding information about the two families and their current activities has been surprisingly easy," Linda said, her voice calm but carrying a note of disbelief. "I mean, it's all available either online or by following Congressman Chambers' lobbying efforts and voting record in Congress. But to get the whole backstory, you have to continue where you've begun… right there, locally."

David nodded to himself, his jaw tightening as her words resonated. "Locally," he repeated, his thoughts already

199

spinning. The knot of apprehension in his gut tightened further as he hung up the call. With each new piece of the puzzle, the stakes seemed higher than ever, not just to uncover the truth about the Whitacre family massacre, but to expose a decades-long cartel of corruption. And all of it from the most unassuming of places: a quiet, sleepy region in middle America.

Downstairs, the hotel's modest breakfast buffet buzzed with low chatter. The air was thick with the scent of sizzling bacon, golden toast, and freshly brewed coffee. The tables were a blend of early risers, hardworking locals who greeted David with a mix of warm nods and polite smiles, and a few watchful eyes, wary of the big-city reporter poking around their small-town secrets.

David spotted Jerry and Mark sitting at a corner table, engrossed in a quiet but animated conversation. He approached them, his notebook tucked under his arm.

Jerry glanced up as David slid into the chair across from him. "We have got a plan?" he asked, his tone casual but expectant.

David leaned forward, his voice carrying a spark of adrenaline. "More than a plan. I've been in touch with Linda, and we're onto something much bigger than just a murder investigation. This is turning into a full-blown political quagmire. The Von Stook family isn't just some relic of the past; they're making a move for a new nuclear power plant right here on the Missouri River. And they've got Congressman Chambers in their pocket."

Mark, mid-sip of his coffee, raised an eyebrow. "A nuclear power plant? That's not small potatoes. So… do we have a lead or something actionable?"

"Linda's tracking down sources," David replied, his tone shifting to one of calculated determination. "In the meantime, we start here. Right here. This town holds the threads we need to unravel." He turned to Jerry. "I want you to talk to locals. See if anyone, besides Emile, might have noticed that the two Chambers kids were harassing the Whitacres in the days leading up to the murders. Focus on former employees, neighbors, or anyone who might be willing to talk. Someone must know something."

Jerry gave a small nod, already mentally preparing his approach.

David shifted his gaze to Mark. "We also need historical context. Track down anyone who might have records or firsthand accounts of the Von Stook family's earlier dealings. There's a retired politician who might be useful. Mark jotted down notes on his phone, glancing up briefly. "Got it. What about you?"

David leaned back slightly, his eyes narrowing as he considered his next move. "I want to talk to Emile Fletcher again," he said decisively. "There's more he hasn't told us. I felt it when we met him at the Pour House. He's holding something back, something he feels compelled to share, but he needs the right nudge. And if we're turning our focus to local history, who better than Emile?"

The group fell silent for a moment, letting the plan sink in. The stakes were clear, and the timeline was tight.

Later that night, the three gathered again in David's room, the small table between them cluttered with notes, maps, and a list of potential contacts. The names ranged from former coal miners to mid-level bureaucrats, each representing a potential piece of the sprawling puzzle.

David ran a finger down the list before circling Emile Fletcher's name. "Alright," he said, setting down the pen. "Emile it is."

# Chapter 18

## A Very Certain Murder

The next evening, the Pour House thrummed with its usual vigor, a bastion of routine amidst the uncertainties of life. The golden glow of stained-glass lamps spilled across battered wooden tables, creating a kaleidoscope of shifting colors that softened the sharp edges of the room. The scent of fried food and stale beer mingled with the faint tang of tobacco smoke, wrapping around patrons like an old, familiar blanket. Laughter rippled through the air, interspersed with bursts of animated conversation, while the occasional clink of glasses punctuated the hum. Regulars clustered near the bar, their easy camaraderie built over countless evenings spent in the comforting haze of the establishment.

David stepped through the door, pausing briefly to take in the scene. The lively atmosphere washed over him, but he wasn't there to partake in its warmth. His focus was sharp, his purpose clear. His gaze scanned the room, landing on the familiar figure of Emile Fletcher seated in a corner, partially obscured by shadows. Emile, ever meticulous, was absorbed in the simple act of wiping condensation from his beer mug, his thick gray hair slightly askew as though the weight of untold stories had ruffled it.

"David!" Emile's voice carried an unexpected exuberance, his hand waving him over with an energy that seemed at odds with his otherwise reserved demeanor.

David crossed the room, sliding into the chair opposite. "Good to see you, Emile," he began, his tone steady yet insistent. "I hope you have a moment. I'm still digging, and I know I'm being presumptuous, but I have this feeling, there's more to tell. You told me not to hesitate if I needed answers, so here I am."

Emile leaned back, his lips curving into a faint, knowing smile. "That's what I said, isn't it? Well then, what do you want to know?"

David exhaled, gathering his thoughts. "I've made progress, but I need something more. Not just stories… something concrete. The power dynamics, the undercurrents driving this place, and how it all connects to the recent events. I need the missing pieces."

At that, the lightness drained from Emile's face, replaced by a shadow of something heavier. He gripped his mug as if anchoring himself. "You've got me thinking, David. I've been restless since our last talk, turning things over in my mind. There's something I've kept locked away for years... decades, really. Maybe it's time."

David leaned forward, his voice gentle but unwavering. "Look, whatever it is, I'm here to listen. I'll keep your confidence. No one will ever know it came from you unless you say otherwise."

Emile stared into his mug for a long moment, the weight of his thoughts etched in the lines of his face. "One night back in 1959, I was about fifteen, and two friends and I sneaked out to the Stookton Brickworks. Back then, it was the stuff of legends... stories swirling around that fueled our teenage curiosity. We wanted to see it for ourselves."

David's brow furrowed. "What did you find?"

Emile looked at David with a somewhat forlorn expression, and his voice softened a bit, gaze darkened, his voice growing quieter, "Well, the place was creepy... haunting. Imagine a dozen or more domed brick kilns, their open mouths glowing with flames so intense you could feel the heat from fifty yards away. Thick black smoke churned out of smokestacks, blotting out the stars. The air shimmered with heat, and the whole yard was bathed in this unearthly red-orange glow. It was hell, plain and simple.

"The workers..." He shook his head. "They were covered in soot, their shirts soaked through with sweat. Boys not much older than me, and men who should've been enjoying their twilight years. They shoveled coal endlessly, their movements mechanical, desperate. Over it all, a foreman's voice cut through like a whip, screaming at them to shovel faster. It was brutal."

"How old were these workers, would you say?" David pressed.

"Every age," Emile said grimly. "Teens to old men. Most of them were poor whites or black men, descendants of slaves who had escaped Arkansas and Mississippi after the Civil War. They had nothing else, nowhere else to go."

Emile paused, a haunted look settling over his face. "We were hiding behind a coal pile, trying to stay out of sight. That's when we saw him… Andrew Von Stook, Peter's son. He was with Wesley Kleg, one of the foremen, and another man I didn't recognize. They were arguing, but the roar of the kilns drowned out most of it. Then Andrew shouted something that's burned into my mind: 'Then you'd better by God take care of it!'"

David sat up straighter. "What happened next?"

"They came back," Emile said, his voice barely above a whisper, "with a cart. A small one, like they used for gravel and tools. But this one didn't carry tools. It carried bodies. Three of them. Black men, from what I could tell in the dim light. Their skin was covered in soot and dirt. We froze, lying flat behind the coal pile, terrified of being seen.

"They rolled the cart right past the workers. Not one of them even looked up. It was like it didn't matter, like it was routine. Then they pushed it up the gravel path toward one of the glowing kilns. And... they threw the bodies in. Just like that. Like they were garbage."

The weight of his words hung heavy in the air, silencing even the muffled din of the bar around them. David leaned back, his mind racing. "Emile... this could be everything."

Emile looked up, his eyes glassy and distant. "I've carried that night with me for almost eighty years. If it helps you, take it. But know this, David, the truth won't make any of this easier."

Emile stopped talking and let the weight of silence fill the space between them. He stared into the middle distance, his lips pressed tightly together as though suppressing the torrent of emotions threatening to escape. After a moment, he grabbed his glass, the amber liquid sloshing slightly, and knocked back a gulp of beer so large it seemed almost desperate. Even after the glass hit the table with a dull thud, he remained silent, his thoughts clearly elsewhere.

David leaned back in his chair, his expression clouded with thought. He took his time, trying to fully absorb the enormity of what Emile had just revealed. Finally, he broke the silence, his voice tinged with disbelief. "My god, Emile. That's unbelievable. Did you or either of your friends ever speak of it again?"

Emile shifted his gaze to David, his eyes glistening with a sorrow so profound it seemed to reach back through decades. His voice, though steady, was heavy with regret. "You know, that's the thing I have regretted my whole life. My two friends with me were Tommy Shuck and Mike Warren. And that night, the three of us made a pact that we would never speak of it again, not to the authorities, not to our parents, not even to one another. Ever. We were kids, we were frightened, and all of us understood: you don't go up against the Von Stooks. Who the hell would have believed three kids, anyway? Still, it's haunted me my whole life."

David leaned forward, the intensity of the conversation pulling him in. "So, whatever happened to Tommy and Mike? Are they alive?"

Emile sighed, the sound heavy and world-weary. His shoulders slumped as if weighed down by invisible chains. "No, they're both dead. And that haunts me too. Although we kept our pact never to speak of it, Tommy had all kinds of health and emotional problems after that night, all the way through high school. I think I've always known it was because of the torturous secret we kept. Then, in 1961, a year before graduation, Tommy dropped out of school and joined the Army. By July of that year, he was in Vietnam. He was part of the first U.S. military force Kennedy sent over there, and he didn't last six months. He was killed in action just three days before Christmas. Then, *son of a bitch*! Six years later, when Mike was twenty-four, married with two kids, *he* was killed in Vietnam. It was awful."

Emile's voice cracked slightly as he finished speaking, and he looked at David with a pleading expression, his eyes searching for understanding. "I don't know what you must think of me. Like I said, the guilt of never having reported it has haunted me my entire life. I guess we thought we could somehow erase it by burying the secret ourselves. I'm not proud. I still feel its burden to this day."

David sat back in his chair, his brow furrowed in concentration. He tried to process the gravity of Emile's admission, the threads of tragedy weaving their way through decades. "This is invaluable information for our backstory, Emile, but I don't see how it relates directly to the murders of the Whittacre family."

"I'm not saying that it does. But don't you see? Everything ties back to the Von Stook family," Emile replied, his voice rising slightly with urgency. He shook his head as though trying to dislodge a painful memory. "Going back to Victor, his father Andrew, and his grandfather Peter, it's literally a legacy of corruption and evil. And now we have the sons of Congressman Chambers, all part of the same family and business coalition who possess the same cruel and vicious traits. I cannot emphasize enough how powerful they are even now. Andrew is long gone, but Victor has taken up the mantle, controlling Chambers just like his father and grandfather, controlled Congressman Keeling. And if Congressman Chambers's sons did have anything to do with the murder of the Whittacres, they did it with impunity and no fear of retribution because of who they are."

David studied Emile carefully, his gaze searching for any cracks in the old man's composure. Emile seemed genuine, a man of good character, weighed down by a lifetime of guilt and regret. But a nagging question burned at the edges of David's thoughts, refusing to be ignored. "Emile, I have listened carefully to everything you've told me, and frankly, I am gobsmacked by it. It's fascinating. But..." David paused, choosing his words with care.

"But?" Emile's voice carried an edge of uncertainty.

"But given the experience you have just related, knowing what you know about this place, and the things you've seen, why, after finishing college, did you come back here?"

Emile's gaze turned inward, his expression clouding as he considered the question. After a long pause, he answered with measured deliberation. "David, I've asked myself that question a thousand times. I don't know. Looking back on it, I thought if I came back here... well, maybe I could make a difference. Or maybe it was just to be near my family, who had lived and worked here and sacrificed to provide the opportunity for a first-rate education. Or maybe, maybe, it was my way of paying penance for all the years I kept that awful secret. I don't even remember now. But here I am. Old and retired, and this place is still as rotten as an aging corpse."

David stared at the old man, who suddenly seemed smaller and more fragile. The lines etched into Emile's face appeared deeper, his weariness more pronounced. "Alright, Emile. All I can say is, you have my attention. I need to gather more evidence and more stories like yours. Where can I begin?"

Emile leaned in, his earlier weariness momentarily replaced by a spark of determination. "If you want to dig deeper into Stookton's history, you should start at the Chambers County Library. Rumor has it they possess a tome called 'The Chronicles.' It may be buried, but it speaks to the history of this area… dark events and decisions made long ago, particularly concerning the Von Stook family."

"The Chronicles?" David repeated, the intrigue evident in his tone. "What's so special about it?"

"It's a ledger or a book of some kind. Rumors of its existence have been floating around for years. Supposedly, it's a record of events that dates all the way back to the late 1800s when this area was just being settled. My advice is simple: don't just search for facts; find the stories behind the facts."

"So, these Chronicles. Do I just walk into the library and say, 'Hey, I'd like to see all the dark and evil secrets of your town's past?'" David quipped, though his curiosity was genuine. "If they are just local lore, and no one is sure they exist, how do I find them?"

"David, to tell you the truth, I really don't know. I've heard about these old documents my whole life." Emile tilted his head, considering the question. "But there *is someone* you need to meet who can be of real assistance. There's a Dr. Lydia Brookes… she's a professor of history at Chambers Heritage Community College. I've met with Dr. Brookes several times so she could pick my brain about local history. You should speak with her; I think the two of you could help each other."

"Dr. Brookes," David echoed, mentally filing away the name.

"She might have access to further resources and contacts. She's been working on a book about the history of this area. She could certainly tell you more about *The Chronicles*. Between her academic perspective and your investigation, meeting her may have mutual benefits," Emile urged, leaning forward with quiet intensity.

"Chambers Heritage Community College?" David asked, jotting down the name in his notebook.

"That's right. It's across the river just north of Stookton. A beautiful little campus, and she practically lives in her office, so she'll be no trouble to find. You should talk to her." David snapped his notebook shut with a decisive motion, leaning back and exhaling deeply. "Wow, Emile, you sure know how to get a guy's wheels turning! This has been a lot. I'm having another. But no beer. I'm ready for a real drink." The waitress soon approached with a vodka tonic and a dirty martini, setting the glasses down gently on the table. The two men fell into a companionable silence, the weight of the conversation lingering in the air. Emile lifted his drink, taking a slow, thoughtful sip, his gaze drifting somewhere far beyond the walls of the bar.

"You know, David," Emile began after a moment, his

213

voice quiet and reflective, "I'm an educated man… a man of science. Geological surveys, soil analysis, and all of that. And you… you're a man of logic. Get the facts, check the facts. Always searching for the truth. Right?"

David, intrigued by the shift in tone, leaned in slightly, his curiosity piqued. "Alright. So we agree. We aren't just handsome devils; we're also sharper than a whip. But what the hell are you talking about all of a sudden?"

Emile placed his glass down gently, his eyes locking with David's. His expression was unusually grave. "I was just wondering how open you might be to another, completely different dynamic to the history of Stookton and the brickyards?"

David arched an eyebrow, swirling his martini glass idly. "I'm not sure, Emile. Right now, it's gonna take two or three of these dirty martinis to wash down the present dynamic. What are you talking about?"

"There are rumors," Emile said, his voice dropping. "Stories of hauntings. Ghosts."

"Really," David replied, his tone heavy with sarcasm as he took a sip of his drink.

"Now, wait a minute, David. Aren't you the guy who told me the first time we met that it never hurts to have a conversation? So, let's have a conversation."

David hesitated, his journalistic instincts wrestling with his natural skepticism. Emile had been nothing but forthright so far, and dismissing him outright would be a mistake. Besides, he knew from experience that even the wildest stories often had a kernel of truth.

"Alright, Emile," David finally said, setting his glass down. "I don't have another live shot until noon tomorrow, and I decided about halfway through your story that I wouldn't leave this place until I needed a designated driver. So, let's talk. I'm all ears."

Emile leaned forward, his voice dropping to a conspiratorial whisper. "Okay. But keep an open mind. Let's start with the brickyards... particularly the one here in Stookton. They say the spirits of the workers haunt the area... men who toiled and suffered only to meet untimely ends. Others speak of specters in the old Von Stook estate. Victims of wrath and cruelty tied to the family's cursed legacy."

David's expression betrayed his skepticism, though he couldn't help but be intrigued. "And you believe these sightings are connected to the crimes of the Von Stook family?"

Emile nodded, his eyes darting around the room as if to ensure no one else was listening. "Not just the Von Stooks

215

per se, but the evil forces that may have influenced this area for centuries. Over the years, children have heard whispers in the brickyards after dark and seen shadows moving along the cliffs above the old shale pits on the Coal Road. And there are stories about two young women who were murdered on that road back in the 1930s. I once heard someone say that Andrew Von Stook had even been a person of interest.

"And the estate… it's avoided not only because of what some claim to have seen, but because of the palpable dread it invokes. People describe lights flickering in the windows at night, screams that come from nowhere, and the sensation of being watched."

"What sort of things?" David pressed, leaning forward despite himself.

The weight of Emile's story seemed to hang in the air, weaving itself into the dimly lit ambiance of the bar. David felt the contrast keenly, the lively chatter of patrons around them, and the growing gravity of the tale being shared.

"David," Emile began, his voice quieter now, as if afraid the walls might hear, "my father was a man of science, and he did not suffer foolishness or entertain unfounded stories. But there was one night, back in the 50s, that stayed with him until his final days."

David leaned in slightly, drawn by the deliberate cadence of Emile's words.

"It was during a brutal snowstorm, the kind that silences everything with its ferocity. The roads were barely passable, and the whole area shut down for days afterward. That night, my father was called to the Von Stook Mansion to treat Andrew's groundskeeper, Buddy Spencer, who was in the advanced stages of pneumonia."

Emile paused, taking a slow sip from his glass as if trying to steady himself. "My father returned home around 2 a.m. I'll never forget it. I was just a boy, maybe 10 or 11, and I woke up early the next morning to the sound of my parents out in the den whispering. Their voices carried that frantic edge, the kind that sticks with you, even when you can't make out all the words.

"I crept closer, just enough to catch snippets of my father's account to my mother. He said that while he was treating Buddy, he kept noticing movement in the dimly lit halls, shadows flickering just at the edge of his vision. Each time he turned to look, nothing was there. He mentioned lights in the windows of long-unused rooms, faint and fleeting. And he swore that when the wind howled through the woods surrounding the estate, it carried voices, murmurs that seemed almost human."

Emile's gaze dropped to his glass, and his voice softened further. "The next morning, when he came down for breakfast, he was a different man… quiet, withdrawn. He didn't speak of the night again. The only clue to how deeply it affected him came when I saw him reach into his medical bag, pull out a tranquilizer, and down it with his morning coffee. The one and only time I ever saw him do that. 'Just a bit of a headache,' he told us, but he carried that silence with him for days after."

David glanced around the bar, the din of laughter and clinking glasses now seeming distant and surreal against the eerie weight of Emile's recollection.

"You see, David," Emile continued, his voice steady but shadowed by reverence and unease, "I think Stookton's stories are like those ghosts. They show themselves to those who seek them and stay hidden from those who don't."

David tapped his fingers against the edge of his glass, his expression unreadable. "When I talk with Dr. Brookes, you think I should ask her about these hauntings?"

Emile nodded, his demeanor certain. "She's been gathering stories, facts, and rumors for years. If anyone can separate truth from tale, it's her."

David studied Emile's face, searching for any hint of embellishment or jest. "Why are you telling me this?"

Emile's eyes met his, the sincerity in them unmistakable.

"Because these stories are a part of this place, as much as the bricks of its buildings or the people living in them. Stookton is built on layers, David. If you want to uncover its truths, you'll need to see the ghosts, too… whether they walk among us in flesh or linger as shadows."

A thoughtful silence settled between them, the bar's liveliness fading to an almost forgotten backdrop. For a moment, it felt as though the weight of Stookton's history itself had joined them at the table, quiet and watchful, waiting to see if its secrets would finally be heard.

# Chapter 19

## Welcome Wagon

The sun had slipped below the horizon, surrendering the sky to an enveloping blackness streaked with faint remnants of twilight. As David stepped out of the Chambers County Library, the chill of the evening wrapped around him, sharp and unforgiving. His mind buzzed with the weight of the confrontation that had unfolded inside the austere building.

The library loomed behind him like a fortress, its towering shelves within more akin to battlements than a haven of knowledge. The air inside had been heavy with the mingling scents of aged paper and varnished wood, each steeped in a history the building refused to share willingly. It was there, amid the oppressive silence and dim yellowed lighting, that he'd encountered Evelyn Cook.

Evelyn, the head librarian, carried herself with an air of authority that bordered on the combative. Her sharp gaze had followed David like a hawk circling its prey. "Mr. Archer," she'd said, her voice brittle and cutting, as if each word could flay him alive. "This is not some playground for national news correspondents. Stookton's history is not for you to dissect." Her tight, gray curls bobbed slightly as she shook her head with conviction, each movement underscoring her disdain.

David had tried to hold his ground, gesturing toward the towering stacks surrounding them. "But surely, you of all people must understand…"

Her interruption had been swift and uncompromising. "I understand perfectly well," she snapped, her brow knitting into deep furrows. "This library is for the residents of this town. We do not assist outsiders looking to uncover buried secrets."

Her words hit David like a slammed door, yet he pressed on, his voice steady despite the racing of his heart. "I'd only like to access your archives, Ma'am. The *Chronicles of Stookton*, from what I've heard, could provide invaluable insights."

The mention of the Chronicles seemed to stoke something fierce within Evelyn. She leaned forward, her face lit with a fire that was equal parts derision and warning. "The *Chronicles*? You believe in legends, Mr. Archer? Folklore spun from fear and half-truths? You're wasting your time. You're not welcome here. Leave your fancy equipment behind and try your luck somewhere else. You're not a state resident, and you certainly have no business in our histories."

221

Her dismissal had cut through the room like a blade, the finality of her words punctuated by the echo of David's footsteps retreating through the library's cavernous halls. The heavy wooden door creaked shut behind him, its sound more like a tolling bell than a simple exit.

Now outside, the night felt oppressive, the cool air biting through his jacket. A shiver crept up his spine, lingering at the base of his neck like a phantom's touch. He glanced back at the library's imposing structure, its facade illuminated by pale streetlights, casting stark shadows that seemed to move with a life of their own. For a fleeting moment, David felt as though the building itself was watching him, its stony exterior concealing secrets it would never willingly relinquish.

The sound of footsteps behind him broke his thoughts, soft but deliberate, a rhythm that sliced through the stillness. His pulse quickened, a drumbeat of unease hammering in his ears. Without turning, he picked up his pace, his focus narrowing on the parking lot ahead.

Then he saw them.

Two men, silhouetted against the faint glow of the horizon, their forms large and imposing. They moved with the precision of predators, their figures blending into the shadows like they belonged to the night itself. David's breath caught, his legs stiffening for a moment before instinct pushed him forward.

The night seemed to close in around him, the air thick with an unspoken menace. Each step he took seemed to echo louder than the last, his heartbeat roaring in his ears as the distance to his car felt impossibly long. The men didn't speak, didn't call out…yet their presence loomed, heavy and undeniable, like a dark omen hanging over him.

"Hey there, TV star," one of them drawled, his voice low and gravelly, like stones scraping together. The dim light from a flickering streetlamp revealed his face, a cruel smirk twisting his features as though malice had carved them. "We're the welcome wagon."

David turned slowly, his breath steady despite the churn of fear clawing at his chest. He forced himself to stand tall, projecting an air of calm confidence he didn't quite feel. "I'm not here for a party," he replied, but the slight tremor in his voice betrayed the truth.

The second man stepped closer, his figure a shadowy monolith under the weak glow of the streetlamp. His eyes gleamed with a predatory glint, the kind that spoke of trouble long before words followed. "The next big story coming out of Stookton could very well be an obituary. Yours, in fact." The threat hit like a cold wind, sending shivers racing down David's spine. The primal urge to run surged through him, but he fought to maintain his composure. "You don't scare me," he said, his voice firm but thin, trying to sound defiant. "I'm just trying to report the truth."

The first man let out a dark chuckle, his shoulders shaking with mirth that didn't reach his cold eyes. "That's the problem, ain't it? We don't take too kindly to truth-seekers poking around our town. You don't know what you're asking for."

"Or who you're poking at," the second man added, stepping so close that David could feel the oppressive heat of his breath. The acrid scent of stale cigarettes and sweat rolled off him, mingling with the faint diesel fumes wafting from the nearby trucks.

"What are you suggesting?" David asked, swallowing hard to force the words past the tightness in his throat.

"Just a friendly warning," the first man said, his voice dropping into a menacing murmur. "Stookton has a way of swallowing people whole. The night here… it reveals more than you might want it to."

A bead of sweat trickled down David's temple, cold against his heated skin. His shoes felt glued to the asphalt as though the very ground sought to trap him. He glanced over his shoulder toward his car, a distant beacon of safety, and the reassuring weight of his keys in his pocket became his only lifeline.

"Listen, I'll leave," he said quickly, before his bravado could betray him further. "I'm not looking for trouble. Just reporting."

"Then be smart," the second man sneered, taking a deliberate step back. "Get in your car and drive right out of Stookton. You're not welcome here, and you're definitely not equipped to handle what's waiting in the shadows."

The smirk on the second man's face lingered as he withdrew, a smug satisfaction dancing in his eyes. "You think those dusty old books can help you? If folks like us wanted to keep things buried, they'd stay buried. The Chronicles you're after... best leave them alone, trust me."

Their words hung in the air, heavy and charged, even as they melted back into the shadows. David's body moved on instinct, his feet breaking into a brisk jog toward his car. His pulse pounded in his ears as his fingers fumbled with the keys, the cold metal slipping against his sweat-slick grip. Finally, he unlocked the door, and the soft blue light from the interior spilled out like salvation.

He climbed in hurriedly, slamming the door shut behind him. For a moment, he sat frozen, his breath shallow and uneven as he scanned the darkened street. But the men were gone, swallowed whole by the night as though they'd never been there at all.

Yet, their voices lingered, a haunting echo etched into his mind. The weight of their warnings pressed on him, urging him to flee, to abandon the search and leave Stookton's secrets buried.

But beneath the fear was something stubborn and unyielding… a fire that refused to die. Whatever lay hidden in this town, David had to uncover it. The Chronicles of Stookton were more than just a story. They were the key to exposing truths long buried in the shadows of this sinister place.

As he drove away, the faint flicker of streetlights slipped past in rhythmic intervals, casting fleeting pools of light into the darkness. His thoughts whirled with determination and unease, each turn of the wheel pulling him deeper into the heart of Stookton's mystery.

# Chapter 20

## Collaboration

The sun was now just rising, and spreading a soft light over the old stone buildings, as David was graduating, and coming nearer to the Chambers Heritage Community College, and with that, these buildings seemed to awaken under the touch of the sun.

Generally, the campus appeared serene and nearly lethargic, and few students were strolling over the walkways, some carrying coffee in their hands, others wearing backpacks over their shoulders.

Going under the arch, David experienced the world opening up to him. The expansive campus stretched out with its neat lawns that were a beautiful green patch with some bright flowerbeds scattered throughout. Flurries of crimson, gold, and violet hung in the morning air, and the colors changed during the day like a kaleidoscope with the sunshine shining through the leaves.

His eyes were attracted to the neoclassical structures on the main road. The main academic hall was in the center of it all; it was a stately but friendly building. The polish of its red-brick walls was rich, and contrasted with white- framed arched windows blazing in the sunshine. Above this, the clock tower was rearing, A graceful spire with its face inscribed in gold, with its hands purpose-loving. The chimes could be heard far off, but as if it were a heartbeat along the campus.

The student union was busy with life to the right. The patio of the cafe was a world of youth, and the swirl of freshly baked coffee and pastries filled the air with laughter and spirited talk. Students sat in groups on wrought-iron chairs, some reading textbooks, others waving their arms and talking about their dreams and goals.

David turned his attention to the huge quad, which is a green oasis in the center of the campus. The lawn could not have been greener, carefully tended as it was, and it beckoned careless groupings as well as meditations. Turning walks led off the quad, and were lined up with wooden benches on which a few early risers sat, thinking something or attending to their machines. The figures of great historical personalities were on guard, and with flickering morning sunshine, their surfaces of polished bronze glowed.

David parked his car in a small lot behind a grove of oaks, sat back, and allowed the atmosphere to fall upon him. The atmosphere was cool and fresh and had the faint scent of earth and the flowers that were growing. He shut his eyes for a second, the sound-world enveloping him, the chiming tower clock, the twittering leaves, and the hum of college life, far away.

***

The Chambers Heritage Community College library was a haven of the mind and silent cogitation. Its ceilings were high, arched above his head, and its beams were carved in fine detail, and the shelves were in rows, stretching away into the distance, each filled with the brunt of wisdom. Dust motes danced listlessly in rays of sunshine streaming through deep, leaded-glass windows and falling in a soft, diffused light across the polished wooden tables.

And when David came in, there was awe with his anticipation. There was the dim odor of books, of mustiness and of ink, and the quietness was rather sacred.

"David!" There was a sharp, decisive voice, and he looked about and saw Dr. Lydia Brookes walking at a brisk pace his way. She was a beautiful woman, her auburn hair as it fell through the light of the library windows, catching the sun, which gleamed in her face, which was marked with acuity. Her green eyes glowed with an intelligent alertness, the type that took little notice, and her fitted blazer made a fine emphasis on her calm but easy manner.

"Thank you, Dr. Brookes," said David on meeting him, with a sincere handshake.

'Of course," she said, her handshake was strong, her smile was friendly but businesslike. "Emile Fletcher mentioned you were in town covering the Whittacre murders. It's a chilling story... unthinkable, really. Please, have a seat."

David sat in one of the comfortable chairs in the library, which had a plush covering that was comfortable but supportive. "It's grim, no doubt about it. The network requested that I apply to remain in town a couple of days longer to do some digging, in order to determine whether I should be able to form any context. People are even talking of making this a documentary."

Dr. Brookes nodded, upon which she sat down and contemplated him from a chair opposite him. "This part of the world is not lacking in history. I have been reading and rereading it ever since I was three years old, I started working on it, and I keep finding new strands. I hope to take it all and make a textbook out of it, one that will one day be a part of the curriculum here."

David turned forward, his voice garrulous. "Precisely

230

that is why I came to you. Emile replied to me that you are the authority as far as the history of this region is concerned. Anything you can say will be priceless."

Her lips turned into a demure smile. "Well, I'll do my best to help. The history of this region is rich; however, it is also tied in a lot with shadows that most people would prefer not to talk about. Let's see where we can start."

The gentle atmosphere of the library appeared to close in on them as their discussion commenced. After which, they were enveloped in a sense of common mission. It was a time when wonder and determination met in the case of David, and the initial steps of discovering the mysteries of Stookton have been made.

"I do not think I am all that informed," Dr. Brookes said with a small shrug. "But as I was saying just now, I have been digging into the history of this place quite some time now. Regrettably, a good deal of what I have been seeking after is not only difficult to get at, but it is not desired by anyone to talk about the past around here." Her head was there in the air, as though she were revolving, as she hesitated. "There's a complicated legacy. There is a current of corruption, accidents, people who just vanish, and a degree of power and influence that is extremely uncomfortable to a great many."

231

David lifted his eyebrows and drew forward. "No, I am learning all right, you see," he said, a little drolly. "And even as regards asking questions, I have already been firmly instructed not to come and go. Seems like there are individuals who believe that my news crew and I are better suited to do our reporting in another place."

"Really?" Her face changed to a curious one as Dr. Brookes asked her. "What happened?"

David laughed, but he was laughing rather out of bitterness than out of happiness. "Let's just say there were a few gentlemen last night who kindly escorted me to my car. I was driving out of the library, and they made it easy to understand that I could be much healthier as I did my research at a very distant place. It seems that they thought that no one had ever attempted to intimidate me before. He grinned sarcastically. I would think I should be accustomed to it by now."

Dr. Brookes was a wide-eyed unbeliever, and her features were astonished and disgusted." It is not surprising, David, as disgusting as that is. And I know we would not have to go too far to guess who conceived that little welcome-party." Her voice stopped, and her face relaxed as she looked up at him more soberly. "You were at the library, she asked, nearly as though she were checking him."

David nodded. "Yeah. I entered rather casually with the thought that I would enquire whether I could have access to their archives. I was attempting to better understand what Emile described as the 'Chronicles.' It was at that moment I was allowed the... honor of meeting the head librarian, Mrs. Evelyn Cook."

"Oh, yes, Mrs. Cook," said Dr. Brookes with a shake of the head. "She's a gem, isn't she? Let me tell you, the reception that she gave you was an embrace and a kiss in comparison with the reception I received the last time I spoke with her. She actually called me 'Princess Snoop.'"

David laughed, shaking his head. "Well, then, Dr. Brookes, I was not so much surprised by her reaction to me. The media does not appear to receive the respect that we once did. I suppose the attitudes have changed."

She nodded thoughtfully. "Alright, before we proceed any further, would you please refer to me henceforth simply as Lydia?" she asked. Then her voice had changed slightly and was no longer official but on a personal level.

"Lydia, it is," David returned with a pleasant smile, thankful at the diversion of their talk.

Before proceeding, she smiled wryly at him. "And as to the Chronicles... not, perhaps, the best place to begin where you are mainly concerned with digging into the history of the area. The fact is that some of these antiques and records are present, hidden somewhere in different corners, even in the library. The bulk of that which has survived is irrelevant or, to be quite honest, useless. I've seen them myself. They are mostly full of folklore and rumors... tales that have been handed down throughout the generations." Lydia paused for a moment, and the chuckle that came to her mind was cursory and ridiculing. "I've gone through some of them. There is even a page on the best method to make Amish bread, and another one indicating that menstruation is the sign of the beast. The stuff that has been written down over the years is nonsense. The 'Chronicles' are now a myth rather than a fact."

David raised an eyebrow, manifestly interested. "So, where do I begin then? What's the real history? Where are the buried bones?" His voice was more solemn now, as he leaned forward a little, as though he were planning to get down into something deeper than historical records.

Lydia hesitated a moment to think of what he was saying, and looked thoughtful. "You must peep behind the curtain to know the real history of this place. The 'Chronicles' will not take you anywhere significant. You have to pay attention to the faces, to the faces of the people, the ones who have been governing since the very inception of the town, the families whose names are inscribed in the walls of the town. But even that can be tricky." She sighed, and her eyes clouded with some unspoken thought. "Just be careful. You had better keep some things covered up."

Lydia stood motionless a little, her face flushed to one of quiet seriousness. Her eyes were fixed; there was a certain weight in her voice that could not be misinterpreted. "You know, your choice of words, David, is interesting." She hesitated and looked him full in the face, and her voice gained something more of deliberation. "You did not intend to take it literally, but there are buried bones. Literally, this project you are undertaking, the activity I have been practicing, and the things we can discover should we choose to consolidate our assets... that is no joking matter, and not a little frightening. Some will have rather that we should go away."

David looked at Lydia, and a slight change in the atmosphere was noticeable between them. This is when he finally understood that it was not a simple murder case; it was something more. The woman who was before him was more than an intellectual lady; she was a willful, educated, and possessed that quiet intensity which indicated that she had witnessed things few others had observed. There was a tincture of warning in what she said, yet there was an appeal as well. His intuition, which had been sharpened with the years of his pursuit of leads, had told him that the suspicions of Emile were correct. And this tale was much more than anybody had ever thought.

His voice was seriously low as he leaned forward a little. "Lydia, let's do this," he said in a very determined voice. "And what you have learnt, starting at the very beginning, tell me everything. I will make notes, keep in mind what you have told me, and perhaps, perhaps, we shall see how to do a favor to each other and discover the truth." He stopped to add, "I can get myself some very strong stuff. One of the most skilled researchers at the network is Linda Carr. And you see, she can be taken with fact-based information such as that you have unearthed. Where might we go with this story?"

Lydia sat thoughtfully silent, with the burden of his words sinking in. Years had she held her research close to her chest, and had been very careful to guard the information she had collected together, as she could one day bring it into the light in her book. But that something about David, his seriousness, his frank inquisitiveness, and even the fact of danger which he appeared to be welcoming, made her change her mind. Was it that she suddenly felt an attraction to him, or that she had been frustrated by the years of

236

resistance and intimidation she had been resisting? Perhaps it was both. It was something, but her subconscious told her that she could trust him. She had to be assisted, and this could be the appropriate time.

"David, it is a lot," she said, finally, and her voice was less deep but still had an element of apprehension. "The news I have got, the study... there is too much to digest, yet... who knows, we can. Let's work together."

She made David lift his heart. It had not been the kind of speedy consensus he had anticipated, but he was delighted by it. "Lydia, that's excellent. Where do we start?" He was very much excited, though he restrained his tone and concentrated.

Lydia shook her head and gave a little laugh. "Well, not here, not right now. I must go teach a lesson in half an hour. She looked at the clock on the wall and, looking back at him, she smiled in a mischievous manner. 'What is your plan for the remainder of the day?"

David gave a sigh, rather disappointed that they should have to stop their conversation, but soon got on again. "Pretty crazy, actually. I should go back to my crew and work on a live shot of an update on the murders of Whittacre during the past hour of *America This Morning*. Then I've got another live portion for the 6.00 evening news. My colleagues and I will then go out seeking the closest watering hole to relax."

The laughter of Lydia was light and contagious. "Well, when you have nothing on at about eight, I have a bar that is very well stocked in my place. Have a cocktail, it may be a pleasant, easy method of settling down to a long tale. And... I will explain to you what the actual source documents were and my location. Well, some of them. They're called the *Angelorum*."

At the reference to *Angelorum,* David took an interest, and he nodded enthusiastically. "I'll be there. And thanks, Lydia. I would like to know more."

She hastily wrote the address and phone number before taking her notes and briefcase and getting ready to go. "I will meet you this evening," she wrote, then smiled as briefly and sincerely as possible. She did not utter another word, but was up and off the chair with a purpose in her walk towards the door.

He observed her as she went, and an admiration and expectation that were both awe and pleasure grew within him. He was not able to stop feeling an increasing excitement as he left the library and walked back to the hotel and his crew. And not only had he struck a vein of invaluable material to make up a story which he was sure was going to be monumental, but the very presence of Lydia was haunting him. Something about her there was, about her smartness, her fire, her enigmatic charm, which he could not shudder.

Driving away from the campus and back to the hotel and his crew, David could smile at himself. "Oh, this is getting interesting, he said to himself with a voice that was full of excitement and a slowly rising feeling of anticipation."

# Chapter 21

## The Angelorum

David Archer stood on the doorstep of Dr. Lydia Brookes's bungalow, his pulse quickening with something he could not quite name. The late afternoon sun stretched across the quiet street in streaks of gold and shadow, as though even the day itself hesitated on the edge of night, holding its breath for what was to come. Lydia's house stood dignified and timeless, a place that seemed to carry secrets of its own. Ivy crept like patient fingers over the brickwork, curling around the windows as if determined to shield what lay inside. In the front garden, bursts of color swayed softly in the wind, blooms that danced with deceptive innocence, masking the storm of history Lydia was about to unleash.

With a bottle of wine tucked carefully under his arm, a peace offering, a gesture of trust, David knocked. The sound rang sharp and hollow in the stillness, and for a fleeting second, he wondered if even the walls of the house were listening. When the door opened, there she was... Lydia, radiant against the warm glow behind her. Her presence carried both the ease of a trusted friend and the gravity of

240

someone burdened by knowledge too heavy to bear alone.

"David, welcome," she said, her voice rich with warmth yet tinged with something unspoken, as if her words were only half of what she wanted to confess.

She stood there in quiet elegance, dressed in a cream sweater and navy trousers, her hair cascading around her shoulders in waves that caught the fading sunlight. David smiled, masking his curiosity with practiced charm as he handed her the bottle.

"I come bearing gifts," he said lightly, though the weight of the moment clung to his tone.

She returned his smile, softer, gentler. "Much appreciated. Come in… there's much to talk about."

Inside, her home radiated character. Bookshelves brimming with stories of the ages lined the walls, while a modest fireplace seemed to invite confidences that could only be whispered in firelight. A faint scent of cinnamon lingered in the air. David sank into a plush armchair, acutely aware of how easily this sanctuary could transform into a confessional.

They sat together, the soft veil of evening light spilling through sheer curtains, wrapping the room in a muted glow. Lydia placed the wine on the table but left it unopened. Instead, she fixed her gaze on David, her eyes shimmering with both fear and determination.

Her voice lowered, thickened with gravity. "If we're really going to understand Stookton... its secrets, its shadows, we can't stop at just the scandals of the Von Stook family. That's just the surface. What I've uncovered reaches back to the very foundation of this town, back to the soil, the shale, the blood and bones it was built on. I think..." Her words faltered, her breath quickening. "I think this place was cursed from its birth."

David's brows furrowed, but he didn't interrupt. He could feel her words pulling him into a darker current, and some part of him dreaded where it might lead.

She leaned forward, her tone hushed yet urgent. "Yesterday, I mentioned the Angelorum. Do you remember?"

"Of course," David replied, his usual wit subdued. "You have my undivided attention."

Lydia inhaled deeply, steadying herself before she continued. "The Angelorum weren't simply writings. They were early church elders entrusted with chronicling the community's life from the moment they settled here. Their records, their warnings, everything they feared... it all still exists. Hidden." Her voice trembled as she spoke the next words. "They lie in catacombs beneath what remains of a church five miles from here. A church that was built not just for worship, but as a reliquary for their documents. And when they dug those catacombs, they struck shale, the very resource that later fed Von Stook's empire of brickyards. Do you see, David? From the beginning, this land demanded a price."

Her hands trembled slightly as she gestured, as though her body itself resisted the memories she had unearthed. "I've been there before. It's... suffocating. Like the walls themselves are alive, pressing against you, waiting to see if you belong. But in those shadows rests the truth of this town."

David leaned forward, heart pounding, every muscle taut with anticipation. "Go on," he urged, his voice low.

Lydia's eyes flickered with something between dread and exhilaration. "The Angelorum weren't just chroniclers. They were part of a sect, an offshoot of the early colonists. They called themselves *The Awakened Ones*. In the late seventeenth century, they broke away from the rigid doctrines of New England and came here, to the Midwest, carrying with them beliefs that blurred the line between devotion and damnation. These weren't settlers in the ordinary sense, David. They came chasing revelations, visions. They believed this land was chosen. But chosen by what, or by *whom*, that's the question that haunts me."

"The Awakened Ones?" David repeated, his voice catching somewhere between curiosity and dread. "Who were they?"

Lydia's face darkened, her tone tightening with gravity. "A sect," she said slowly, "known for its suffocating piety, its relentless fervor, and its merciless discipline. Their worship was fire and brimstone, and their laws were iron chains. Anyone who strayed, even by a whisper, even by a thought, was condemned. David, there were executions for those found to be 'outside the will of God.'"

Her words hung in the air like smoke, thick and choking. David felt the sting of them settle on his skin.

The fire popped in the hearth, a sharp crack against the silence, sending sparks spiraling upward as though echoing the cruelty Lydia described. The flames painted her face in shifting tones of amber and shadow, each flicker making her look like a figure caught between light and confession. Outside, the wind pressed against the house, wailing low through the eaves, a restless chorus, a ghostly prelude to what she was about to unveil.

Lydia's eyes lifted to his, lit with intensity, yet rimmed with sorrow. "The Angelorum is their record, David. The church leaders kept meticulous accounts: confessions,

244

accusations, and punishments. It's all there. A ledger of humanity's darkest impulses, preserved under the guise of faith."

David leaned forward, tension coiling in his chest. "And you've found these chronicles?" His words came out tight, the anticipation almost painful.

"I've found fragments," Lydia admitted, her voice strained by both triumph and frustration. "Reams of notes, copied from brittle pages. Records stretching back to the 1800s, some more intact than others. But even in fragments, the story is unmistakable. What I've pieced together hints at a hidden network, something sprawling, intricate, concealed not just here in Stookton but reaching into Shale Pointe, a small community just across the river on the Missouri border. And just as with Stookton, it has a dark history. The Von Stooks have a brickyard, there is a Shale pit, some coal mines, and all of them are infected by the same virus as is found here."

David sat motionless, alert, his journalistic prompting skepticism, concomitantly telling him that this was no ordinary story. If true, this was the kind of stuff that could topple legacies, the kind that demanded blood to stay buried. "So," he said at last, his voice measured, "the Angelorum isn't just history... it's a vault of secrets."

"Exactly," Lydia whispered, her gaze flickering toward the shadows, as if afraid the walls might be listening. "They chronicled everything... every meeting, every betrayal, every judgment. Kings and killers alike found their way into those pages. The powerful, the feared, the fallen. All of them."

She rose, moving toward a desk crowded with precarious stacks of folders. From one pile, she retrieved a folder thick with yellowing papers and handed it to him with trembling hands.

"Here," she said. "This is only part of what I've gathered. But you'll feel it when you read them, David, the weight of centuries pressing down on ink and parchment. We will need all of this, and more, to uncover the truth."

David accepted the folder, its heft settling into his palms like a burden. As he opened it, the musty smell of old paper drifted upward, as though the past itself exhaled into the room. As he scanned the brittle notes, unsure if he was holding evidence or folklore.

"You see," Lydia pressed on, her voice trembling now, "the Angelorum makes something very clear: the Awakened Ones did not come to live in peace. They came to conquer. When they arrived, they found remnants of a thriving Native American community here... peaceful, sophisticated, untouched by European corruption. And instead of coexistence, they saw demons. They saw enemies. They believed God had sent them here to purge the land."

Her voice grew harsher, her face tightening with disgust. "Their Bishops, their Elders, declared the indigenous people to be obstacles to God's will. Pagan spirit-worshippers. Demonic. And the sentence for such opposition was elimination. Swift, brutal, final."

David froze, the word slicing through him. "Eliminated?" he echoed, scarcely believing it.

Lydia's eyes gleamed in the firelight, filled with conviction. "You have no idea. The pages are soaked with it… accounts of massacres, of villages burned to ash, of women violated, children slaughtered, entire tribes erased. These zealots… these Awakened Ones… marched with the King James Bible clutched in one hand and a torch in the other, proclaiming God's will as they destroyed everything in their path. They wrapped cruelty in scripture, brutality in prayer."

Her voice broke slightly, though she pressed on, unyielding. "What they did here was no different than the witch burnings in Europe, or the bloodshed in colonial America. Only here, it was swallowed by the earth itself, hidden beneath the shale and the brick, until no one

247

remembered. Whole peoples were annihilated, and the town was built on their ashes. And I believe this whole region lives in the shadow of those secrets."

"Well," David said hesitantly, his voice heavy with unease, "that's not so different from what we're seeing in today's culture. Politics, education, so many of our most trusted institutions are being twisted by fanatical religious fervor. What used to be the 'lunatic fringe' in this country just a few years ago... now they're the ones driving the bus." Lydia leaned forward, her expression tightening, the firelight reflecting in her eyes like embers of conviction. "David, that is so true. And as a professor of history, I see it more and more. That thread, it isn't new. It's woven into the very fabric of who we are, stitched through centuries. What we're watching play out today is the same poison that first seeped into Stookton generation ago."

Her words fell heavy between them, the crackle of the fire filling the silence as she stared into the flames. It was as though she was gathering her strength by articulating he theories.

"I believe the authors of the Angelorum," she continued, her voice steadier now, "knew exactly what was happening. They watched their leaders drape violence in scripture and cloak cruelty in piety. They couldn't stop it, not openly, but

248

they could bear witness. They became an order of sorts, a secret society, scribes of truth in the shadows. "The Angelorum," this collection of documents, became a rebellion. It was their way of preserving honesty for those who would come long after. A hidden chronicle to ensure that what was buried in silence would not be lost to time."

David raised his hand slightly, as if to steady the conversation. His eyes narrowed in thought, and he let the silence stretch before he spoke again. "Alright… wait. So in your research, when you think about where all of this leads, how do you hope to use it? What's the endgame for your book, Lydia? Where are you going with this?"

She didn't hesitate. Her words came sharp, charged with purpose. "I believe from the moment this fanatical sect set foot in this region, they sought only one thing: power. Everything else was a disguise. Their religion was just a weapon… justification for murder, corruption, for greed and control. And those seeds, David, were planted deep. They grew. They infected the generations that came after, blossoming into atrocities that still echo today. Look at the Von Stook family. Their grip on this region isn't an accident. It's the poisoned fruit of that first planting."

David studied her, his journalist's eye scanning every flicker of emotion in her face. "Your research is incredible," he said softly. "You've done more than anyone could have imagined."

At that, Lydia sighed, her shoulders sinking under the invisible weight of years. "I've worked hard, David. Harder than you know. But there's more. Always more. And I haven't yet reached the heart of it."

David tilted his head, his curiosity sharpening like a blade. "So, we're not just unearthing Stookton's secrets, the scandals of its present, but the historic echoes of an entire region? Hidden truths that bind the past to the now?"

"Precisely." Lydia's voice softened, and for the first time, there was admiration in her eyes. A recognition that David understood, perhaps better than most, the enormity of what she was uncovering.

A silence fell then, thick, almost reverent. The fire snapped in the hearth, and both of them sat still, as if the very walls of the bungalow leaned in closer to listen. David felt a gnawing in his gut. There was something Lydia wasn't saying, something she was holding back.

Lydia broke the silence suddenly, rifling through the worn stacks of papers on her desk, her fingers moving with a kind of restless desperation. "Most of what I've found so far, David, is old, very old. Documents dating back to when the Awakened Ones first came west from the colonies. Those records tell their brutality plainly enough. But there's a void I can't bridge, a silence in the archives that covers the years from the early 1930s through the years after World War Two."

She stopped, her hands frozen on a folder, her gaze turning inward. The firelight caught the moisture in her eyes. "That period... it's sealed, locked away by time or by deliberate hands. But I know something happened here... something dark. Just before the war, and during it. Something that no one has ever been able to prove. And it's not just academic curiosity that drives me to it, David."

Her voice dropped lower, trembling with a rare vulnerability. "Someone very close to me may have died trying to uncover it. Their name is in these documents. I think they came too close. And the truth swallowed them whole."

David's throat tightened. The words hit with the weight of confession.

"That's why I'm here," Lydia said. "That's why I took this post at the college. Why I decided to write this book. It isn't only for history, David, it's personal. I'm not just chasing Stookton's story. I'm finishing something someone In my family started long ago. And I will not stop until the silence breaks."

251

***

As David steered his car away from Lydia's house and back toward the hotel, his thoughts wouldn't settle. The evening's conversation circled in his head like a restless bird. From the very first moment he had met Lydia, a question had nagged at him: *What was a woman like her doing here?* Teaching at a modest community college, of all places, and burying herself in the history of a town most maps barely acknowledged. It didn't make sense.

Lydia carried herself with an elegance that felt out of place in Stookton. She was refined, sharp, and unmistakably Ivy League; her education clung to every syllable, every measured pause. David knew she could have commanded a post at any top university in the country, yet she had chosen obscurity.

And then there was her remark that evening, delivered so quietly it seemed almost accidental. *"I'm in Stookton to finish something someone near to me started a long time ago."* He chose not to probe further. She would tell him when she was ready. But her words wouldn't leave him. They gnawed at him during the drive, burrowed deep, demanding explanation.

Tomorrow, they were meeting again in her office. He wouldn't let the moment slip past this time. Before anything else, he needed to know what Lydia *wasn't* saying.

# Chapter 22

## Lydia's Secret

David sat alone in Lydia's office, waiting. The room breathed with a quiet personality all its own. Late-afternoon sunlight slipped through the slats of tired blinds, cutting the space into alternating bars of gold and shadow. Books were everywhere, shelves groaning with worn monographs, towers of dog-eared paperbacks stacked on the floor, piles of student essays kept from collapse only by a brightly painted ceramic mug.

The desk was modest, half-buried beneath notecards scribbled in Lydia's elegant hand, an open planner filled with neat but hurried entries, and a cold, abandoned cup of tea. A spider plant sagged from a cracked saucer in the corner. On the wall hung a crooked diploma, and beside it a faded flyer advertising a long-past lecture on river trade in 1840. The room radiated contradiction: an Ivy League brilliance contained in an office that seemed almost willfully ordinary.

The door opened suddenly. Lydia entered with an armful of folders pressed against her chest, her hair swept into a hurried knot.

"You're early," she said. Her voice came softer than she meant it to.

David gave a half-smile. "What can I say? I like to be ready."

She set the folders down and glanced at the teacup, then at the overstuffed mug of pens. For a moment, her composure faltered. "I… sorry," she began, fumbling slightly. "I should've warned you. I got held up with a student, and then the printer decided to revolt, and…" She waved a hand, embarrassed. "I didn't mean to leave you sitting here."

David shook his head. "Don't apologize."

Lydia dropped into the chair behind her desk, tapping the end of her pencil against a yellow legal pad. She let out a slow sigh. "So," she said at last, "where were we?"

David leaned forward, letting his gaze hold hers longer than necessary. "Lydia, I don't get it. I don't get *you*. What are you doing here, at Heritage Chambers Community College, in a place like Stookton, Illinois? You could have tenure anywhere."

"I *worked* at that level," she interrupted. Her tone was quiet but edged with finality. She had expected this moment. "I had the office where the coffee was French roast, the

255

debates were sharp enough to draw blood, and the pay was three times better."

The campus bell tower tolled in the distance, deep and resonant. Lydia glanced toward the window. "But I didn't come here for gourmet coffee or notoriety. Stookton doesn't have the Bolshoi Ballet or the Guggenheim. That's obvious." She hesitated, her words thick with weight. "There's another reason I'm here. One you won't find on a faculty bio, and one that will never appear in a press release."

David leaned closer. His voice dropped to a low urgency.

"Then tell me. What are you saying, Lydia?"

She inhaled slowly, steadying herself. "Back in April 1945, just days before the end of World War II, American soldiers liberated Dachau Concentration Camp. Among them was a journalist, Jake Cohen. While documenting what he saw, he discovered evidence that Stookton Brickworks, owned by Peter Von Stook, had supplied the bricks used to construct the furnaces."

David stiffened, his throat tightening. "You mean the furnaces…"

"Yes," Lydia said grimly. "The furnaces used to burn the bodies of Jewish prisoners."

The silence in the room pressed heavy against them both.

She continued, her voice sharper now, carrying the edge

256

of long-buried anger. "Jake Cohen swore he would expose the collaboration. After returning to the States, he came here, to Stookton, in October of 1945. He intended to uncover more and publish a series of pieces in *Life Magazine* that would reveal everything. But before he could release a single word, he vanished. Disappeared without a trace. No body, no articles... just silence."

Her eyes locked with David's, unblinking. "I've been chasing his trail ever since. Every scrap of evidence, every whisper, every forgotten file. My work here isn't about tenure. It's about finishing what he started. About finding the truth, they buried with him."

David's brow furrowed, the weight of Lydia's revelation hanging between them like a gathering storm. "But wait a minute," he said slowly, his voice taut. "How do you even know about Jake Cohen? How do you know who he was, or that he ever came to Stookton?"

Lydia's gaze fixed on him, her expression solemn. Her voice lowered, each word deliberate. "David... Jake Cohen was my grandfather."

The silence that followed was thick, pressing against the walls of the office. David sat back, stunned into stillness. A dozen questions formed at once, but none reached his lips. He simply waited, sensing there was more she needed to tell.

257

Lydia drew a breath, her eyes softening with memory. "All my life, I heard whispers from my grandmother, fragments of a secret my grandfather carried back with him from Europe. She used to say Jake had seen something during the liberation of Dachau, something the world *needed* to know. But he never told her the details. Only that he couldn't speak of it until he knew more.

"In October 1945, just a few months after returning from covering the war for the American Press International, he told her he had to leave for a few days. He said it was research, gathering information for a series of articles he planned to publish nationally. She trusted him, of course. He was a seasoned reporter; travel and separations were nothing new for them. But that trip was different. He left in early October, and... he was never seen again. My grandmother went to her grave never knowing what happened to him."

David leaned forward, his voice hushed but urgent. "But Lydia, how did *you* find out? How do you know about Jake's connection to Stookton Brickworks... or that he even came here?"

Lydia dropped her eyes to her folded hands, pausing as if to steady herself. When she spoke again, her tone was weighted with both grief and conviction. "Three days after I completed my master's degree at the University of Chicago, my grandmother died. At her graveside service, an old man approached me, disheveled, weary, but with eyes sharp as glass. His name was Dick Mercer. He told me he had been my grandfather's news editor back in the 1940s. It was Mercer who had sent Jake to cover Dachau."

Her gaze lifted to David, holding his. "Mercer said that when my grandfather came back from the war, he carried a shadow with him. He hinted to Mercer, as he had to my grandmother, that he had uncovered something at Dachau that would shatter Americans if exposed. But he refused to share the details until he did more research. He asked Mercer for a two-week leave. 'I need to chase this down,' Jake had said, and Mercer agreed. A few days later, Jake left Chicago and vanished into silence."

David opened his mouth to interrupt, but Lydia lifted her hand quickly. "Wait. I'm coming to the most important part. "Just before my grandmother died, Mercer had been asked by the current editor to clean out his old files from the bureau. Buried under mountains of yellowed newsprint, he stumbled across a box, an entire archive my grandfather had left behind. Inside was a letter addressed to him, along with stacks of documents. Jake had laid out in those notes what he had discovered: Stookton Brickworks' complicity with Nazi Germany.

"According to Jake, the Von Stook family and many in Stookton and nearby Shale Pointe Stookton weren't just business partners; they were Nazi sympathizers, tied to the American Bund. In the 1930s, that movement had millions of followers right here in the U.S. People disillusioned by the Depression, terrified of communism, clinging to the idea that America should be a 'Christian nation.' Many of them looked to Hitler as a model. The Von Stooks were among them. But exactly what role they played, what their dealings with Germany really were, that remains hidden."

David exhaled slowly, shaking his head. "So the key to your grandfather's disappearance... all of it was sitting in a newsroom box for decades?"

"Amazing, isn't it?" Lydia said softly. "After Mercer gave me those files, I spent months combing through them. Page after page, I pieced together fragments. My grandfather had discovered corruption, brutality, exploitation of workers, and a tie between this town and the Nazi regime. The specifics, though, he never wrote down. Only that he was coming here to uncover the truth in full. Whatever he found..." She shook her head, her voice tightening. "He never had the chance to reveal it."

The room was quiet except for the faint tick of the clock. David stared at her, troubled. "Lydia, it's fascinating. But I don't understand why one of the most powerful regimes in the world, at that time, would care about a little town in the American Midwest. Why Stookton?"

Her expression darkened. "I don't know. Neither did my grandmother, nor Mercer. That's the riddle my grandfather was trying to solve, the one that likely cost him his life. I believe he witnessed something darker than we can imagine.

Stookton has always hidden its sins under the veneer of small-town respectability. The more I dig, the more I find whispers of cover-ups, families burying the truth to protect legacies. And I believe the Von Stooks are at the very center of it."

David shifted in his seat, the tension palpable. "And your book... that's what you're hoping to uncover? To finally tell what he couldn't?"

Lydia's eyes blazed, a spark of fire cutting through the heaviness. "I want justice. Justice for Jake Cohen, for the victims silenced in Dachau, for every life destroyed by lies and collusion. I want to drag what's been hidden into the light."

David let the silence linger before speaking again, his voice low. "So... where do we go from here?"

Lydia leaned forward, her words deliberate, almost urgent. "David, you and I are chasing the same beast. You're

261

trying to expose the truth about the Whittacre murders for your documentary. I'm trying to finish the book my grandfather never got to write. And both roads lead to the Von Stook family. To Stookton's buried past.

"To prove it, I need to go back into the catacombs. To find the entries of the *Angelorum*. They may hold the key to understanding the connection between this town and Nazi Germany. But I can't do it alone. I need your help."

She paused, her gaze fixed on him. "That, David… that is our next step."

# Chapter 23

## Best Intentions

When David returned to his hotel room, the atmosphere felt charged, almost combustible. An electric tension clung to the air, thick as fog before a storm. His mind buzzed with Lydia's revelations: the legacy of her grandfather, the Von Stook family's sinister past, and the promise of the Angelorum hidden deep in the catacombs beneath the old church. He could hardly wait to tell Mark and Jerry. But as soon as he stepped inside, he realized his team was equally restless, hunched over the table littered with notes, empty coffee cups, and scattered photographs, the overhead light casting hard shadows across their faces.

Mark Allen, the seasoned photographer, leaned back in his chair, a grin tugging at the edge of his mouth, though his eyes betrayed urgency. "David… you're not gonna believe this."

Before David could even sit down, Jerry Marsh, the field producer, cut in, his words tumbling out fast. "We got a call. From Emile Fletcher."

David blinked, the name landing like a stone. "Emile?"

"Yeah," Jerry said, leaning forward, his voice dropping a notch. "He claims he's got new information. About the Whittacre murders."

"But..." Mark interjected, his smirk fading into a grim line. "The guy's scared out of his mind. Shaking. Said he has evidence. He's on his way here, right now. Wants to go live with it tomorrow morning on *America This Morning.*"

The words hung in the air, sharp and unsettling. David was still processing when a soft knock rattled the door.

For an instant, all three men froze, exchanging wary glances. Jerry, closest, rose slowly, his hand hovering over the handle before pulling it open.

There stood Emile Fletcher, or rather, the ghost of him. His face was ashen, his forehead slick with sweat that caught the light in trembling beads. His shoulders slumped under an invisible weight. The jovial, loose-tongued old man David remembered had been replaced by someone hollowed out, brittle.

"Emile," David said quietly, stepping forward, his voice laced with concern. "Come in."

The door clicked shut behind him, the sound unnervingly final.

"I... I heard them." Emile's voice was raw, a whisper frayed at the edges. He shuffled inside, clutching a brown

264

paper bag like a lifeline. "Robert Lee Chambers and A.J. Chambers. The congressman's boys. They were bragging about... about the massacre."

The words detonated in the silence, leaving the room heavy, suffocating. Mark shifted in his chair, Jerry's jaw tightened, and David felt his stomach drop.

"Bragging?" Mark repeated, incredulous, his brow creasing.

"Yeah," Emile rasped, fumbling the bottle from his bag and taking a burning swig of Jack Daniel's. His hands shook so hard the liquid sloshed behind the Cardinal uncomfortably, across from the Pour House on Dewey. "They were in the alley, talking to some other fellas. Loud, cocky... like they wanted the whole damn world to hear. They didn't care. They were proud of it."

Jerry leaned forward, his voice sharpened with gravity. "Did they say anything specific? Names? Details?"

Emile nodded slowly, his body trembling as if the memory itself scalded him. "They said how easy it was. How nobody would suspect them. Jesus Christ, David..." His voice cracked, breaking into a desperate rasp. "What if they saw me? What if they know I heard?"

His breathing hitched as he took another long swallow from the bottle, then lowered his head, grief carving deep lines into his face. "I came to you because I don't know where else to go. I can't..." his voice faltered. "I can't carry another secret like this. Not again. I told you once about that murder I kept quiet about when I was a kid. It's haunted me every damn day since. I won't go to my grave with this one. Not this time. I'm talking."

He slumped into a chair, the room closing in around him. The silence stretched, taut and suffocating, before Jerry broke it, his tone cautious, almost pleading.

"Emile, as a field producer, I have to ask you straight. Are you certain you want to do this? To go public? The Chambers family, the Von Stooks, these people have reach, power. Once you speak their names on live television, there's no going back. It could be dangerous."

Emile lifted his head, his eyes wide, glassy, desperate. "If I stay quiet, I'm already dead. If they find out I knew, I'm a target anyway. At least this way, the spotlight's on me, maybe it buys me some protection. And maybe..." His voice broke, a shuddering breath escaping as he gripped the bottle tight. "Maybe it redeems me. For all those years of silence. For the boy I once was, who didn't speak up."

David was torn. His chest tightened as he looked from Jerry to Mark, then back to Emile, whose trembling hands betrayed his desperation.

266

"A live interview?" His voice was steadier than he felt. "Guys, I know we have a job to do here, but this isn't just about ratings or breaking a story. We all understand what kind of risk this is for Emile. And..." his voice dropped lower, weighted with the gravity of the moment, "...we're starting to understand what these people might actually be capable of."

The words hung heavy in the air, and a chill swept through the room. It wasn't just the draft seeping through the windows; it was the dread of unspoken truths, the knowledge that this town thrived on secrets, and that those secrets were protected by people with power and no conscience.

David turned his gaze back to Emile, whose haunted eyes pleaded for direction. "If we decide to go this route, we'll protect you. But first, I have to check with legal back at the Chicago bureau. We need to know what the implications are for the network... and what kind of personal protection we can secure for you."

Jerry, always the scrupulous one, leaned forward, his voice sharp but edged with concern. "Guys, we need to be damned sure what we're stepping into. We're talking about a couple of kids overheard mouthing off in some alley, but those kids happen to be the sons of Congressman Phillip Chambers. A man lobbying for a fourteen-billion-dollar

267

contract to build one of the largest nuclear plants in the country. If the Chambers family feels threatened, they'll bury us. And given what we've been digging up about the power base here in Stookton and Shale Points, we cannot take this lightly."

Jerry placed a hand gently on Emile's back, grounding him. "If we do this, I need at least forty-eight hours to get my ducks in a row with the network. I won't let this story implode before it even breaks. That being said..." his voice softened but carried a dangerous clarity, "...there's an upside. The moment you step into the light, those guys hiding in the shadows lose their cover. You make yourself visible, and suddenly it's a hell of a lot harder for them to silence you."

Emile clenched his fists, his knuckles whitening, his trembling replaced by a stubborn resolve that carried the weight of decades of silence. "Then let's do it," he said, his breath ragged but steadying with each word. "Let's go to the police... and then let's go live with David. No more running. No more hiding."

# Chapter 24

## More Questions

The next morning broke dark and bitter over Stookton. The sky sagged under the weight of bruised gray clouds, swollen with snow. A hush lay over the town, smothering sound in a thick white blanket that covered rooftops, roads, and fields in a shroud of silence.

David pulled his coat tighter as he crossed the icy path to Heritage Chambers Community College. The red-brick facade, glistening with frost, stood as both a beacon and a warning, history, knowledge, and power woven into one imposing structure. Its windows reflected the bleak sky, and for a moment, the building looked less like a college and more like a watchtower keeping secrets of its own.

Inside, Lydia's office was a cluttered labyrinth of thought and obsession. Books leaned precariously, threatening collapse, while maps peppered with pins and scrawled notes plastered the walls like evidence in a detective's war room. The smell of old paper, coffee, and damp wool clung to the air. This was not just an office; it was Lydia's mind made visible, a battlefield of past and

269

present locked in uneasy dialogue.

Lydia herself stood out like a deliberate stroke of charcoal on a canvas. Her bomber jacket clung to her frame, its dark tones amplifying the warmth of her loosely tied hair. Slim black trousers and ankle boots gave her the aura of someone perpetually straddling two worlds: academia and excavation, intellect and earth. She looked up as David entered, a spark of wry amusement in her eyes.

"Ready to get your hands dirty?" she asked, her tone teasing, but beneath it lay a thread of steel.

"Always," David replied, a faint smile tugging at his lips. He admired the way she balanced gravity with levity, her resilience shining through her carefully measured composure. He suspected it was what kept her from being swallowed whole by this town's history.

They set off in Lydia's olive-green Land Rover, its tires crunching over the snow-packed lot. The vehicle moved with steady determination down the winding road that unspooled from Stookton, each bend revealing the stark beauty of isolation. Frost-laced fields stretched endlessly, broken by clusters of skeletal trees whose ancient branches groaned under the weight of ice.

"This place seems so peaceful," David said, his eyes tracing the quiet landscape beyond the window.

270

"Nature." Lydia's voice cut through the silence, almost bitter. "The great concealer."

The Land Rover jostled as she turned onto a gravel lane, the road narrowing until it was little more than a scar carved through towering oaks. Then, through the tangled canopy, it emerged: the old church.

Its roofless silhouette loomed like a skeletal hand clawing at the sky, the spire a blackened finger of accusation pointing heavenward. As they drew closer, the ruin revealed itself, a mosaic of charred stone, creeping ivy, and broken majesty. Gargoyles, once fierce sentinels, had eroded into grotesque caricatures of themselves. Their hollowed faces, streaked with snow and shadow, seemed to leer down at the intruders. Lydia pulled the Land Rover onto an embankment overlooking the ruin. The tires crunched to a stop, and for a moment, neither spoke. The engine ticked as it cooled, the sound unnervingly loud in the otherwise oppressive silence.

The old church waited, silent, wounded, and alive with secrets.

Gathering their backpacks, they set out, boots crunching into the snow as they descended a steep, unforgiving slope toward the ruin. The flakes fell heavier now, swirling around them in a frantic dance, carried on the biting wind that rattled the skeletal branches above. Each groan of wood sounded like bones grinding together, a macabre symphony echoing Lydia's words.

"This place," Lydia began, her voice half-swallowed by the icy breeze, "was once a sanctuary... a refuge for those seeking divine solace." She paused, her eyes tracing the broken silhouette of the church below. "But now..." Her voice trailed off into the silence, the unfinished thought heavier than anything she could have spoken.

The air thickened as they descended the winding, leaf-strewn path, the oppressive quiet amplifying every step. Their footfalls crunched rhythmically against the frozen earth, the cadence underscoring the anticipation that coiled tighter with every yard closer to the ruin.

"There it is," Lydia whispered, her breath rising in pale plumes.

The old church loomed in front of them like a sentinel abandoned by time. Its skeletal frame of charred stone and ivy-clad walls rose defiantly against the ashen sky. Shadows clung to its hollows as though unwilling to relinquish whatever secrets it still guarded.

They stepped through what remained of the entrance, where proud wooden doors had once stood. Now the arch gaped open like the mouth of some stone beast, waiting to devour trespassers. Crossing the threshold, David felt the outside world fall away, replaced by a suffocating silence that seemed to vibrate through his bones.

The air inside was damp, earthy, tinged with smoke, the lingering ghosts of fire. Shafts of dim light pierced the grime-coated stained glass, the fractured images of saints and angels casting distorted, spectral figures across the blackened floor. Charred pews lay toppled, brittle remnants of faith reduced to ash. The high ceiling arched overhead like the ribcage of some long-dead giant, their flashlights sending jittery beams over faded murals, half-obscured but still whispering fragments of forgotten devotion.

Lydia's flashlight cut a narrow path through the dark. "This way," she murmured, her voice reverent, cautious, as if afraid of waking something long asleep. She led David toward a spiral staircase, its iron rail cold beneath her hand. The steps wound downward into a blackness so complete it felt alive.

As they descended, the air grew colder, denser. A distant drip echoed through the cavernous silence, each drop ringing like a warning bell in the void. David's voice broke the hush, hushed yet awed. "It's like stepping into another world."

At the bottom, the passage opened into a low chamber. The beam of Lydia's flashlight swept over crumbling stone

273

shelves stacked haphazardly with crates, boxes, and bundles of brittle parchment. Dust stirred in the air, thick and alive, glowing like embers in the thin light.

"This is it," Lydia said, her voice laced with both excitement and gravity. She reached for an ancient folio, lifting it with care, her fingers reverent as though touching relics of saints. "These are the records of the Angelorum."

David leaned in, his breath catching as he traced the faded ink and fragile fibers of paper. Here was a history hidden, waiting, its truths preserved in silence. The Angelorum had chronicled everything, the light and the darkness, and now, perhaps, the key to Stookton's deepest secrets waited among these shelves.

"Somewhere in these documents," Lydia whispered, her eyes fever-bright, "is the record Jake Cohen never lived to bring to light. The files from the '30s and '40s, and the Von Stook clan. This is where I found the older papers before. This is where the truth should be."

David brushed dust from a nearby crate, revealing a label faded almost to nothing. Lydia swung her light onto it, her voice tightening with urgency. "Remember, David… we're looking for anything tied to the years before, during, and after the war. And especially any reference to Jake Cohen."

The air in the catacombs was charged, the silence so thick

it pressed against their skin, as though the past itself resisted being disturbed. Shadows shifted in the corners, moving with the breath of their flashlights.

"Help me with this," Lydia said, her tone steady but her hands trembling ever so slightly. She pulled at a weathered tome wedged into the shelf. Its spine cracked with a brittle sigh, and a cloud of dust erupted into the cold air, swirling around them like ashes rising from the grave.

David stood beside her, peering over her shoulder, his breath shallow in the frigid air. "Do you think this could be it? The evidence we've been chasing?" His voice was low, reverent, like a man speaking in a cathedral, careful not to disturb the ghosts that seemed to press in from the shadows. "Only one way to find out," Lydia murmured, though her heart thundered in her chest. With trembling fingers, she opened the brittle book. Its pages were yellowed, edges curled and fragile, the ink neat and purposeful as though every word had been meant to endure eternity. Her eyes skimmed the lines and suddenly froze. A chill bolted down her spine.

"Lydia," David breathed, his voice barely audible, "look at this."

She turned, pulse racing, as he pointed to a page filled with contracts and signatures. His flashlight illuminated the scrawled words, shipments from *Stookton Brickworks* bound for destinations in Germany.

"These are from the late 1930s," David whispered, his expression darkening with each word.

Lydia's hand flew to her mouth as comprehension struck. "Oh my God, David... furnaces." Her voice cracked, and for a moment she thought her knees might give way. "They were sending bricks... for the concentration camp furnaces."

The words felt like poison on her tongue.

The silence thickened, heavy as lead. David's jaw tightened as he traced a trembling finger over the faded ink. "And here," he muttered grimly. "The signatures. Peter Von Stook... his sons... half the family. It's all here, Lydia. This is what Jake uncovered. He *knew*. He was trying to prove it."

Her throat constricted as anger and disbelief warred inside her. "They weren't just sympathizers," she whispered, her voice breaking. "They were collaborators. They had blood on their hands... American hands feeding the machinery of genocide."

Lydia rifled through the pages feverishly, parchment crackling beneath her touch. Each line revealed more: ledgers, correspondence, coded memos. Then suddenly she stopped, her breath catching. "David... look!"

276

He leaned in, his flashlight steady as she pointed to a passage. The script was deliberate, almost reverent. "A journalist," David murmured, recognizing the cadence of someone chronicling events with purpose.

Lydia nodded, eyes glistening. "The Angelorum recorded his arrival. Fall of 1945. He came to Stookton, investigating the brickyards. They even wrote of a man who asked too many questions. David... this was Jake."

David flipped through more pages, his brow furrowed. Mentions of Jake grew sparse, then disappeared. The trail went cold in the ink just as it had in life. "He was building the case," David muttered, almost to himself. "Tying the Von Stooks, their empire, and their Nazi ties together. But whatever he found after this... it never left Stookton. Someone silenced him."

For a long moment, they stood in silence, surrounded by the echo of dripping water and the weight of history pressing in on them like a tomb. The documents in Lydia's hands felt heavier than stone. They were holding evidence of atrocity, and the ghost of a man who had died to reveal it.

David's eyes lingered on her as she gently slipped the journals and crumbling pages into her backpack. Her tenacity, her courage, her relentless hunger for truth, it both awed him and terrified him. Still, a question gnawed at him, and he could not swallow it down.

"Lydia," he said carefully, his voice low and urgent, "there's one thing I can't wrap my head around. Why? Why in God's name would one of the most powerful regimes in the world, the Nazis, enter into some unholy alliance with a small Midwestern town?"

Lydia's lips curved into the faintest, almost haunted smile. She had expected this. "Ah, David. That," she said softly, "is where things get very interesting." Her eyes glinted with both triumph and unease. "Tomorrow, I'll take you to see my mentor, Dr. Paul Jacobs. He's the only one who can help us piece this together."

She glanced around the catacomb, shivering as the shadows seemed to pulse closer, pressing against the circle of light. "But right now? Let's get out of this tomb. I've got a date with a dirty martini."

David exhaled, a strained laugh escaping him, breaking the tension for a moment. "Now *that's* the best idea I've heard all night, Doc."

# Chapter 25

## A History Lesson


David Archer and Dr. Lydia Brookes stepped out of the crisp, biting cold of the evening and into the warm, cloistered quiet of Dr. Paul Jacobs' office. The air inside was heavy with the scent of aged paper and pipe tobacco, a world apart from the wind that had chased them through the streets. The space was an academic sanctuary: dark wood shelves lined every wall, packed to overflowing with leather-bound volumes and battered paperbacks alike. A globe sat in the corner, its surface faded and worn, oceans the color of old parchment, while framed maps of pre-war Europe hung alongside black-and-white photographs of rallies, protests, and long-forgotten faces.

Behind a broad oak desk sat Dr. Paul Jacobs, a man whose very presence seemed to carry the gravity of history. He was in his late sixties, with thinning silver hair, a neatly trimmed beard, and piercing blue eyes that seemed to see past the moment and into the marrow of events themselves. He looked up from the spread of yellowing papers on his desk as they entered, and the faintest smile touched his lips.

"Ah, David. Dr. Brookes. Please… come in." His voice was warm but laced with solemnity, as though he already anticipated the weight of the conversation to come. Rising slowly, his movements precise, he extended his hand first to Lydia, then to David. "David, I've seen you on television more times than I can count. And Lydia has told me all about your… persistence." His eyes twinkled briefly before darkening again. "Persistence is what history requires."

They exchanged greetings and settled into the two worn leather armchairs across from his desk. David placed his recorder carefully on the armrest, as if afraid to disturb the gravity in the room. Lydia leaned back, her eyes roaming across the shelves, clearly both at home and reverent in this place.

"Dr. Jacobs," David began, his voice steady but edged with curiosity, "thank you for agreeing to see us. I've been going through these records Lydia and I uncovered, and I'm trying to wrap my head around what they mean. The Von Stook family, and Stookton itself, working hand in glove with Nazi Germany. It feels impossible, but the evidence is undeniable. What I need to understand… what I need you to help me understand… is how this was even conceivable. What drove Americans, families like the Von Stooks, to sympathize with or even collaborate with the Nazis?"

280

Jacobs lowered himself into his chair again and folded his hands, his gaze distant for a moment. His expression shifted, softening into a mournful one. "It was a dark chapter,

David. Darker than most Americans care to admit. Fascism didn't just arrive from across the Atlantic; it found fertile ground here. The German-American Bund, the Silver Legion, the Black Legion..." He shook his head slowly. "These groups had real followings. They weren't fringe. They were neighbors, businessmen, ministers, teachers."

Lydia leaned forward, her voice clear, her conviction shining through. "Paul, why don't you explain to David what we've discussed before, how it wasn't just about economics, though economics was part of it. There were deeper societal wounds, deeper prejudices being fed."

Jacobs steepled his fingers and inhaled deeply, choosing his words with the precision of a surgeon. "You must picture America in the 1930s. The Great Depression wasn't just a financial collapse; it was a collapse of confidence, of stability, of faith in the system. People were desperate, hungry, and frightened. When you combine desperation with latent prejudice, you create the perfect tinderbox. Anti-Semitism was already widespread. Anti-immigrant hostility was simmering. All the Nazis had to do was strike the match.

Their rhetoric… anti-communist, anti-Jewish, pro-order, resonated far more deeply than we'd like to think. Far too many people nodded along."

David's brow furrowed, his pen scratching furiously across his notepad. "But why? Why would Americans, supposedly proud, free people, buy into such an ideology? It doesn't add up."

Jacobs gave a slow, almost sorrowful nod. "Some saw the Nazis as a shield against communism. Others believed in the myth of racial superiority and white supremacy as a divine right. And here's the part that unsettles most: the marriage of these ideas with religion. Christianity, twisted and bent into alignment with Nazi ideology. Crosses flying side by side with swastikas. Preachers in pulpits speaking of purity, discipline, obedience, while quietly justifying racial hatred. It was a perverse fusion of faith and fascism." His eyes flicked to Lydia, then back to David. "And it wasn't just in Germany. It was here, in Detroit, in Chicago, in small towns like Stookton. Hundreds would attend rallies, cheering, saluting, believing they were participating in something righteous."

David set his pen down and leaned back, shaking his head as if trying to clear it. His voice carried both disbelief and horror. "So what you're saying is… it wasn't some accident,

282

some isolated group of lunatics. It was systemic. It was woven into communities."

Jacobs' face hardened. "Exactly. That's why we must talk about it. That's why uncovering the Von Stook documents matters. It tears away the illusion that this was all safely contained overseas." He paused, his voice dropping to a low, almost conspiratorial tone. "It wasn't. It was in our backyards."

The silence that followed was heavy, thick with the ghosts of the past pressing in. Lydia finally broke it, her voice sharp with resolve. "David, this is only the beginning. Paul can tell us about the Bund, about the structures that enabled men like Peter Von Stook to thrive in shadow. But the rest... the rest we'll have to piece together ourselves."

David turned to Dr. Jacobs, his recorder's red light glowing faintly. "Alright then. Let's go deeper. Start at the beginning, Professor. Tell me everything you know about the German-American Bund."

Dr. Jacobs sat back in his chair, fingers moving deliberately as he packed his pipe, tamping down the tobacco with the ritual of a man who had delivered countless difficult truths in this very office. The faint scratch of the pipe tool seemed to punctuate the silence before he began, his voice low and deliberate.

283

"Well, the German American Bund was one of the most notorious fascist organizations to gain traction in this country during the 1930s and into the early 1940s. It's a part of American history most people would rather forget, or pretend never existed. But it did. And it thrived." He paused, eyes flickering briefly toward the photographs on his walls before locking back on David and Lydia.

"You must understand... antisemitism wasn't some fringe attitude back then. It was woven into the very fabric of society. Jews were scapegoated, cast as the enemy not only of Germany but of America as well. Bund members promoted the dangerous lie that Jews were conspiring to control politics, economics, the press, even Hollywood. To Americans out of work, beaten down by the Depression, and searching for someone to blame, Hitler looked like a strongman who stood up to a supposed common enemy. For those on the brink of despair, fascism began to look like an answer... an intoxicating one."

David leaned forward, his pen still against his notebook but unmoving, his voice edged with disbelief. "But Dr. Jacobs, that still doesn't explain what Lydia and I have uncovered. We're not just talking about rallies or rhetoric. The Von Stook family, their brickyards, their coal and shale mining businesses, they were in business with the Nazis.

284

This wasn't symbolic support. This was trade, money, contracts. How could a Midwestern community… a family like the Von Stooks… become so entangled with one of the most brutal regimes in human history?"

Jacobs studied him carefully, his piercing blue eyes narrowing, as though measuring how much truth David was prepared to handle. Finally, he leaned forward, pipe resting in his hand like a gavel. "David, you need to remember, this wasn't happening in isolation. During that period, right-wing organizations weren't just popular; they were woven into mainstream American life. The Ku Klux Klan, for example, boasted over a million members by 1932. And these weren't just nameless faces in white hoods… they were senators, congressmen, bankers, factory owners, even clergy. These were community leaders, people others trusted. Their influence normalized extremism. Their numbers gave it legitimacy."

Lydia shifted uncomfortably in her chair, the weight of his words pressing heavily in the room.

"But," Jacobs continued, his tone grave, "with visibility came scrutiny. The louder the Bund and the Klan became, the more Americans began to question their true motives. Newspapers covered them, critics pushed back. Yet, in the meantime, alliances were already being forged in the

285

shadows."

David looked down at his notes, his mind racing to connect the dots. He finally lifted his head. "Alright, but if suspicion was already growing, how in God's name did they still manage to strike deals with companies like Stookton Brickworks and the Von Stook enterprises? How did ideology transform into something as tangible as trade?"

Jacobs' gaze darkened. He set the pipe aside, lacing his fingers together. "Well, David, that's the heart of it. Trade with Germany in the early 1930s was not illegal. It wasn't unusual either. Many American companies, proud, respectable names, had dealings with the Reich before Hitler's true designs were laid bare. Ford Motor Company, for example. They had a subsidiary in Germany, Ford-Werke, that produced vehicles later used by the German army. They weren't alone. German emissaries traveled to the United States throughout the 1930s, courting businessmen, offering lucrative contracts, dangling profits in front of struggling industries.

"But here's the distinction: when the tide began to turn in the late '30s, when the truth of Hitler's ambitions grew harder to deny, most American companies broke ties. They wanted no part of what was coming. But others, those who shared Nazi sympathies, those seduced by ideology as much

286

as profit, they stayed. They doubled down. And the Von Stooks…" His voice hardened. "…the Von Stooks were among them. Stookton Brickworks. Stookton Mining. Chambers Railway. These weren't just companies doing business. These were businesses run by men who believed in Hitler's vision. Peter Von Stook adored him. He remained a Nazi sympathizer until the day he died. Their alliance wasn't just transactional, it was ideological. Dark, brutal, and, in their eyes, inevitable."

The room fell silent. The shadows cast by the lamplight seemed to grow longer, stretching across the shelves, as though history itself was reaching out from the walls. The faint groan of the old wood echoed like a sigh from the past. Lydia's voice broke the stillness, soft but firm. "Dr. Jacobs… do you think it could happen again? With what we're seeing today, the nationalism, the xenophobia, the fear being stoked, are we staring down the same patterns repeating?"

Jacobs' eyes grew grave, his jaw tightening. "Lydia, it's not a matter of *if*. It's already happening. History doesn't repeat itself neatly, but it rhymes… loudly. The same scapegoating, the same rhetoric, the same willingness to sacrifice truth for the illusion of strength, it's alive and well in modern America. And what frightens me most…" He

287

fixed David with a hard stare. "…is that the media, your profession, has not spoken out loudly enough. You, of all people, must see the parallels. This is not a time for timidity."

David felt a shiver crawl across his skin, an unease that wasn't just academic but visceral. The lamplight flickered against the spines of old books, casting the room in an almost funereal glow. The weight of what they had uncovered, the documents, the history, the warnings, pressed down on him like a stone.

And though they would leave Dr. Jacobs' office later that night, David knew the shadows of that conversation would follow them, clinging, insistent, whispering of dangers not buried in the past but stalking the present.

# Chapter 26

## Linda Goes Fishing

The rain in Stookton had a way of erasing distance, blurring the hard edges of the town into a watercolor of gray and shadow. Roads that were two lanes in daylight became wet, endless ribbons at night. The glowing neon light over the front door of the Pour House Bar and Grille appeared as smeared paint on the slick pavement. The flashing intersection light at Dewey and Carter streets pulsed like a slow-beating heart. Inside the Pour House, the air was thick with the sour scent of spilled beer and damp coats. David sat hunched at the bar, the condensation from his too-tall glass dripping slowly onto a coffee-stained napkin, each drop falling like a metronome for his thoughts.

He turned the glass absently, staring into the amber liquid as if it held answers. Emile Hirsch agreeing to speak on camera. The pages from *The Angelorum*, documenting the Von Stook family's collaboration with the Nazis, atrocities not whispered but etched in ink. And tomorrow: the national live shot with Emile, a moment David had chased but now weighed like a stone in his chest. Reporting on the Whittacre

289

murders had been his assignment. He hadn't anticipated stepping into a labyrinth of Stookton's buried sins. He thought of the meeting he had just left with Dr. Jacobs and Lydia, the professor's voice still in his ears, comparing extremism to a deadly virus, invisible until it was too late.

The sudden ring of his cell phone snapped him back to the present, a sharp, insistent sound that cut through his thoughts. The screen glowed: "Linda Carr." She was CNC's chief researcher, the woman who could trace a man's mortgage from ten years back and name the vendor who supplied his feed corn, someone who made secrets appear like ghosts summoned from thin air. David answered before the second ring.

"Linda," he murmured, his voice low, almost instinctively, as though the walls themselves might be listening. David tuned out a country song drifting in the background.

"David? Are you sitting?" Linda's voice was sharp, quick, the sound of a woman fueled by coffee and deadlines, always a few steps ahead of everyone else in the room.

"What's up?"

"I just got a call from someone claiming he has hard proof on Congressman Phillip Chambers's involvement with the Stookton Nuclear Power Plant, doing business as Clayburgh

Valley Power Corporation, now being referred to as CVPC."

David's jaw tightened, his knuckles whitening around the glass. "Go on."

"There's a lot," Linda said. "Ledgers. Wire transfers. Contracts marked to hide kickbacks. Audio of at least one conversation where Chambers tells a contractor to 'make sure we don't have any surprises.'"

David stared at the bar top, watching a rivulet of beer run like a crack in the wood. "Who is it? Name, job? Why now?"

"He won't identify himself unless he speaks to you... only you," Linda replied. "He's seen your live reports. He called from a burner; it's probably already in a dumpster. He said he'll come forward if... and only if... you're the one he talks to."

David scrubbed his thumb across the glass of his battered notebook, smudging an old coffee stain. "Why me? I'm out here. I can't get back to Chicago tonight."

"He said he's been waiting for you," Linda's voice softened slightly. "Said something about 'stories only want to be told once.' Then he asked if you were safe in Stookton."

A bird shrieked outside, high and sharp, making David instinctively shift further up the bar, away from the window. He glanced out at the rain-slicked streets and saw the silhouette of the Von Stook brickyard rising against the

291

horizon, a dark tooth gnawing at the sky. The wind caught a paper bag and sent it skittering across the pavement like something trying to flee. "Watching me how?" he asked.

"Don't know," Linda said. "He claims he's been followed. He asked about protection. I told him about the bureau contacts, the legal teams. Even with that, he's adamant. It's you or nothing."

David felt something drop into his stomach, cold, heavy. "Linda... Is this guy credible? Why call you and not the FBI or the NRC?"

"No way, David. He's a whistleblower, genuine. He said too many people are compromised in D.C. and in Stookton. He named names. Said there are people on Senator Chambers's influence list who could make a complaint disappear."

Silence stretched between them, taut as a wire. David could hear the rain spattering against the windows, each drop a muted drumbeat against the glass.

"Unbelievable, huh?" Linda said, finally. "That a small community like Stookton could foster that kind of influence? But every community has its congressman. They all go to Washington to serve."

David exhaled slowly, staring at the dark reflection of his face in the beer. "Linda, as usual, this is great stuff," he said.

292

"Well, I appreciate the accolades, but you haven't heard anything yet." Her voice dropped, conspiratorial. "Check this out. Our whistleblower sent me an index of documents, scans. Their origin's unproven, but they're damning. Bank identifiers. Wire trails leading to shell companies owned by the Chambers and Von Stook interests. Payments dated over the last decade, before Stookton Nuclear Power even existed on paper."

David gathered his thoughts, every muscle taut with the weight of what Linda was telling him. His voice came low, measured, but burning with intensity. "Alright... Linda... this is incredible. Tomorrow morning is the live shot with Emile Hirsch. He's going to go on national television and say he overheard the Congressman's kids bragging about murdering the Whittacre family."

"Holy *shit*!" Linda cut him off, her voice sharp with shock. "I heard Carl Meyer down in the newsroom whispering about that earlier today, but I thought it was newsroom gossip. Everyone here is on pins and needles waiting for your live shot. Dammit, David... be careful tomorrow."

David exhaled slowly, steadying himself. "We're ready. Believe me. Thanks to everyone back at the bureau, we've kept Emile under wraps, safe, quiet, away from prying eyes.

So far, nobody's gotten close."

"Remarkable," Linda responded. Then her voice tightened, clipped. "David, there's another problem. Right after my call with the whistleblower, my office line lit up. Anonymous number. I answered... and there was nothing.

No voice. Just silence. Like someone was listening in. Monitoring. Either on my end... or yours."

David straightened on his barstool, scanning the rain-slick windows of the Pour House, his eyes catching the distorted reflections in the glass. He lowered his voice to a whisper. "Alright. From now on, you arrange the meeting with our whistleblower. And for safety... let's give him a name. From this point forward, we call him... 'Moonlight.'"

"Moonlight?" Linda repeated, half incredulous.

"Yeah. If Chambers's two little darlings get dragged in for questioning, you know damn well he'll call a presser. My gut says he'll come back from D.C. to do it here... Stookton, his home turf. The timing couldn't be worse. This town is crawling with cameras and satellite trucks, reporters stacked on every corner. It's a hive buzzing with coverage. So before I hit Chambers for a reaction, we *must* get to Moonlight. He's the key."

Linda's voice snapped back, quick and pointed. "So let me ask you something. Are you seriously considering blindsiding Chambers with the Stookton nuclear scandal at the same press conference about the Whittacre murders?"

"I don't know yet," David admitted, the weight of both stories pressing down on him like twin anvils. "Depends how it all breaks tomorrow. But whatever Moonlight brings me… it's going in my back pocket. Insurance."

Linda was silent for a beat, then her tone turned dry, almost amused despite the tension. "One more thing. Why in the hell are we calling this whistleblower 'Moonlight?'"

David allowed himself the faintest smirk. "I don't know. Just sounds cool."

After Linda's call, David sat for a while, staring at the beer he had not touched, his reflection fractured in the golden liquid. His mind reeled with everything Linda had just laid on him. Proof. Wire transfers, whispers of surveillance, and the looming chaos of tomorrow's live shot.

Finally, he shoved back from the bar. He had to get back to the hotel, back to his crew, to plan every angle for *America This Morning*. But first, he'd call Lydia. She needed to hear everything, every detail, before the storm broke.

\*\*\*

Lydia hadn't hesitated when David suggested a drink.

By the time she pushed through the door of The Pour House, the place was already throbbing with noise. Reporters and camera crews had claimed every corner of the only bar in Stookton, their laughter too sharp, their conversations clipped with tension. The air reeked of spilled whiskey and stale smoke, the kind of smell that clung to your hair and followed you home.

She spotted David in the back, tucked into a shadowed booth beneath a green-shaded lamp that cast a sickly glow over the table, as if it were interrogating them both. Beyond that small pool of jaundiced light, the bar dissolved into gloom, where secrets could settle and stay unbothered. Outside, rain ticked against the window like fingernails, steady, insistent.

David rose half a beat when she approached, then sank back down. He looked wired, as though every nerve had been rewired for the hunt. Lydia slid into the booth, brushing the damp from her coat sleeve, her eyes alive with the same fever.

"David," she said softly, "I'm glad you called. Long day or not... I couldn't wait. You need to see what I've been digging up in the Angelorum."

She set the battered accordion file onto the table with the care of someone laying down live explosives. The cardboard was stained with age, its edges curled, its papers the brittle yellow of unearthed bones. Her hand lingered on it, fingers hooked like a lock holding back the blast.

David leaned closer, the lamp casting sharp planes across his face. "What's in it?"

Her voice dropped, carrying urgency edged with dread.

"Margin notes. Cross-references. All pointing to a private archive no one's ever seen. Hidden inside the old Von Stook mansion."

David let out a low whistle. "The mansion? I thought Chambers…"

"No. When Victor built his palace, the old house was sold off. Different family now. But pieces of the Angelorum, whole sections, were stripped out and stashed before the sale. According to this," she tapped the folder, "somewhere in that mansion is a vault. A place where they sent what they couldn't burn."

The words seemed to thicken the air between them.

"Disappearances. Land transfers. Shady bequests. Payoffs disguised as 'donations.'" Her voice tightened, each word like glass under pressure. "The ledger even lists visitors and shipments. And David…" she paused, her eyes flicking to the window where storm clouds had gathered like a verdict. "It mentions names. A ledger of who took what…

297

and who was silenced. If it's true, if the vault exists, it's not just corruption. It's the town's black heart in one locked room."

Thunder rumbled across the horizon, deep and deliberate, like drums heralding a march no one wanted to witness.

David sat back, pulse hammering. He could feel it, the hook of a story that threatened to rip everything open. The rain began in earnest, sluicing down the windows in frantic diagonal streaks, as though it wanted to get inside and add its testimony.

Lydia's eyes, sharp and haunted, found his. "My gut says it's there, David. The vault. Inside the Stook mansion."

The word *vault* lingered like a ghost between them, louder than the storm, heavier than the whiskey-stained air.

David's chest tightened, the exact sensation of curiosity when it sharpens into hunger. He wasn't just chasing a lead now. He was circling something dangerous, something that wanted to stay buried.

And he knew, without saying it, that tomorrow would be too late to turn back.

# Chapter 27

## Live Shot

Morning came too quickly for David. Normally, the start of a broadcast day filled him with energy, but after seventy-two relentless hours, fatigue clung to him like a second skin. Stookton didn't help. The town wore its gloom like a funeral shroud, gray skies pressed low against red-brick facades, leeching color from storefronts that usually looked quaint in the sunlight. The sour tang of coal smoke and the sulfur stench from the Brickworks drifted through the streets, searing the throat with every breath. The cold was raw; David's exhalations hung in the air like smoke signals, swept away in a heartbeat by a restless wind that tore at faded banners advertising an autumn festival no one would remember after today.

He checked his mic, hearing his own voice echo in his earpiece. Across from him, Mark Allen wrestled the tripod against the gusts, cursing when the wind snatched his CNC NEWS cap and sent it tumbling down Main Street. Jerry Marsh, steady as stone, clutched his battered clipboard, muttering the morning rundown one last time. Their stage

299

was set directly outside the Cardinal Lounge, the uncomfortable place where Emile claimed he had overheard the Chambers boys. Jerry insisted on the spot for impact, to remind the audience: this was where the story began.

The townspeople had already started to gather. Across the street, shop doors cracked open. Curious eyes lingered at the edges of the crowd. An elderly couple pressed their faces against the bakery window, fogging the glass. Two uniformed officers drifted back and forth in the street, their stiff pacing betraying an unease they tried to hide.

Besides David, Emile Hirsch looked like a man carrying his own gravestone. His coat hung too loose on his thin frame, and his shoulders curled inward as though bracing for a blow. He shifted his weight from foot to foot, his lips moving soundlessly, rehearsing words that seemed to splinter each time they touched his tongue.

David leaned in, clipping the lavalier to Emile's lapel. His voice was calm, but his eyes carried the intensity of command.

"Emile, I need you steady now. You're about to make history. We're live in ten. Listen, you'll be fine. Just breathe. I'm right here."

Emile gave a stiff nod, but his throat bobbed as he swallowed hard. He tried again, whispering fragments under his breath.

"They were over by the..." he faltered, his voice breaking. His eyes darted toward the small crowd forming.

Courage flickered for a moment, then slipped away again. His hands trembled, clutching nothing, as if trying to hold the memory still.

"They bragged. Right here. Chambers' two sons. They bragged it was them."

The words seemed to taste like poison in his mouth.

"Thirty seconds," Jerry's voice cut in, flat and professional, his fingers tapping a nervous rhythm against the clipboard.

David straightened, slipping into his broadcast smile, the polished mask every anchor wore before the red light blinked on. In his ear, Mike Brannon's baritone rolled from the CNC studio in Chicago: *"...and now we go live to Stookton, where correspondent David Raines has breaking developments."*

David turned slightly, microphone in hand. "Mr. Hirsch, for the record...tell our viewers what you heard. Where were you, what did you see and hear, and when did this take place?"

The crowd hushed. The wind dropped as if the town itself was straining to listen.

Emile's gaze locked on the Cardinal Lounge's front step, the very step he'd sat on that night. His voice came slow at first, unsteady, then hardened into something raw and deliberate.

"I was right there. Rolling a cigarette, ready to walk home. It was after midnight, and the Cardinal had just closed. Chambers' boys came out, laughing, with two other fellas. They walked to the alley out back. I heard their names, clear as day. I heard them say Mary Whittacre. Her children."

His breath hitched. He squeezed his eyes shut, as if that might erase what came next.

"They bragged they'd made sure nobody would talk. Said it like it was funny. Like it was nothing."

His voice cracked on the last word. The crowd shifted uneasily.

Suddenly, Emile doubled forward, gagging on the memory. His knees buckled, and his hand shot out, gripping David's wrist with desperate force. The cameras caught it all: the confession, the collapse, the town holding its breath. The camera hummed steadily, its glass eye unblinking as David held the moment, letting Emile recover. Every second of pacing mattered now; the rhythm could mean the difference between confession and collapse.

"And these were the sons of Congressman Phillip Chambers? Robert Lee Chambers and A. J. Chambers? You're saying you heard them admit to being involved in the murders?" David's voice was soft, coaxing, the tone of a surgeon guiding a hand through delicate work.

Emile's nod was faint but unmistakable. "Yes. I heard them say they went inside the house. Said they'd covered everything, and that being the Congressman's boys would keep them safe. Told their friends, 'you're part of the Chambers family... you got a ticket to ride.' That's the way they said it. Like it meant nothing could ever touch them." His voice cracked into a whisper. "I kept it quiet because... because I'm not a Chambers. Or a Von Stook. And in this town, that means you're vulnerable. I've seen too much. But I can't live holding this inside anymore."

Behind them loomed the courthouse, its clocktower rising into a dark, bruised sky, the town's symbol of justice standing mute and indifferent to the words unraveling beneath its shadow.

David pressed. "Did you hear names? Where exactly were they standing? Could you identify them now?"

Emile's hands shook visibly, the microphone trembling on his lapel. "They called each other by nicknames: 'Bobby-Lee' and 'A.' That's Robert Lee and A.J. They were just beyond the alley, in the shadow of the courthouse. And I know those boys, David. Watched them grow up. Always swaggering, always bullying, like they owned Stookton. It was them. No doubt."

David's earpiece crackled, Jerry's voice from the control truck. *"Standby. Toss coming back to you. Follow-up ready."*

Jerry raised his hand, silently counting down. *Three... two...*

Then...

A sound. Too sharp, too clean. Not a firecracker, not really. A crack that split the air.

For a split second, David felt something zip past his ear, a wasp's sting in flight, then the bang registered, rolling through the square.

Mark flinched at the tripod, his head snapping toward the courthouse roofline.

Emile's eyes went wide. His lips parted as if to speak, but a second report shattered the air.

And in that instant, Emile's body convulsed. A grotesque marionette dance, strings cut, limbs jerking in betrayal of his will. David's mind caught the sound, the angle, the precision: a sniper's shot, surgical, cold.

The next bullet landed true. It punched just below

Emile's collarbone, the impact twisting him forward. David saw the small red bloom on his shirt spread, dime-sized, then quarter, then dollar, spilling life outward in a grotesque flower. Emile collapsed, face-first on the pavement.

The square exploded.

Screams fractured the air. Some dropped to the ground, arms over heads, while others bolted in every direction, a panicked flock scattering before a predator. Uniformed officers drew weapons, radios howling, their boots pounding toward cover. Sirens, faint at first, wailed closer with each second, the sound of order trying desperately to catch chaos. David dropped beside Emile, his palm pressed to the old man's wrist. Nothing. Just the hot rush of blood pooling, the metallic tang hitting his nostrils and forcing him to turn his face away.

The camera never looked away. Mark's lens caught it all: the confession, the shots, the collapse. Its red tally light blinked on, steady and merciless, as if it were a heart beating through the carnage.

In David's headset, Jerry's voice ripped through: "We're live…assassination…keep rolling, keep rolling!" His words collided with the storm of sirens closing in.

Emile lay sideways, eyes glassy, mouth slack, forever silenced. A man who had dared to name names, cut down the moment he said them.

The message was unmistakable. Someone powerful wanted this story buried.

And they had just written the warning in blood across the courthouse steps.

# Chapter 28

## Fallout

The Chambers County courthouse lights sputtered and hissed above, their harsh fluorescent glow slicing across the marble steps like interrogation lamps trained on the guilty. The horde of scandal-hungry reporters swarmed like vultures, eager to feast on the remains of tragedy and mayhem. Their unintelligible shouted questions blending with the frantic snapping of cameras. When the great oak doors finally creaked open, the crowd surged forward with the force of a storm breaking against a seawall. As was his practice, David had maneuvered his way to the front of the mob, pen in hand, and Mark with his Sony poised to capture the first images as the big doors swung wide. David had been waiting for this moment, ever since the press conference detonated twenty-four hours earlier, exposing truths that shredded the illusion of Stookton's untouchable elite. The arrests of Robert and A.J. Chambers had seared themselves into public memory, two heirs dragged from privilege to disgrace, their hands bound in steel, their faces masks of arrogance cracked under flashing lights.

Now, their father emerged.

Congressman Chambers stepped into the daylight, a towering figure dressed in his customary navy suit, the fabric gleaming with wealth that felt suddenly sinister. His eyes flicked across the mob like a trapped animal sizing up its hunters. Every camera flash burst against his face like muzzle fire, illuminating the strain etched deep into his features. His family name, once a pillar of respect, now trembled under the weight of whispered treachery. The ghosts of his great-grandfather's legacy hovered, but they no longer lent him strength; they pressed down like chains.

"Congressman!" David's voice ripped through the din.

"What is your immediate response to the charges against your sons?"

Chambers adjusted his tie, chin lifting in rehearsed dignity, though his hands betrayed a faint tremor. "This is an impossibly difficult time for my family," he began, his voice even, too even, words polished in backrooms and spoken with practiced sorrow. "Robert and A.J. are innocent. Innocent until proven guilty."

David didn't wait. He drove the knife deeper. "But given the severity of the accusations, how do you plan to defend them? What's the strategy leading into trial?"

The Congressman faltered. His composure cracked, the

question slicing through the armor of his performance. His eyes clouded with something raw, panic, perhaps, or fury restrained by thin threads. "My sons have always served this community loyally," he said sharply, bitterness clinging to his tone. "This courthouse itself stands as a testament to our family's sacrifices. My great-grandfather fought for this land."

David leaned in, his words sharpened to a point. "And yet, Congressman, what about your dealings with the Stookton Nuclear Power Station? Many wonder if your connections there influenced your sons' behavior."

The crowd froze. The noise collapsed into silence, sudden and suffocating. The mere mention of Stookton hung in the air like the toll of a funeral bell.

Phillip's mask shifted, the corners of his mouth tightening, a flicker of rage betraying him. For a heartbeat, the statesman veneer slipped, revealing the brittle man beneath. Then he barked, "My family has always put the community first. I won't have our integrity questioned on the courthouse steps by baseless rumor!"

David's blood thundered in his ears. He pressed harder. "Is it baseless, Congressman? What about your relationship with Victor Von Stook? Whispers of collusion, corrupt bidding... are these just rumors too?"

309

Gasps broke across the crowd. Reporters leaned in like wolves scenting blood.

Phillip's eyes burned with fury. His voice rose, strained and venomous. "I will not dignify these lies with a response. You've crossed the line, Mr. Gardner. You think you know my family... you know nothing."

David met his gaze, unflinching. His voice cut with the force of conviction. "What I know is that voters deserve truth. And truth has a way of clawing its way to the surface, no matter how deep it's buried."

The standoff pulsed in the cold air, the tension snapping between them like a live wire. Reporters shouted, their frenzy swelling. The Congressman's face glistened with a sheen of sweat, his breathing harsh. At last, he snapped:

"I have nothing further to say."

He spun on his heel, his entourage closing ranks as he stormed towards his car. But the damage was done, the silence he left behind roared louder than any denial. The questions hung in the air, unanswered and damning, circling like vultures over a battlefield.

David exhaled, his pulse thrumming with the intoxicating rush of revelation. He knew, with bone-deep certainty, that this was only the beginning. Stookton's darkest days were not behind them. They were just

310

beginning to break.

***

Hours later, Phillip Chambers found himself standing in the lion's den, the office of Victor Von Stook. The room was a shrine to power: mahogany desks gleamed beneath low, golden lamplight, leather chairs exuded the stench of old money, and a wall of glass framed the city skyline like a trophy. Victor sat behind his desk with unnerving stillness, a faint smile ghosting at the corners of his mouth, as if savoring the moment. His composure was poisonous, the sort of calm that threatened violence without needing to raise its voice.

"Phillip," Victor drawled, his tone almost playful, though his eyes cut sharp as razors. "What a spectacle you've made. Your sons in handcuffs, your name in ruin, headlines splashed across every paper. Do you even grasp how dangerous it is to stand before me now... this unprepared, this desperate?"

Phillip's jaw clenched. His hands pressed against the polished desk, knuckles whitening against the slick grain. "You think I don't understand? My family is under siege. I came here because I need your support. Your influence could..."

311

"Influence?" Victor leaned forward, voice dropping into a growl. "You want me to sweep your sons' sins under the rug? To resurrect a legacy already half-buried in the mud, they dragged it through? They've disgraced you, Phillip. And in doing so, they've disgraced me."

Phillip's face flushed, a storm of anger and fear colliding behind his eyes. "You can't wash your hands of this. You've benefitted from my position, from my loyalty. The Nuclear Power Station contract, we both know what's at stake. If my family collapses, your enterprise burns with it."

Victor's laugh was low, mirthless. He steepled his fingers, tilting his head like a predator appraising wounded prey. "Do not confuse mutual benefit with loyalty. You've brought chaos, Congressman. I've had to wade through fire to cover my own tracks because of your recklessness. And now you come to me, hat in hand…like a beggar."

The words stung, slicing through Phillip's thin defenses. But desperation sharpened his tongue. "If this scandal grows, and it will, the press will start digging deeper. They'll find the ties between your business and my family. They'll drag us both into the flames."

Victor's eyes narrowed. The air seemed to constrict, suffocating, as his voice turned to steel. "Careful, Phillip. You speak as though you hold a knife to my throat. But don't forget... I'm the one who taught you where to cut."

Phillip inhaled sharply, then leaned forward until their faces hovered dangerously close. His voice was hoarse but steady. "And don't forget... I know about the whispers. The House Committee sniffing around your friends at the Nuclear Regulatory Commission. One word from me, and those whispers turn into subpoenas."

The silence that followed was thick and deadly, charged like a storm before lightning strikes. The threat coiled between them like a viper, waiting to strike.

Victor's expression darkened, his calm shattering into something rawer, uglier. "You wouldn't dare."

Phillip didn't flinch. "Try me."

For a moment, it seemed the air itself might ignite. The two men locked eyes, a brutal contest of willpower, Phillip's desperation clawing against Victor's cold dominance.

Finally, Victor leaned back, the predator's smile creeping once more across his face. "You've grown teeth after all. But remember, snapping at the hand that feeds you is a dangerous habit. If you force my hand, I won't hesitate to make sure you choke on your own ambition."

Phillip straightened, his chest rising and falling with the weight of the standoff. The office felt colder now, the shadows longer, as though even the walls conspired against him.

"We're bound together whether we like it or not," he muttered, voice taut with defiance.

"Bound?" Victor's laugh was guttural, almost inhuman. "No, Phillip. Parasites bind themselves to their host. Partners build. Choose carefully which one you want to be."

Victor flicked his wrist in dismissal, as though brushing dust from his sleeve, and Phillip felt the dismissal like a blade. He turned, the heavy silence trailing him to the door. Each step was a reminder that the ground beneath him was cracking, that every move now was a gamble with ruin as the prize.

Behind him, Victor's voice cut the air one last time, cold and final:

"Pray you don't make yourself my enemy."

As Phillip exited into the darkened corridor, the weight of legacy and betrayal pressed down like a storm cloud ready to break. The game had changed. The rules had sharpened. And the first casualty, Phillip knew, would not be a body; it would be a soul.

# Chapter 29

## A Day in the Park

The morning sun washed over Chambers Heritage Community College in soft gold, its stately brick facades glowing as though untouched by the ugliness of the world beyond. Students moved like currents across manicured lawns, laughing, rushing, pausing in small knots of chatter. Professors strolled beneath maples just beginning to bud, their voices carrying in the crisp air. To an outsider, it looked like a place of promise, ambition, and youth.

But to David Gardner, driving beneath the college's stone archway, the place felt haunted. The echoes of yesterday's horror, Emile's last words, his collapse, the red bloom spreading across his chest, clung to him like a second skin. Even here, on this picture-perfect campus, he couldn't shake the image.

He parked by the old library, its ivy-clad walls standing sentinel over the generations of minds it had shaped. For a moment, he sat in the car, fingers drumming the steering wheel, torn between anticipation and unease. Lydia had asked to meet. Emile's death had gutted her, he knew, but

315

she also carried something, information, discoveries from her work on the *Angelorum*. And though he wouldn't admit it aloud, the thought of seeing her stirred something he couldn't afford to dwell on.

Inside, the library smelled of parchment and time. Dust motes floated in shafts of pale light slanting through high windows. And there she was, Lydia, alone at a table near the back, framed by glass and shadow, surrounded by scrolls, thick binders, and yellowed documents.

She looked flawless, as always, in a navy blazer, khaki slacks, hair immaculately set, but her eyes betrayed her. Tired, rimmed with shadows. David's chest tightened at the sight of her.

"Oh, David," she said softly, standing halfway before sinking back into her chair. "I'm so glad you came."

He smiled faintly, trying to mask his own exhaustion. "Of course. How are you holding up, lady?"

Her sigh seemed to carry centuries of grief. "I don't know. The murders of Mary Whittacre and her sons, Emile's death, and everything I keep uncovering about Stookton, it's as if the ground here is poisoned. And yesterday..." Her voice faltered. "Yesterday was senseless."

David nodded grimly, sliding into the chair across from her. "I won't sugarcoat it. My world's full of brutality, but

316

what's been unleashed here?" He shook his head. "It's beyond anything I've seen. Stookton's not just corrupt… it's cursed."

Lydia sat in silence for a beat, then leaned forward, her voice trembling with both grief and conviction. "When I met Emile, I felt this… kinship. He carried the same awareness I did… that shadow over this town, heavy and unrelenting. He always urged me to keep pushing, to finish my book, to defy the darkness. And in the end, he lived by his words. He stood up. He paid the ultimate price."

Her voice cracked. David reached across the table, took her hand gently, and for a long moment they sat in silence, two people bound together by grief and the weight of truths too big to contain.

Finally, Lydia straightened, withdrawing her hand only to pull a fragile document from the pile. The parchment crackled as she unfolded it, her eyes sparking with urgency. "The more I study the *Angelorum,* the deeper this goes.

These aren't just scattered stories or myths. There are accounts, records, from the Civil War, and even before. And the most chilling are from the time of Peter Von Stook and his son, Andrew."

David leaned in, pulse quickening. "For example?"

Lydia smoothed the paper flat with delicate fingers. The

ink, though faded, was still legible. She drew in a breath, then began to read aloud.

Saturday, May 16, 1936

*A day of profound sorrow and unspeakable horror has befallen our community. The life of an honest and most revered Black man, Zebediah Coal, was ended in the most hideous fashion on the lawn of Stookton's city park. When Zebediah reported his suspicions to Sheriff Ted Betts about Congressman Richard Keeling's possible involvement in the deaths of two local women, a furor swept through the community like wildfire.*

*The two young ladies, one a schoolteacher at McKinley Elementary and the other a nurse at Stookton Hospital, were at first believed to be victims of the vicious and most despised Andrew Von Stook. But no arrests were ever made. Zebediah, a worker in Stookton's shale pits and later in those awful brickyards, was frequently approached by other laborers who trusted him, and there were rumors.*

*When the Von Stooks heard their hand-picked and groomed-for-service Congressman Keeling was at the center of the stories that Zebediah chose to take to the sheriff, his death warrant was as good as signed. With no trial, evidence, or discussion, he was dragged from his home by a mob fueled by rage, bigotry, and hatred, and taken to the large oak tree at the very center of our town's otherwise beautiful old park. A rope was thrown across a low-hanging branch, and before God and all that is holy, they hanged him by the neck until he was dead.*

*His cries echoed through the town square, a sound that will forever haunt this town. Peter Von Stook himself watched with a cruel smile upon his face. May God forgive us all.*

Elder Scribe Abraham Hayes, The Angelorum David's response was sharp, almost a bark. "Unbelievable."

Lydia sifted through the mountain of notes and folders, her fingers trembling slightly as she shook her head. "It is unbelievable," she echoed, her voice heavy with a mix of awe and dread. "And these old documents are riddled with it. But... listen to this. After reading late into the night, the first thing I did this morning was head straight to the library, then the county courthouse. I scoured every archive, every public record, page after page... and there is nothing. Not a single record anywhere of a double homicide in May, or in any other month of 1936."

David's instincts snapped to life, his eyes narrowing with determination. "Alright," he said, his voice carrying the weight of command. "Give me the sheriff's name again, and the exact date from the Angelorum entry. I'll put Linda Carr

319

on it. If she doesn't dig up something, I'll buy drinks for the next six months."

Linda, her pen scratching frantically across the yellow legal pad, looked up, her brow furrowed. "There are plenty of references to Sheriff Ted Betts. He even received several citations for meritorious service. But not one word... nothing... about investigating a double homicide. According to these records, he came here from St. Louis, served until early 1937, and then... silence. He vanishes. No trace of him, no trace of these murders."

David leaned back, his expression grim. He let the silence stretch for a moment before speaking. "So, for any documentary I'll be doing, and for the credibility of what you're going to publish, we're facing a mountain. Too many blanks, too many shadows. Filling them in won't be easy."

"You're right," Lydia said, her tone quickening as if the urgency was pressing down on her. "And here's what makes it worse. Remember, I told you that when Victor Von Stook was young and took the reins of the empire, he sold the old Von Stook mansion?"

David leaned forward, eyes lit with curiosity. "Yes. You said it was going to be an exceptional story. So... tell me." "Early in my research, I uncovered two articles, one in the Stookton Herald, another in the Stookton Chronicle, from the summer of 1961. They reported that the mansion had been purchased by a young lawyer named Michael Douglas Hart. At just 33, he was appointed as a district judge for the Seventh Circuit Court in East St. Louis. The man was brilliant, highly respected, and breezed through Senate confirmation. The articles described how he and his wife wanted to raise their children in a small town. So they came here, to Stookton, and bought the old Von Stook place. After all, it was conveniently close, just twenty-five miles from the Seventh Circuit."

David slapped the table, his enthusiasm cutting through the tension. "Finally! Something concrete. Something we can verify, something to anchor the story and maybe... just maybe... help us piece together the town's recent past."

Lydia's eyes gleamed with a dangerous kind of excitement. "Exactly. And remember this, many of the Angelorum documents and entries were torn out, hidden away somewhere in that mansion. What if Judge Hart found them? What if he knew? Imagine what secrets he might have uncovered, imagine what truths were locked away within those walls."

# Chapter 30

## Loose Ends

The three days following Emile's assassination, and the explosive press conference with Congressman Phillip Chambers, had been nothing short of a storm. But this wasn't the usual media circus, the kind that blazed hot for a few hours and fizzled into gossip. No... this time, the chaos had teeth.

Robert Lee Chambers, age twenty-one, and his nineteen-year-old brother, A.J., had been charged with capital murder. Six counts each. A grand jury loomed, waiting to carve their fates. And their father? He had slipped into the shadows. Congressman Phillip Chambers, once untouchable, was now a ghost. Even his allies whispered. A national paper ran a savage cartoon: a wanted poster in a drugstore window, Chambers' face plastered across it.

WANTED!

*Congressman Phillip Chambers*

A bystander asked, *"You mean for investment fraud, wiretapping, conspiracy?"*

The journalist replied: *"Maybe. But right now, he's*

*wanted mostly for an interview."*

Carl Meyer and the CNC Network pulled David and his crew back to Chicago, shifting their lenses from Stookton's mysteries to the Chambers family implosion. A ninety-minute documentary would come later. Tonight, David was leaving. But not before one final stop. Lydia.

\*\*\*

The library at Chambers Community College was hushed, sunlight spilling through the mullioned windows in fractured gold. Beyond the glass, the town moved at its usual sluggish rhythm, as though the murders, revelations, and betrayals of the last two weeks had never happened.

The Angelorum lay between David and Lydia like a living thing, its weight almost palpable. A silence pressed in thick, unyielding. Their eyes met, and in that moment, something deeper passed between them. Feelings unspoken. Longing deferred. But not now. Not here.

Finally, Lydia closed the book with a soft thud, her palm lingering on the cover as if to trap its secrets inside. "A lot has happened, David," she said quietly. "And there's still so much we don't know. Maybe so much we'll never know."

David reached across the table, enclosing her hands in his.

His voice was steady, anchoring her. "Let's not lose ourselves in the fog. You still have a book to publish. I'll be back in a couple of months with Mark and Jerry, and we'll keep digging. More pieces will fall into place. We're a hell of a team, Lydia."

Her eyes softened. "David, I've loved this. As horrifying as it all is, I've loved working with you. Your confidence, your encouragement… it's been a lifeline."

"The feeling's mutual," David said. And he meant it.

Lydia hesitated before her voice broke the silence again. "You know… one of the reasons I came here, why I threw myself into this whole 'Stookton mystery,' was my grandfather. I promised my grandmother I'd find out what happened to him. The Angelorum says Jake Cohen came here in 1945. Whoever wrote those entries… someone knew."

"Between now and when I come back, Linda Carr will be working the case," David reassured her. "She'll turn over every stone. She'll find the threads."

"I know," Lydia said. But her voice cracked with something deeper, exhaustion, or obsession. "I think about those two young women murdered in their thirties. Zebediah Coal's lynching. What he really knew about Congressman Keeling. Was it Keeling who killed those girls? And what about the missing Angelorum documents? What did they contain? David, it's consuming me."

"I know," David said softly, his hand squeezing hers. "It's overwhelming. But we'll do what we always do: research, verify, connect the pieces. The truth will come."

She exhaled slowly, eyes fixed on the old book as though it might answer her. Then, her tone shifted. "There's something else I've never told you. Something Emile confided in me about the mansion itself. Strange stories. Unexplainable things that happened there."

David raised a brow, skepticism creeping into his voice. "He mentioned it once to me too. But you know me, Lydia. I deal in facts. Things I can document, sources I can verify. Ghost stories don't hold up under a camera lens."

Lydia leaned in, her voice firm, charged with conviction. "After three years of digging into Stookton, Stookton, the Von Stooks and their allies, there's one thing I'm sure of. There is a curse on this place. Think about it. This is a community in the heart of America that forged a covenant with Nazi Germany. They weren't just collaborators; they built their prosperity, their wealth, their power on blood. Innocent blood. Whatever incident, or chain of events, set it all in motion, it's still here. Still poisoning this town. Stookton is built on a foundation of murder. The whole damn town stands on a grave."

# Epilogue

## Saturday, August 12, 1961

Michael eased the luxurious SUV up the long, tree-lined drive to the Von Stook mansion. Maples and oaks arched overhead, their limbs knitting into a living tunnel that swallowed the car's engine note and left only the hush of leaves. Olivia pressed her face to the window, breath fogging the glass. "Oh, Michael... I've forgotten how beautiful it is," she whispered, as the house slowly revealed itself across the rolling lawn like something reclaimed from another century. At thirty-three, Michael Douglas Hart wore pedigree and promise easily, Harvard polished, a high-flying St. Louis litigator turned newly appointed district judge.

He had engineered the move with chess-player efficiency: twenty-five miles from the Seventh Circuit, close enough for hearings, far enough for Emma's school plays and Claire's soccer games. Olivia, Radcliffe-bred and luminous, sketched column inches in her head even as she marveled at the turrets. Their daughters, eyes wide, leaned between the front seats, voices a chorus of delight. "Which bedroom is mine?" Emma demanded. Claire, eleven, translated wonder into mischief. "It's like a spooky story house... there must be hidden passages!"

The mansion rose three stories in red-brown brick, a last gasp of the Gilded Age, cornices carved like lace, a slate crown sliced with ornate dormers, and a turret that kept watch over the town below. Narrow windows punctured the facades; dark eyes set in a weathered face. The porch columns vanished into shadow; hand-turned spindles were worn as if generations had smoothed each one with the same palms.

The heavy front door swung inward with a brass knocker that had lost its shine. The entry hall stole the breath out of them: cathedral high, cathedral narrow, oak paneling that smelled of resin and memory. A spiral staircase coiled upward like a helix of iron and shadow, balusters scrolling like black vines, the railing burnished glossy by decades of hands. Light from transom windows pooled on a parquet floor, making the dust dance like a constellation of tiny ghosts.

They spilled into the house, Olivia with a delighted laugh, the girls scattering down corridors that sighed under their footsteps. Thirteen-year-old Emma's eyes glittered as she took in the soaring ceilings and ornate moldings. Claire pressed her palm to a wall and pretended she'd found a secret latch. Their chatter filled the rooms with new life, an incantation against the hush that had settled in the old bones for decades.

Michael followed slowly, savoring the echo of each step. He watched his daughters run, felt Olivia's hand slip into his, and for a moment, the mansion seemed to promise only fairytales and afternoons of study. Then he cleared his throat, a careful, practical sound. "Let's explore carefully," he said, the admonition soft but certain. "This house is old... some things might be... surprising."

Emma and Claire darted down the upstairs hallway, their laughter echoing against the walls as their footsteps thudded across the old wooden floor. The corridor stretched long and narrow, lined with stern-faced portraits in gilded frames and heavy velvet curtains that swallowed the afternoon light.

Emma slowed suddenly, her eyes locking on something at the far end. A massive portrait loomed there, an elegant older woman in a sweeping gown of deep burgundy, her silver hair pulled into a regal twist. The painted eyes glinted strangely in the dim light, following them with a gaze that was both serene and unyielding.

"Whoa," Emma whispered, her voice barely carrying as she stepped closer. "She looks... important."

Claire edged beside her, frowning. "Important? She

329

looks alive. Like she's staring right at us."

Before Emma could answer, the massive frame groaned. Slowly, impossibly, the painting shifted on hidden hinges, swinging away from the wall with a muffled creak. Dust billowed into the hallway. Behind the canvas, steel glinted, a thick, dark vault door embedded in the wall like the mouth of something ancient and hungry.

Both girls stumbled back, their hearts hammering.

"Did you see that?!" Emma gasped, clutching her sister's arm. "It moved on its own!"

Claire's eyes widened, her voice trembling with awe. "It's a secret door... and behind it... Dad, there's a vault! There has to be something inside!"

Adrenaline drove them downstairs. Bursting into the parlor, breathless and flushed, they found their father in an antique armchair, thumbing through a dust-coated book.

"Dad!" Emma blurted out, words tumbling over themselves. "You won't believe this. We found something upstairs. The big portrait at the end of the hall... it opened like a door! And there's this huge vault behind it!"

Michael Hart looked up sharply, surprise flickering across his face. "A vault? Are you sure? Where?"

"At the very end of the upstairs hallway," Claire said, nodding furiously. Her eyes shone with urgency.

Michael set aside the book and the box he had been carrying, rising with measured caution. "Show me."

The three of them climbed the creaking staircase, the girls racing ahead while Michael followed with slower, deliberate steps. When they reached the hallway, Emma pointed, her voice a whisper edged with awe.

"There. It's still open… just like we saw."

Michael stepped forward, the shadows deepening around him as he studied the vault. The metal was thick; the kind forged for secrets not meant to be shared. He ran his hand along its cold surface, frowning.

"Incredible," he murmured. "This house has been standing for over a century. God only knows what's hidden inside these walls."

Emma's eyes gleamed with mischief and curiosity. "Shouldn't we open it? What if there's treasure? Or something valuable?"

"Wait a minute, ladies," Michael cautioned, his tone steady but firm. "We don't know what's in there. Whatever's behind that door has been sealed away for a reason. It could be dangerous."

Claire tugged at his sleeve, her eyes pleading. "Please, Dad? Just a peek? It's like… like we've discovered a real adventure."

Michael studied his daughters, their faces alight with excitement. Finally, with a reluctant sigh, he gave a faint smile.

"Alright," he said, his voice low. "But we'll be careful."

Emma and Claire tore down the upstairs hallway, their laughter echoing in the cavernous old house. The long corridor stretched ahead of them, its walls lined with stern-faced photographs and heavy velvet curtains that dulled the afternoon light.

Then Emma froze. At the far end of the hall loomed a massive portrait, a woman of unmistakable authority. She was painted in full length, wrapped in an opulent gown, her silver hair swept into an elegant crown. Her eyes, sharp and unyielding, seemed to follow them as they moved.

"Whoa," Emma whispered, stepping closer, her voice hushed as if afraid to wake something. "She must have been someone important."

Claire squinted, unease tugging at her. "Important? She looks alive… like she's watching us."

Before Emma could reply, the silence was broken with a low groan. The portrait shuddered, then began to swing away from the wall on hidden hinges. Dust spilled into the air. Behind it stood a massive steel vault door, its surface dark and unwelcoming, like the sealed entrance to some long-forgotten crypt.

The girls leapt back, their hearts hammering.

"Did you see that?!" Emma gasped. "It just moved... by itself!"

Claire's eyes were wide with awe. "It's a secret door. And behind it... a vault. There has to be something inside!"

Breathless, they raced downstairs, nearly tumbling over each other in their haste. In the grand parlor, their father sat in a deep armchair, an ancient book open in his hands, dust rising from its pages.

"Dad!" Emma burst out, her words tumbling in a rush. "You won't believe what we found. The big painting upstairs, it opened like a door! And behind it was this huge vault!"

Michael looked up sharply, startled by their urgency. "A vault? Are you certain? Where exactly?"

"At the end of the hall," Claire said, nodding, her eyes bright with both fear and excitement.

Michael set the book aside, the weight of his daughters' urgency still lingering in the room. Without a word, he rose and followed them up the staircase, their small footsteps echoing ahead of him. At the end of the dim hallway, Emma pointed with trembling excitement.

"There! The painting... it moved aside, just like we saw."

Michael stepped forward, his eyes narrowing as he examined the hidden vault door now revealed in the shadows. The steel surface was thick, cold, and foreboding, a relic of another time. He brushed his hand across the metal, feeling the chill seep into his palm.

"This…" he murmured, almost to himself. "This house has secrets."

Emma's curiosity flared. "Should we open it? What if there's treasure, or something important inside?"

Michael hesitated, the air heavy with the weight of possibility. "We don't know what's behind that door," he warned. "It could be dangerous. Locked away for a reason."

Claire tugged at his sleeve, her wide eyes pleading.

"Please, Dad? Just a peek. It's like a real adventure."

Michael looked at them, two faces glowing with excitement and innocence, eager for mystery rather than afraid of it. He sighed, the corner of his mouth curling into a faint smile.

"Alright," he said softly. "But we move carefully. If this house holds secrets, we must respect them."

He pressed his hand firmly against the vault's handle. The hinges groaned in protest, a deep metallic growl that echoed through the hall. Slowly, the heavy door creaked open, and beyond it yawned a darkness so thick it seemed to swallow the light. A breath of stale, ancient air escaped, carrying with it the scent of dust, iron, and something faintly unsettling, something that had been waiting.

The threshold stood before them, like the mouth of the mansion itself, daring them to step inside.

*What started in blood... will end in shadows.*

**Coming soon...**

# Blood Foundation – Shadows

Printed in Dunstable, United Kingdom